I0687039

# The Takeover

## Erin Pickett

Published by Between The Cornfields Publishing, 2023.

THE TAKEOVER

**First edition. July 18, 2023.**

ISBN: 979-8988077800

Written by Erin Pickett.

---

1. http://www.mannisondesign.wordpress.com

2. http://www.jenarcollins.com

*To Dave*
*Whether we're fighting bedtime with the kids, mosquitos at the lake, or if the*
*words in this book jump off the page—there's not another person I'd rather have*
*by my side.*

# Chapter 1

My husband's phone conversation just outside our bedroom door taunts me more than the mound of laundry we had been folding together before his ex-wife demanded his attention.

"I'll be there," he says. "I've got a few days to clear my schedule ... Yeah, I can manage the whole weekend ... No problem at all."

I slam the dresser drawer closed, catching my finger inside. "Dammit!"

Clint slips quietly through the door. "That was Christa," he explains.

Yanking open the sock drawer, I prepare myself for a fight. "Sounded like you agreed with whatever she wants. Again."

He sighs, taking a stack of shirts to the closet. "Apparently Sidney is in a play. Opening night is next Thursday. She wants me to stay for all four performances over the weekend."

I hand him a neatly folded pile of boxers. "You can't do that," I say, though I know he already agreed.

"I told Christa I would be there. I'll get Harry to cover the shifts at the shop and if you're working maybe the kids can stay at the Gillman's after school."

I cross my arms, a swell of emotions washing over me. "Tanner's birthday party is Saturday afternoon."

He freezes, a lone sock dangling from his hand. "His birthday isn't for another two weeks."

"Remember we decided to have it early? The bait shop is hosting that fishing tournament the weekend of his birthday."

He runs fingers through his thick, blonde hair. "What if we move Tanner's birthday party to the weekend after?"

I shake my head. "We can't do that six days before. I've already sent out invitations."

"Well, you didn't invite the whole town, did you? Surely it won't be too hard to call and make adjustments."

I bite my lip, inhaling slowly. "Clint, just go see the play on Thursday or Friday and be home by three on Saturday for your son's party."

He hangs his head. "Sidney is expecting me to be at every performance."

"I think she'll understand."

"I can't back out now."

"You'd rather tell your five-year-old that you're going to miss his birthday?" He bats his long lashes—ones I think God wasted by giving to a man—and his lips droop as he pouts pitifully in my direction. "Oh no. That's not going to work. *I* am not telling the kids."

He blinks seductively. "Please? You know I can't handle disappointing them."

"So don't. Go to opening night and be home for Tanner's party on Saturday."

Clint stretches his arms over his head. "The thing is, they're doing a special parent's night thing on Saturday. Sidney really wants me to be there."

I rub my fingers into my temple. "It's Tanner's birthday. Besides, it's not like Christa told you in advance. I'm sure they've known for weeks this was coming up."

"Christa said they got busy and she forgot."

I roll my eyes. "That's always her excuse."

"Are you sure we can't reschedule Tanner's party?"

I slap my hands against my thighs and list our plans for the next three Saturdays. "But, yeah, let's make everything revolve around Christa and her schedule."

He flops onto the bed. "There you go making it sound like I'm choosing her over you. Again."

I throw my hands on my hips. "Aren't you? Why don't you ever invite us along for these things? We could all drive up there on Thursday and see the play. I'm sure I could find someone to cover my shift Friday and we can celebrate Tanner's birthday *with* his older siblings for a change."

"We can't afford the cost of a hotel room," he argues.

"Not that I want to stay in your ex-wife's house, but wouldn't she have room for us?"

He shakes his head. "Christa's house is full of expensive things. If Tanner or Ella broke anything we couldn't afford to replace it."

I release an exasperated sigh. "I'm trying to compromise here, but it sounds like you don't want us to go. Normally when someone divorces and remarries, they blend their families together. I'm tired of being the only one who tries. It's like you and Christa have zero respect for me at all." My eyes drift to the nightstand drawer where divorce papers have been hidden for months.

"You're overreacting. Nobody is trying to stop you from being involved with Sidney and Jett."

I forcefully cross my arms. "Seriously? I can count the number of times they have been to our house. I've even offered to drive the three hours to get them. I feel like an outsider. *I* am your wife, but it always seems like Christa calls the shots. Maybe we should have asked her before we planned Tanner's party. You didn't even tell her about it; just said you'd clear your schedule. Why is she always more important?" Tears well in my eyes as I sit beside him on the bed.

He drapes his arm over my shoulder. "She's not more important."

I shrug it off. "Then why do you seem more interested in keeping her happy than me? And why are the kids suffering because of it?"

Clint stands, shoving his hands in his pockets. "Why does it always turn into a big fight every time I go see my kids?"

I push to my feet, squaring up to him. "Don't make it sound like this is about you seeing your kids. It's about you choosing to do what Christa wants while completely ignoring how that affects me or the kids."

He reaches for my hand. "That's not true. I'm just trying not to make Christa mad."

I pull my fingers slowly from his grasp. "Right. Because it's better to have an angry wife than an angry *ex*-wife."

"You know she likes to use her father to intimidate me. Last time I told her no, he threatened to close the bait shop. And he has the connections to do it. I'm just trying to keep the peace."

"How about you stand up to him? Stop giving them all the power."

He eases onto the bed. "It's not that simple."

I step to the nightstand. "It really is." With a deep breath, I gather my courage and open the drawer. "I had these drawn up, though I hoped things would change and you'd never see them. But it's clear now that this is the only way to open your eyes," I say, handing him the divorce papers.

He cautiously opens them. "What is this?"

"They're divorce papers. I want you to read them carefully before you make your decision. The drive to Middletown should give you time to think about it. You either sign those or stand up to your ex and her father. And that's just for starters. I want my needs to come before Christa's. I'm not asking you to give up time with your older kids, but I need to know that you can manage special events for everyone. And, dammit, consult me before committing to things."

He slaps the papers onto the bed. "You want a divorce because of a birthday party?"

I inhale deeply. "You think that's what this is about? No. It's about the time you missed seeing Ella in the Fourth of July parade because Jett had a baseball game. You were gone four days that time. Then you spent a week with him when he got his permit and you missed Ella's first day of school. There was the Thanksgiving you missed with us so Jett and Sidney got to see their grandparents on their mother's side who were in town from Cape Cod. I still don't know why you had to be there for *that*. There was Memorial Day when Ella was two that had something to do with Sidney, but I don't remember what. It's about you not caring that you're missing stuff with our children because Christa thinks you need to be there with them for trivial things. It's like she always finds a reason to pull you away when our kids need you. If we all worked together, there would be time for all the children. It's been building for a long time, Clint. I can't do it anymore."

"All of my kids need me. Besides, the rational thing to do would be to discuss it, not let it fester until you see a damn lawyer."

I throw my hands in the air. "I've *tried*. It seems like this is the only way left to get your attention."

"If I go see Sidney's play, you're divorcing me?"

I shake my head. "No. If you miss Tanner's party, I'm divorcing you. Maybe then you'll show up. I've given you a reasonable solution. The choice is yours."

"And I've told you Christa's father will close the bait shop if I don't keep her happy."

"Figure it out. Stand up to him. Or simply explain that it's Tanner's birthday. I'm sure he's not completely heartless."

Ella's head peaks through the cracked door. "I was wondering if we could get some twisted ice cream."

"That's a great idea!" Clint opens his arms, inviting Ella onto his lap. His eyes sweep past mine as he shoves the papers into his back pocket. "We'll talk more about this later."

# Chapter 2

Clint raps his fist against the steering wheel as we crawl to a stop on County Road 111.

Our eight-year-old, Ella, giggles from the backseat. "He's waiting for it to turn green."

"Stop signs don't turn green," I remind her.

"Damn tourists," Clint mutters to the red Prius blocking our lane. "Connecticut's a left turn, pal."

"Those 'damn tourists' pay most of your bills," I chide him, staring out the window at the leaves swaying in the late summer breeze.

"Not that one, Lexi."

I force a smile his direction. "No, not that one, but the ones who do will be gone soon."

"They'll be back in a few months when the lakes freeze." Clint's store, Boats 'N Bait, depends largely on tourism and I hate when he treats them like the nuisance they tend to be in the summer and winter months. "I'm going to see if they need help," he says. Clicking the latch on his seatbelt, he steps out of the vehicle and draws himself up to his full six feet.

In the back seat, Tanner and Ella, have no clue I'd just given their dad the divorce papers that hid in my nightstand for months. Tanner's dirty-blonde hair is in disarray and his six-year-old face is smudged with dirt, but that's nothing new. Dirt clings to him the way it does to all boys. Ella swings her legs while her piercing blue eyes look around, a clear sign she's eager to get the ice cream her dad promised. I couldn't refuse one last trip as a family, but now my stomach churns as I watch Clint knock on the window of the vehicle in front of us. I wonder what he's thinking. Is he delaying the end of the marriage or contemplating a way to save it? I use the precious seconds it takes him to storm back to our truck to convince myself that I made the right decision.

"Nobody's in there," Clint says, slamming the shifter into drive. "Nut must've broken down and not had the sense to pull off the road." He swerves angrily around the vehicle, flipping it the finger as we pass.

"Maybe they couldn't," I suggest as he swings a left onto Highway 10.

"That's what they get for driving a hybrid," he snarls.

"As opposed to this gas guzzler?" I tap the armrest on the door of our fifteen-year-old Dodge diesel.

"Won't find us on the side of the road."

We're pulling into the parking lot next to a black Camaro at Caroga Creamery before I can make a sarcastic comment about being on a first-name basis with our mechanic. Not that it's hard to be on a first-name basis in Caroga Lake, a town with a population of less than a thousand, not counting tourists at any given time.

The door to the creamery faces West Caroga Lake and Clint flings it open, rocking it hard against the hinges. If Clint really wanted to delay the dissolution of our marriage, he would've driven the ten miles south out of the Adirondacks to Dairy Queen. I usher the kids in first as he holds the flimsy screen door open, eager to get back home and discuss what happens next.

Ella races toward the counter and skids to a stop before reaching it. There are no employees or customers in the building and the place is deathly silent except for the soft-serve machine which sputters the last bits of melted brown and white liquid onto the floor. The place smells like the first meal I made Clint—burnt. Clint's worried expression matches my own. He leaps across the counter in one swift movement, crushing a sugar cone in the slosh. Flies flock to half-eaten food on two of the eight tables inside the small building, but there's not a soul in sight. Smoke seeps into the dining area as I pull Tanner's hand away from the cold fry he was about to grab.

Clint turns off the machine on his way back from the small kitchen. "Lexi, there was food still on the grill."

"It's like everyone just disappeared," I breathe, wondering if we missed The Rapture.

Clint hops back to our side of the counter. "Let's get out of here."

"I want ice cream," Tanner screams as I fight to get him strapped in.

"I just remembered I have the best ice cream at home." I sigh, relieved I had managed to find Edy's on sale the other day.

"We should call the police," Clint nearly yells over Tanner's wailing.

I reach for my phone as I climb in the cab. "I don't have any reception."

"Use my phone." He tosses it and pulls onto the street without so much as looking for traffic.

"You don't have signal either."

Clint runs his fingers through his thick blonde hair. He turns right to take us the ten miles to the nearest Sheriff's Office.

Ella taps her finger on the window. "Why are there Xs on all the doors?"

Clint and I study the houses lining the next block. Sure enough, they all have spray paint markings on the doors.

Clint slams his foot on the accelerator. "I haven't seen a single vehicle since we left the creamery."

A few minutes of eerie travel pass as though it's been hours.

"I think we've found them," I say, pointing ahead to the first ever traffic jam our town has seen. Cars line the shoulder as if they pulled over for an emergency vehicle and forgot to take off after it passed. Clint eases forward to get a better view of the obstruction. A line of men fills the roadway. Dressed in black from head-to-toe, they march toward us. Clint's hand flies to the shifter, but before he can flick his wrist upward, rifle barrels point directly into the cab windows. Red dots light the inside of the truck like a Christmas tree. Clint's eyes dart to the rearview. With the slightest jerk of my head, I tell him not to plow through the swarm of men surrounding us. We'd be dead before we made it ten feet. Defeated, he places the vehicle in park.

Ella's screams pierce our eardrums as gloved hands open all the doors at once. A thick arm yanks me from the truck. I stumble as one of them leans over Tanner's booster seat. Pushing the intruder out of the way, I fumble with the sticky latch and scoop my son into my shaking arms. He clings to my neck, soaking my clammy skin with his tears. A gun jabs into Clint's back as Ella shrieks. He whispers into her ear as he carries her, coming to stand beside me. His small action gives me one last shred of hope for our marriage, though that isn't important right now. The men circle us, leading us to a military truck where they search us for weapons. They pluck our phones and IDs and throw them into a box among hundreds of others.

A masked man, whose eyes are dark as coal, yanks my six-year-old's arms off me and firmly plants him in front of Clint. He motions for Ella to come to me as my son flails his arms and legs, trying to fight his way back. I step toward him, but one of the men blocks my path, pointing a gun at my head. I freeze as Tanner's cries rip my heart to shreds. Another man grabs him and forces him into Clint's arms. I reach for Ella and wipe her tears away as Tanner's cries fill the air. At eight, Ella understands more of what is going on. She's a critical thinker and I'm less worried about her than Tanner. He's too young to understand why he can't have his mommy. He has always been a momma's boy and I've never been unable to help him. We are pushed into separate trucks nearby and I can still hear Tanner's lament as I look around at the tear-stained faces of the women and children already seated inside. Ella clutches me tightly, but not so much that I can't sense her bravery. She's trying to be strong for me and that hurts as much as Tanner's cries which soon get drowned out by the roar of the truck's engines. I wish I had stayed up to play trains with him last night instead of sending him to bed crying, I think as Ella curls up against me. As we begin to move, the woman next to me whispers about World War III until she is finally told to stop scaring the children by a mother who is also comforting a young girl.

The truck couldn't have driven more than the distance across town when it stops. Scared for what comes next, I suddenly feel safe in this dusty, smelly truck. A tall, gun-wielding man opens the flap and motions for us to move. I notice a small girl, probably a year or two older than Ella, cowering in the corner. Her blonde pigtails and glasses look familiar. I reach out to her. She slowly comes to me.

"Savannah?" She nods and wipes her nose on her arm. "I'm Lexi. I went to school with your mom."

"I saw you at the bait store," she whimpers.

I nod as another masked man points his gun to a single-file line and motions for us to join it. I grab Ella and cling to her with an intensity I've never known. I fear if I let go, I may never see her again. Savannah grasps my other hand as if I'd just become her best friend or maybe her last chance.

A dozen M-16s usher us between two rows of long buildings with garage doors lining the sides. "MB's Storage" is stamped on each one. The place was nothing more than a vacant lot a few months ago and nobody seemed to know anything about the owners or what they were doing with the space. It was as if everything just appeared overnight. How could we not have noticed this? The line stops as a man with a clipboard scribbles notes and barks orders in a language I don't recognize. Women are shoved into units with guns to their backs while their daughters scream in terror. Ella is no exception. The door slams behind me and three other women, trapping Ella on the other side. The distinct click of a lock sends a shiver down my spine. Taking in my new surroundings, I identify my roommates. Cindy Clark from the hardware store, Misty Timmons, the school principal, and Jackie Thornwood, the homecoming queen my senior year. I slam my fist into the wall, pulling back a throbbing hand. The best way for me to help Ella is by staying calm and figuring this out.

A tiny sink sits in one corner, a metal toilet in the other. Four cot-sized beds hang from the wall. Jackie stares at the blue flannel sheets in disgust. Once again, I can't help but wonder how all this was organized right under our noses without anyone talking about it. It's possible the changes were made in the middle of the night and, since it's on the outskirts of town, nobody really noticed. It surely isn't important *now*.

"What the hell is happening?" Misty wrings her hands together, pacing the small space. "How did we all end up here?"

"Randy and I were at home talking to our daughter on the phone—she's in her senior year at Purdue University, you know—when the line went dead, and men burst through the door. I told Randy we needed to start locking it, but he insisted we live in a safe town," Cindy says.

Misty nods and shares how she was pumping gas when the place was suddenly surrounded, and everyone was forced into the trucks. Jackie, a single mother since her husband's tragic passing last year, had been on a boat with her young son. They were captured at the marina and separated. I share my story and we start talking about why this is happening and how to possibly get out of it, but nothing makes any sense.

When trays of sloppy sandwiches are shoved through a slot in the door, Jackie is the first to grab it up. We hadn't noticed the opening until now. I drop to my knees in front of it, pushing on the flap. It reminds me of a mail slot in some old houses I've seen. I try to see out of it, but it's too low to the ground so I give up and decide to eat with the other women.

I hold what must be week-old bread and two thin slices of mystery meat. "What are the chances this is poisoned?"

Jackie laughs between bites, but her chewing slows as she questions the thought.

"Surely, they wouldn't go to all this work just to poison us slowly," Cindy says, twisting her nose as she takes a small bite.

# Chapter 3

By the second day in the ten by twenty-foot prison, we've all nearly pulled our hair out worrying about our families. Hell, I'd give anything to fight with Clint about Christa again. I've whittled my fingernails down to the nub with the anxiety of not knowing where my son is and if he's okay. Ella is somewhere nearby, but still unreachable. I don't know how she is or if she's being mistreated, but I won't be any good to either of them if I let this break me. Despite all my pacing and conversing with my cellmates, nobody has a plan. It seems we're all just trapped here, and we don't know why.

I lose count of the passing days in a sequence of naps, mindless chatter, and never-ending conspiracy theories. The only sunlight to guide the days is provided through the slot in the door when food slips through two or three times a day. Caged animals are treated better, I fume silently, guessing we've been locked away for ten days. Could be more. Could be less. Though we've washed our clothes in the sink, my shirt still smells like I pulled it from a stale gym bag. My denim shorts are stiff, and I'd do almost anything for a real shower. A few times we swear there is laughter coming from outside, but as time passes, we convince ourselves we are hearing things.

When the doors finally open, we are herded into the parking lot of the storage facility. It takes a while for our eyes to adjust to the light, but we see now the area has a ten-foot fence with barbed wire around the top and guard stations along the outside. The mom-and-pop's grocery store next door has cars strewn haphazardly across the small parking lot like Tanner's matchbox cars on our living room floor. The thought of him fuels me to get answers and find my way back to him. Men dressed in black patrol the perimeter as women rush to find relatives and friends. With my thoughts on my children, I dash through the crowd, frantic to find Ella. Guards mingle between the mass of women who all seem to have the same question—where are the kids? Several women shake the sturdy gate that blocks us in, but it barely moves as they bombard it.

A hand falls heavily on my shoulder. I turn with a start. "Do you know where my daughter is?" The lady, probably in her mid-forties, searches my eyes from her dark circle-rimmed ones as if I have the answers. She might as well wear a sign that says she's a tourist.

"I don't. I'm looking for my own," I admit.

"She has red hair and more freckles than you can count," she pleads.

"I'll keep my eyes open for her."

"What does your daughter look like?"

Before I can answer, a siren wails and we are ushered back to our cages.

The door slams behind us and Misty immediately quizzes everyone on what they had learned. We don't have much as we go around the room. Nobody knows where the men or children are. She brainstorms as we eat another bland meal and, by bedtime, has assigned everyone a question to answer. Mine is to find out what I can about what is happening. Jackie is assigned to find the girls, Cindy will look for clues on where the men are being held, and Misty is going to try to find a way out.

The sun beats down on the new asphalt, making it unbearably hot during our time outside the next afternoon. The other women mingle as we all try to find answers. I head straight for a guard. Risky, but if it works, more effective than getting rumors. A woman in a yellow sundress with a fresh-from-the-beach tan grabs my arm as I pass. She pulls at strands of tangled hair and yanks me close.

"I heard they are going all over the country capturing small towns and turning the citizens into soldiers."

If she had said these words to me in the grocery store, I would've thought she was describing the plot to a horror film. I whisper my response. "Why?"

"So they have an army to take over the large cities." She releases me and disappears into the crowd.

I lose my nerve to approach the guard and watch the women interact instead. Some are frantic, while others appear disoriented, and a few remind me of zombies. What we need is to become organized, I think as the siren blares and we are ushered into our rooms. They aren't allowing us time to communicate, I note as the door slams behind us.

"That's absurd...right?" Misty asks when I tell them what I was told.

"I heard this is going to be some documentary about brainwashing people," Jackie says with a tiny laugh.

"I heard that they are a new terrorist group trying to make their name known," Cindy adds.

Jackie walks to the toilet and waits for us to turn our heads. "Don't terrorists just strap bombs to themselves and blow people up?"

"If they are terrorists then they are going to kill all of us at some point," Misty says. "What's the purpose of holding us here?"

Jackie flushes. "They could be trying to prove they can take over an entire town."

"Wouldn't it be more impressive if they captured a town bigger than a thousand people?"

"It depends on what their goal is."

"Okay, so let's focus on facts instead of rumors."

Having gone to bed with more questions than answers, I wake to the screeching of a speaker. Jackie hits her head on the top bunk as she jolts upright. Gibberish pours out in a language that has us all shaking our heads. The overhead light hanging between the sets of cots casts a low beam, as breakfast—stiff oatmeal and cold toast—is thrust inside our room. For five days—or so I gauge by the number of meals we are served, which is my new way of telling time—we listen to the same recording. It's worse than the year Ella insisted on listening to "Jingle Bells" from Halloween until Valentine's Day. The light stays dim, and the door remains closed. The only sight of daylight we have is when our meal tray slips through the slot.

Jackie shows the first signs of distress. She sits on her bed and rocks while the rest of us struggle to tune the gruff voice out. Cindy's eyes soon become nothing but a vacant stare as she repeats the recording. Misty and I join hands and tell every story we can think of to stave off whatever overtook our friends. I watch Jackie sink to the floor and claw at it with her fingers like she's been buried alive. Misty turns my head back to hers so we only see each other.

"We can't let it take us too."

"I told Clint I want a divorce," I say, having run out of every other secret I possess. And I certainly can't bring up the children we're all so worried about. It will only send us over the edge.

Cindy climbs onto the top bunk and stands on the bed, crouching to avoid the low ceiling. Misty releases my hands and pulls her down.

"*Qutil*," she whispers and lunges at me. I swiftly plant a right hook on her jaw, sending her to the floor.

"Lexi! You're letting it get to you," Misty says, bending over Cindy's limp body and I admit I may have taken out some anger on her that should've been directed at...Clint...the people holding us hostage...the situation. Jackie laughs and crawls over to Cindy. Hanging her head over Cindy's, she swings back and forth, giggling. Grabbing her by the hair, I pull her head up. Her facial features are sunken, and her eyes are glazed over. Misty splashes water on Cindy and we place the two on opposite cots. If I didn't know better, I'd guess they had never met.

"Me?!" I glare daggers at Misty. "She's the one acting possessed."

"*Hadm*," Cindy says, looking to Jackie, but her gaze seems to go straight through the other woman.

"Destroy," Jackie responds.

"*Qutil*."

"Kill."

The sirens sound as Misty and I stare at each other in horror. We hurry away from our cellmates as soon as there is enough space in the door.

I run into the crowd, glad to be free of the room. The awful recording still plays, but I ignore it and study the crowd. The women move as if in a drug-altered state. They are sluggish and most of them mutter to themselves, their attention drawn to the speakers in the corners of what we now refer to as the compound.

The woman in the yellow dress wanders by as I lull myself to blend in. "I heard one of the guards is sneaking people out. Only question is, which one?"

"Do you know where the men are?"

She cackles and slinks away.

I turn to Misty, but she is nowhere to be found. I mimic the actions of the zombies around me, pretending to stare at the large black boxes like it's the god I've always wanted, but I'm actually using my peripheral vision to find signs of a disloyal guard. The recording stops abruptly, only to resume a moment later from a single speaker. The mass of women turns to face the box making the noise. Playing the part of a pawn, I pivot when the noise is relocated to the speaker facing the grocery store. For the better part of what I believe to be an hour we play this game. My mind focuses on Clint, wondering if I made the right decision, and I almost miss the cues to rotate several times. I am so involved in the terms my lawyer drew up that it takes several minutes for me to be fully aware the children have been released. It takes everything I have not to run to Ella when I spot her in the crowd of children who have formed a line near the fence. They chant the words with the speaker as if they have been programmed to do so. One woman, who is missing a shoe, makes a mad dash for one of the girls and is shot before she can reach her. I gasp. A guard searches the crowd for the noise as the woman's body is dragged from the site. It might as well have been a fictional death on TV judging from the reactions. It's as if I'm the only person who witnessed the brutal killing. Guards swarm the crowd and, once satisfied at their progress, the siren blares and we are ushered back inside like cattle. Smells like a pig pen, though, I think, pulling my stained red tank top away from my body.

Cindy immediately finds a spot on the wall to stare at when we are locked in our cell while Jackie goes back to digging at the tiny broken piece of concrete with her nail.

"I've never seen anything like that," I tell Misty. She smooths every wrinkle out of her bed. "Not even on TV," I add. Unsatisfied with the results, she flings the cover back and starts over.

I try to reach her until our dinner is shoved through the slot in the door before relinquishing the fact that I'm all alone. I cry myself to sleep without touching the cold chicken and lumpy potatoes.

# Chapter 4

I spend the next several days memorizing people when they let us outside. The woman in the yellow dress carefully blends in, but always has tidbits to spew as she wanders by.

"They're going to get control of our country," she whispers the first day.

"Find the guard," she orders the next and "Get out now" she demands on the third.

It's another two days before I catch my break. We're outside doing jumping jacks, as ordered, when the woman next to me doubles over in a coughing fit.

One of the guards hurries over as she bends to catch her breath. "Are you sick?"

The woman nods.

As the figure, drenched in black, examines her, she slips her hand slyly into her hijab, flipping the underside of one corner over. A small white dove is ironed out of sight to the unknowing eye. I stop only briefly and wonder where I've seen that dove and why she's showing it to me.

In the midst of burpees, it dawns on me. The woman in the yellow dress has earrings that match the dove. She's nowhere in sight.

That night, I try to explain my theories to Misty. It's no use. I make my decision in the dim light while trying to fight off the wolves in my room. I know they know I'm not one of them and they are closing in. I don't have much time.

When we are released for more physical activity the next morning, my plan is dropped in my lap. As we are taking our places, the woman in the yellow dress, who has reappeared, drops an earring as she passes me. She pretends not to notice, but I'm certain it's done on purpose. I slide it into my fist as we begin push-ups and slip it into my pocket before we run laps around the perimeter. The woman with the coughing fit from the day before is absent. I'm sure of it. I had been trying to get a head count, but it seems

I keep coming up with a lower number than the day before. Could be a coincidence, but it's the only hope I have, and it's clouded with fear.

Another day passes, another brush with the woman in yellow.

"Tonight," she breathes in passing. She wears a single earring shaped like a dove.

The day lingers like the pungent odor hanging in the air from lack of proper bathing. The familiar recording and children's chanting now has English words mixed in—control, fear, destruction, and weak—but it still doesn't make sense. I continue to tune it out as I work to reassure myself that I can't leave Clint now. Not in the middle of whatever this is. Allies are going to be hard to come by. Even the girl who grew up down the street from me has become a stranger. I anxiously try to figure out how I'm going to stow Ella away for whatever the woman with the dove earrings has planned. I can't leave without her, but can I leave *with* her? I position myself as close to her as I can throughout our rigorous workout, but never get within feet of her. The siren sounds. I'm out of time.

Back in the room, I flop on my bed and cry. The noise attracts the attention of women I once knew like sharks to fresh blood. They circle around me, staring. Jackie picks at my tears and pulls at her eyelids. Outside, the monotoned mantra plays quieter, and orders are yelled in the same gruff foreign language. A tray is slipped inside and the wolves lurch toward it, sending a tiny slip of paper floating to the ground. I wait until they dig into their meals before sliding over and covering it with my foot. Between bites, I move the paper to my hand, stuffing it into my pocket when they aren't looking. Well after they have gone to sleep, I pull it out.

"This nation will remain the land of the free only so long as it is the home of the brave—Elmer Davis." A dove is drawn beneath the quote. I sit, convinced this is not a trap like I had earlier thought. Twirling the earring in my hand, I wait.

# Chapter 5

The metal slot squeaks open in the still of night. I freeze as a hand reaches in, unfolding a single earring in its palm. My hand trembles as I place the matching one next to it. The door creaks open enough for me to slide under. The woman flashes the dove on her headwrap and whisks me away by the arm. We stay along the side of the building as I follow her blindly to the back fence, hoping my instincts don't fail me. I steal a glance behind us and find the other walls still guarded. We stop at a gate made for pedestrian traffic only. She quickly unlocks it and slides a folded slip of paper into my hand.

"I sent your daughter on a mission to guard those trees," she whispers, pointing to the lightly wooded area behind the grocery store. With that she shoves me to the other side of the fence. Without looking back, I make my mad dash for the cover of the trees.

Ella is there, as promised, her vacant eyes glued to a large oak. She's changed from the shorts and tank top she was wearing when we left our house and now dons the black garb of the enemy. I throw myself against her, desperate to feel her arms around me, but I'm left disappointed when she stands there like a statue. I try to drag her into the silence of the night, but her feet are firmly planted.

"We have to go," I tell her.

"Guard tree," she responds flatly.

"Don't you want to see Daddy and Tanner?"

She points. "Guard tree."

*What would Clint do? Find a house and hide out or try to make it home? Would he even look for us there or would he go for his other children? They seem to hold more power over him than we ever could.*

As I stew, I get an idea. I position myself between Ella and the tree, which is difficult because she keeps moving to get a better view. Grabbing her, I force her to focus on me. "They sent me to get you. We have a new mission."

"What?"

"We have to find a house. The address is on this piece of paper." I hold it out for her to see.

"Where?"

I open it and read, "United we stand," but what I tell her is our address. She nods. I find a large stick and we begin walking behind the small string of shops. A hardware store is the third building, and we might be able to get inside to find weapons. We creep along the brick until we come to a back door. I hold a protective arm over Ella as I glance into the dark building.

"We're going to go inside to see if we can find a few things," I whisper.

Ella turns in the direction we came from. "I want to go back. I don't like this mission." She takes a step away from me.

I grab her arm. "They have popcorn, remember?" *Crap. There won't be any made.* "Or you can get candy. We can even take some to Tanner and Daddy."

I hold my stick like a bat and creep toward the gardening aisle with Ella close behind. The light from the moon dances through the overhead windows, creating eerie shadows on the floor. I snatch a hiking bag from an end cap as we pass.

I toss some rope in the bag as we weave through the aisles. "You remember the first time we took you fishing?" She remains silent. "You were so scared to touch the fish. It wasn't long before you were hooked though. Do you want to go fishing again?"

Tossing in some duct tape, I remind her of her first day of school and how she soon became friends with Casey. Still no response. I grab several flashlights, batteries, and some small knives as we come to the gardening tool aisle. Shovels and rakes line the shelves, but machetes, axes, and everything else that can be used as real weapons are missing.

"You were so excited to be a big sister," I tell her as we approach the register for candy and other edible items. "From the day we brought Tanner home, you've always protected him. He's in trouble now and needs our help." I empty the boxes of various candy bars into the bag.

"Tanner," Ella whispers as if she's trying to picture him.

After throwing bottled drinks into the growing bag, I sling it on my back and take Ella's hand. We're almost to the door when a clang on the tile floor halts us. A thin shimmer of light leaks in from the cracked door. I'm certain I shut it behind us but clearly, we are not alone. My palm sweats into Ella's calm hand as I lurch for the tiny opening to the restroom door. Ella's scream echoes into the vacant building as a squirrel scampers into our path. I narrowly avoid tripping over the rodent, but don't stop as I veer our course to the main door.

My heart beats heavily as we cautiously continue our journey along the buildings. If we can make it to the West Lake and follow the shore, we can cross the residential area, the main road, and circle around to get home. I hurry Ella along, acting like a member of the SWAT team, until we are safely concealed between houses, each adorned with a black *X*. We run alongside the edge of a single-story house with paint chipping from the wood planks. We stop to catch our breath behind a bush near one of the doors and I contemplate going in. Maybe they have a gun. I hug Ella tightly, as if it might be the last I ever give her. I know I shouldn't take her in with me, but I can't leave her outside either. Deciding sticking together is the best option, I scavenge the bag for a long screwdriver and pull her inside the unlocked door behind me. I keep the tool in striking pose, though I know it's no match for anyone I may encounter. Tiptoeing down the vinyl floor, I check each room until I stumble across the master bedroom. I ransack the nightstand and turn to the dresser when I don't find what I'm looking for. A jewelry box spews cubic zirconium pieces across the top of the scratched wooden top.

Crouching near the bed, I peer underneath. The outline of a rifle case has me smiling. I eagerly retrieve it and throw the top open. It's empty.

"Damn," I mutter, concealing it.

We leave the house with nothing more than a half-eaten bag of Doritos swiped from the kitchen counter.

We step onto the road as a single beam of light scans the neighbor's yard and a distant humming sound reaches my ears. I whisk Ella into the bush behind me, the roaring hum drawing closer. I curse myself for forgetting 'normal' sounds are no longer normal. A large military-issue truck passes slowly, the light shining against the house as it passes. I clap my hand over Ella's mouth in case she has any notions of trying to rejoin them. A reflection plays off metal at my feet as the beam threatens to reveal us. We wait in the darkness and I bend to examine the object. A machete lies near the base of our hideout, a clear chunk missing from the bush.

When I can no longer hear the hum of the engine, I pull Ella through the shaggy grass and across the road. We would probably be safe to hide in any of the houses on this block, but we'd be stuck come dawn. It's better to keep moving.

Two blocks later I stop in the middle of the street when we come to the park. Ella bolts for the swings before I can stop her. I let her swing for a minute, knowing it will help bring her out of her condition. When the chains start squeaking, I quietly tell her we have to get to Tanner.

"Tanner likes to play in the sandbox," she says.

"Yes, he does. Let's go find him," I reply, hoping she's coming back to me.

As we stand there, exposed, I route a plan in my head for us to make it across the main road. A low humming distracts my thoughts and has me searching frantically for the source.

Ella points to a drone almost directly above us. "They've found me!"

With a machete in one hand and Ella's wrist firmly in my other, I feel like a villain in a bad horror movie as I drag her to the dark house across the street. Her screams drown the sound of the hovering device, making it hard to detect its location. We dart behind a garage and around several large trees to the corner of the next house.

"Quiet!" Ella's shrieks abruptly stop at my command.

The whirring is nearby as, I'm sure, are the men manning the drone.

"There," Ella points. Whose side is she on, I wonder, ducking into the breezeway she discovered. We pause to catch our breath until the device maneuvers its way under the open door. Ella switches back to the other team and waves to it. I release her arm and firmly grasp both hands on the machete.

"Get back," I order gruffly, swinging like a maniac. It eludes the first two strikes, but the third takes it down. I open the door to the house as a louder rumbling grows closer, accompanied with shouting.

Ella smacks her hands together. "They're coming for me!"

I bend to Ella's level. "It's either them or Tanner," I whisper.

Her eyes register a hint of conflict. With a shaking finger, she points. "They have a camper."

Leaving the door to the house open, we dash for the one leading to the garage. A large fifth wheel is hidden inside. Lights from a Humvee illuminate against the back wall through a dusty window. Shadows blink across the beams as men disperse on foot. I scramble with the door handle, only to find it locked. Urging Ella underneath, I rush to the back where the access panel leads to storage under the bed. It opens with a squeak as voices bark in another language just outside the building. I toss our possessions to the side of the empty compartment and motion for Ella to come quickly. She slides in and I'm certain the flap has no more than closed when boots slap the pavement inside the garage.

Ella whispers in the darkness and I pray she isn't as loud as she sounds to me. "We're playing hide-and-seek, Mommy," she whispers.

With my finger, I feel for her mouth and cover it, hoping it convinces her to stay quiet.

A sharp bang against the frail metal door comes after a brief jiggling of the handle. The camper sways as they search. Nanoseconds couldn't go by slower as I wait for the coast to clear. The movement stops but the loud closing of the door never happens. I don't know if they've set a trap or given up, but claustrophobia sets in and I push the bed away from us. After peeking out the tiny windows, I examine the damage to the door. There's no way of locking it or even closing it now. I go back to the bed where Ella stands and pull her from it.

"We'll stay here for a few hours. Let's try to get some sleep."

"Okay, Momma," she says and snuggles into me after I pull the bed into position.

My thoughts turn to Tanner as Ella's breathing shallows. Warm tears roll over my cheeks onto the mattress. Sleep isn't going to come for me. I'm torn between trying to find the rest of my family and protecting what I have left. It's a nasty game of 'What Would You Rather?' inside my head. I've never been good at shutting my brain off and I can't help but think that may be the very thing that saved me from turning into a brainwashed zombie during the awful recording. What did it mean anyway? Why would they change a few words to English and leave the rest in...terrorist code? And what was with the woman who helped us escape? Could she really be the spy she appeared to be? I wish I would've asked what her plan was by letting us go. Maybe I should've stayed behind and helped. Too late now. Our only option is to get to safety, but where is safe? Have they done this all over the country like the woman in yellow said or did they pick a speck on the map to terrorize?

There is no way to be certain, but the thought that we aren't alone is both comforting and terrifying at the same time. Surely the military is all over this. Except, those were our vehicles the men had gotten out of. Did that mean they are friendly? I wouldn't bet my life on it.

I gently wake Ella after a restless few hours, long enough for us to move before the sunrise. Her eyes pop open and, with a vacant stare, she proclaims, "*Sawf taemal balnsbt lana.*"

I firmly grasp her shoulders. "What does that mean?"

"*Hadhih al'ard satakun lana.* It is time *balnsbt lana li'iieadatiha.*"

*It is time for what?* I gently slap her cheeks until the black fades from her pupils. "It's time to go."

"Are we getting our land back now?"

I inhale slowly and picture myself on the beach. The waves lap against my feet as I quietly count to ten.

"*Hadm...qutil...lana...*"

I sit on the bed for a moment and listen as Ella starts at the beginning of the mantra and try to make sense of it.

As she mutters along, I wait for the English words—kill, takeover, destroy. I listen until the end. Twice. Grabbing her hand, I drag her outside the camper and into the garage. She continues to recite as if there will be a quiz.

"Ours. It will be ours," she chants while I force her into the cool night air. I wish I had a jacket, but the chill isn't affecting her in her altered state. She's a complete zombie to the words she speaks. Between the invasion that has turned my hometown into a ghost-town, the starless night, and her frightening monologue, even my bones are terrified. I pull her down the street to the Gillman's, wondering if we've somehow been sucked into one of Stephen King's novels. The vibrant red of the Gillman's front door is tainted with the same sloppy *X* as the rest of the houses we've passed. Ella and I stand on the porch staring at it and I wonder if there is the same marking on our door. The thought of someone violating our home makes me shudder, but there's no time to worry about that now. We will cross that bridge when we get to it and right now, my biggest concern is how to get there. Crickets chirp in the still night air and I have to look at Ella to be sure she has stopped talking.

"Momma, do you think Ashley is okay?"

I bend to hug Ella, thankful her big heart pulled her from the black hole she sank into. It is part of the reason I stopped at the Gillman's. Their daughter, Ashley, is in Ella's third grade class and the two ride the same bus.

"I'm sure her mom is looking out for her."

"We need to help her."

I kiss her forehead. "I know, baby. We will, but right now we have to figure out how. Let's go inside and see if they have a gun we can borrow." Her pupils grow as large as saucers. "While I'm doing that, why don't you go to Ashley's room and see if she has a doll you can take her when we rescue her." I know I'm misleading her, but it's my only hope to keep her from slipping into the darkness I know could consume her.

Her little head bobs up and down as I take her hand and slowly turn the doorknob. It's unlocked, as I assumed it would be. Ella's tiny hand slips out of mine and she flips on the light in the Gillman's entryway. I quickly hit the switch again and whisper, "We have to leave the lights off." She nods and drags me through the room and turns to the right in the doorway. In her haste, she trips over a chair that hasn't been pushed back into the kitchen table. It clatters to the floor with her on top of it. I jump and freeze all at the same time. Ella lets out a whimper and I rush to her aide. I swing open the refrigerator door on my way so I can see if there's any blood. The soft glow of the fifteen-watt bulb casts just enough light into the room. As I dust her off, I notice plates of hardened pasta on the table. Ella's eyes follow my gaze and it quiets her sobs. The family had been eating dinner when they were forced from their home. Though we know the Gillmans well enough that I know they wouldn't mind us being in their home, I pick up the chair and tell myself we aren't the intruders.

"Let's have a race," I whisper, hoping to get her mind off the creepy scene. "You see if you can find a doll and I'll see if Mr. Gillman has what I'm looking for. The first one back to the fridge wins."

Ella takes a long look at the table, complete with a film of spilled milk from a tipped glass, then sprints toward the darkness leading to her friend's room. I leave the fridge door open and hurry to the bedroom on the other side of the kitchen. I can almost hear the clock ticking. I'm not just racing Ella finding a doll. An empty rifle case lies open on the bed, a clear sign I won't find anything easily. After a quick search, I run back to the kitchen. Ella isn't by the refrigerator, and I don't know whether to be relieved or scared. Adrenaline courses through my veins as I slam the door closed on the beeping appliance.

"Ella," I call, heading toward Ashley's room. It's empty as well. I call her name a little louder, frantically searching the back of the house where the office and guest room are located. Empty. My heart stops in my chest as I freeze on my way back to the kitchen. The front door is wide open. I grab a sweatshirt off the rack near the door and carefully close it behind me. Awkwardly slipping the garment on around the machete and pack, I glance in the direction that would lead us to our house—if one knew the correct turns to get back to the main road—and squint to hopefully find a lone girl in the darkness. Nothing. My lungs pound against my ribcage as I turn my head in the way of the terrorist prison. If she has gone straight in that direction, she will run right into it. I make binoculars with my hands like it will magically bring her into focus. When I spot a tiny black speck under the glow of a streetlight, I'm sure my mind is playing tricks on me. None-the-less, I sprint down the street as fast as my five-foot ten-inch frame will carry me. Code Blue, I whisper. Except this isn't work and I'm not racing to save the life of someone else's loved one. This is *my* loved one and if I fail—no, I can't think like that. Shoes. Be thankful you wore a sensible pair of tennis shoes to get ice cream. That's what we do after losing a patient—find something to be thankful for. Everyone who stepped into the hospice room, whether it be to bring food, check vitals, or administer meds, we all write a note on the patient's white board of something we're thankful for and how the patient made us appreciate what most take for granted. It's our way of showing the family their loved one made an impact in their last days and that there is always something to be thankful for. It's one of the major reasons I haven't left Clint yet. I'm still thankful he came into my life.

My soles slap the pavement and, to me, it sounds like a mallet hitting a gong in the deathly silence of the night. I close in on the tiny figure who clearly isn't aware of anything but her mission. She may be my daughter, but I've never been more afraid to approach her. This is uncharted territory and I don't want to make a wrong move. If I grab her from behind and cover her mouth, she may fight and we're now close enough I can see the spotlights shining into the compound. A guard from the watch tower searches the outside perimeter. Like anyone would be crazy enough to approach. Except us. As the light moves closer to Ella, I softly call her name. No response. Usain Bolt couldn't have beat me in the last hundred yards that separate me from my daughter. My feet slam the asphalt in a way I didn't know possible and, as I reach her, I cover her mouth and wrap my arm around her, ducking behind a tree in one fluid movement moments before a light passes us. She flails and kicks so violently that the machete slides away from the tree. I fear when the light scans the area again, it will cast a reflection and reveal us. I wrap my legs around her as I struggle to keep hidden and catch my breath. When she bites my hand, I grit my teeth.

"Ella, it's me," I whisper. I might as well have been the second cousin of my mother's great grandma for all the recognition I get. With my foot, I inch the weapon out of sight as the light starts for us again. Ella goes limp in my arms and I relax my hold on her. Having been the one to teach her that trick, I shouldn't have been surprised when she wiggles an arm free and pokes me in the eye. Instinctively, I double over and clutch my face. If the situation were any different, I would be proud as hell as I watch her run away. But this is worst case scenario. I run straight into the light after her. An alarm sounds the moment I'm spotted, but I have no choice except to fight. I reach Ella at the fence. The light frozen on us; she drops the doll.

"Ella!"

"I wanna go home, Momma," she cries.

"Then, run!" I grab her hand, dragging her away from the boots reverberating against the metal grates of the watchtower row as men rush toward the stairs. Sharp commands pierce the air. The whir of a drone is quickly drowned out by a vehicle, no doubt a military model, coming from behind the compound.

Ella's little feet fly off the road in a way I'm sure makes her look like our neighbor's roadrunner yard spinner in a steady wind. We duck into an alley with the drone overhead and the vehicle not far behind. Combat boots storm the pavement as I try to devise a plan. Buildings line either side of us and, having ridden my bike down every street and alley in the town as a child, I know there is no way out of the narrow gravel lane. By the time we reach the end, we are likely to be met with men clad in black. I yank Ella to a stop just past the side entrance to Deanna's Donuts and whip her back into the two-inch crevice that offsets the door. Twisting the fifty-year-old brass knob, I find it unlocked, because apparently the whole town is unguarded except for the brainwashing stations. Although, the fact that anything is left unlocked isn't a shock in our town, considering everyone knows everyone.

The smell of stale donuts wafts through the air as thick as the flies swarming the smudged display cases. Ella's hand shakes in mine as I make a mental map of the surrounding buildings and streets. The men will have followed the drone to our location and should arrive in a matter of minutes. If we head out the front door, we'll run right into them. Our only option is to leave through the same door we entered. The men in pursuit round the corner as we emerge from the bakery, charging us like we're in a wild west movie. My eyes dart to the bricks, hoping to find the fire escape my childhood friend, Jamie, and I had once climbed on a dare. It was rusty then and I can only imagine how unsafe it is now. All those years ago, we realized—halfway up—that the top bolt wasn't attached, but with boys watching, we couldn't stop. The entire unit had come unattached on one side and swung loose with us three rungs from the top. We finally made it to the roof, but the fire department had had to rescue us, and we were grounded for most of the summer. Judging by the looks of it, they did a shoddy job of repairing it, and that was twenty-some years ago.

"Up the fire escape!" I hoist Ella up and plant her firmly on the highest rung I can manage. Ella moves her head back and forth in the way she does when she's made up her mind she's *not* going to do something. "Trust me," I yell against the slapping on the pavement. The soldiers appear to be struggling not to break formation as they press on at break-neck speeds. Tucking the machete into the straps on the bag, I curse under my breath. I shove Ella's dirty behind up until she begins moving on her own. The men close in with their rifles drawn. Gibberish comes from the back as they anxiously await the order to attack. My breath stops in my chest as Ella clambers upward. Her foot slips off a railing and I'm trying to steady her when fingers grip tightly around my ankle. I scream, kicking fervently. My shoe slips from my foot in the process of trying to break free. Ella stops mid-climb and the look of horror on her face gives me the strength to lean backward with one hand clinging to the creaking metal.

"Go!" I command her while trying to fight the burly man off with my free hand. I try briefly to reach my weapon but it's no use. He bobs and weaves my jabs until sweat beads heavily on the hand clinging desperately to the thin metal rod. My foot finds his nose, a light cracking sound escaping as it makes contact. He curses, his grip loosening as he clutches his crooked beak. I scramble farther up the ladder as hands clamber for my long legs. Ella waits safely on the roof with tears rolling down her face. Men almost fight each other up the ladder as we take the chase a level higher. I drag Ella across the tar-covered surface, peering over the edge every twenty feet. There is a canopy off the flower shop if I remember correctly. Now, if only we don't pass it. The men are on our heels in less than a minute. I give Ella credit, she's moving faster than when she races Tanner for the last cookie. Spotting the faded canopy, I push harder, swinging us over the edge seconds before large hands make a swipe at Ella.

The condition of the aged fabric is an unfortunate oversight on my part. The rip starts slowly and grows until my foot slips through the hole.

"Scoot to the bottom," I instruct Ella as I shimmy inside the tear. Staring into the faces covered in black above us, I drop six feet to a table below. Becoming unbalanced, it topples over and I roll into the fall. "Jump!" I yell over the impending sound of military trucks. She clings to the metal rod, staring at the men with their guns drawn. I stand under her with outstretched hands. She leaps as the trucks stop within feet of reaching us. We are running before she has time to steady herself. Across the street and through a narrow alley, we come to a side street with men close on our heels. They seem reluctant to use their guns and I can't understand why.

We aren't going the right direction to get us home and I try frantically to come up with a plan. There is little chance of hiding with them so close behind. It takes great effort to make it across the streets without checking for traffic, but we manage. We are almost to the edge of town where our hope lies in getting into the mountains unseen. *Why haven't they caught us yet? Surely grown men can keep up with a woman and child. It's like they* want *us to escape,* I think as we sprint along the main street. My left foot throbs as gravel embeds itself into the nicks suffered on the roof, but I push on. A quick backward glance reveals that we are no longer being followed...by people. The glow of a streetlight exposes another drone heading our way. *They must be playing games. Maybe they are trying to see what we'll do, how we'll react to the situation. That must be it.*

Ella interrupts my thoughts as we pass Arthur's Horse Stables at a pace too leisurely for being on the run. "Look at the horsies, Mommy," she says.

I turn so sharply into the stables that it almost yanks her off her feet. She'd been looking at the horses in the ten-acre pasture, but I know we don't have time to catch a horse.

Inside the stable, I grab a bridle off the wall and open the first stall holding a horse. She's a gorgeous chestnut mare, though a little thin from unavoidable neglect, and is clearly anxious to be free. As calmly as possible, I slip the bit in her mouth and throw Ella on her back. She whinnies as I dig into her flanks and guide her into the night. With a drone buzzing overhead, we cross in front of an approaching Humvee and plow through Judge Wheeler's yard. I lean into Ella, clutching her torso as I dig my heels into the mare. Screeching tires scream behind us but we're already across the next road. I want to shout, "The British are coming!" like Clint and I did on our first date, but this is hardly the joke it was when Clint's horse got spooked and took him on a wild ride. The British aren't driving angry armored trucks with automatic rifles they seem reluctant to use. Although, our real-life ghost-town could be similar to what Paul Revere experienced. Forcing my thoughts away from an ancient war and how charming Clint was that day, I formulate yet another escape plan. Bowerman's Apple Orchard should be up ahead with a few carefully maneuvered turns. The sound of hooves pounding the pavement mixes with the growl of the drone as it follows in the sky. All else is quiet. I steer the horse past the Baptist church, and she runs with a fury I've never experienced, as if she realizes what's at stake. She leaps over the immaculate white picket fence of the orchard in a graceful bound. Past the trees is the cover of the forest and, hopefully, our freedom. The trucks have returned and crush the fence like toothpicks as I urge the mare forward. Orders are yelled when they are forced to stop at the rows of trees. We are almost to the back fence when I hear an order in plain English.

"It's a woman and her kid. What can they possibly do?"

"You'll see," I whisper as we leap the fence.

# Chapter 6

After crossing a creek and a section of deserted highway, the mare carries us through a small patch of woods that, if my calculations are correct, should lead us to the back of our house. The drone vanishes, leaving us with only the sounds of coyotes and the occasional owl. My navigation is pretty accurate. We ease out of the forest in the neighbor's yard. Their house is pitch black. They're either asleep or they've been taken as well. I force the horse's gait to a walk and circle around to the front of the house. A giant *X* tells me all I need to know. With a gentle nudge of my knees, I guide the horse to our mailbox, a football field from the abandoned brick ranch. I shove my shoe inside, leaving the toe exposed, and inch the mare to the side of our hundred-year-old farmhouse. We walk the perimeter as I look and listen for signs of trouble. When I'm convinced we won't be ambushed, I steer us in the direction of our large white barn. Jak, the black and white cat who adopted us, strolls inside as if nothing is wrong in the feline world. I stop the horse, who happily munches on the tall grass, and place Ella on the ground.

I dismount and grab Ella by the shoulders. "I want you to climb to the back of the hayloft, you think you can do that?"

"Are we going back?"

*Great. She still wants to be on their side. I'll have to figure that out later. For now, I'll have to improvise.* "I need to run into the house and get some things first." I hand her a rock. "If anyone tries to come in the barn, you hit them with this."

"Why?"

"You get extra points," I lamely explain.

She shrugs and takes the stone. "What if I hit you by mistake?"

"I'll whistle first."

"Hurry," she whispers.

I wait for her to get out of sight and run for the house. It doesn't occur to me to tie up the horse until I'm lifting the faulty screen door off the broken hinge Clint said he'd fix when we have the money, but I figure her empty stomach will keep her nearby for a few minutes anyway. Scanning the four-by-ten-foot walls of flaking paint, I search for—what exactly? The loads of dirty laundry piled around the washer certainly won't do any good. I pull the machete from my back and twist the knob to the inside door. It refuses to open, but that's nothing new. I jab the wood with my foot and let out a small cry, a very real reminder that I lost my shoes. It squeaks open into a dark kitchen. After fooling around under the sink, I find a dim flashlight. I'm going to have to get better about replacing batteries, I chide myself as I make my way upstairs to my bedroom for another hiking bag. The stairs creak under each step and the railing wobbles as my hand slides along it. It, too, needs fixed, but as the kids got older, its priority fell to the wayside. I find I'm holding my breath as I reach Ella's pink bedroom door at the top of the stairwell. Glancing longingly at Tanner's door across the hall, I force myself two doors down to the room I share with Clint.

I kick the cracked door open with my foot; machete poised. Seeing no visible threat, I drop it on the bed and empty the contents of my pack.

My right arm is twisted behind my back and I'm on my knees before I can register someone else in the room. Cold metal presses into the back of my neck and I'm shoved to the floor like I'd just robbed a bank. The dim glow from the flashlight shines under the bed as it rolls across the floor. A set of blinking eyes stare at me.

"Tanner?"

"Lexi?"

I'm released from my hold and whisked onto my back. Clint stares down at me, very clearly as surprised to see me as I am to see him. There is a clink on our hardwood floor as he drops his weapon, whisking me straight from the floor into his arms in a standing position. I let him hold me like a ragdoll as I inhale the pungent odor from his stale shirt. I soak it in happily, slowly convincing myself he's not a figment of my imagination. Finally, he steadies me on my feet and swoops me into a firm embrace. A tiny hand tugs at ours.

"You were gonna shoot me with a flashlight?" I laugh, seeing the Maglite he'd been holding.

"Of course not, I was gonna whack you with it. I didn't hurt you, did I?" He tenderly takes my wrist he'd been twisting and examines it.

"I'm fine."

"I thought we'd been followed."

"How'd you get here?"

Clint steps into the hallway. "Where's Ella?"

I yank Tanner's hand, pulling him toward the door. "Come on. We need to run to the barn and get her."

"Why the hell is she in the barn?" Clint barks.

"I thought she would be safer there."

His lips form a tight line. "As opposed to in the house with someone who could protect her?"

"I was afraid there might be someone in the house."

"So you left her alone in the barn? How does that make sense?" His voice rises, and Tanner wraps his arms around my leg.

Putting my arm around the frightened child, I stare Clint dead in the eyes. "Looks like I was right, doesn't it?"

"Tanner, go out and get your sister," Clint commands.

I grab Tanner's arm before he can bolt out the door. "I don't think that's a good idea. She isn't herself."

"Tanner, get your sister," Clint repeats.

"Clint, it's not safe."

"I'm not going to have her out there by herself."

"She's not one of us right now."

"Tanner—sister—now!"

Tanner, scared to leave and scared to stay, turns to me.

Knowing I'm defeated, I pull him close and hope he can reverse the changes in his sister. "Listen, Tanner, when you get out there you need to whistle so she knows it's safe. Do you know how to do that?" Scrunching his face up, he blows air and spit in my face. "Okay, how about you just say her name quietly? She'll know it's you. And you need to walk so you don't scare the horse."

His eyes grow wide as if I'd just told him a spaceship landed in our yard. Clint glares at me as if I'd just brought home a pet without his permission. "We have a horse?"

"Looks like it," I tell him. I wait until Tanner has left the room to add, "Unless she's run off."

Clint waits for the stomping as Tanner runs down the stairs to subside. "I can't believe you left Ella outside with no way to protect herself."

"It was either leave her hiding in the loft or bring her in here and risk us both being caught." That does nothing to soften his mood. "She has a rock," I admit.

"Great. A pebble goes a long way against a grown man."

"It worked on Goliath." Odd that I remembered the one Sunday School lesson from the one time my grandma took me to church.

"This isn't the time to be a smart-ass. We're not in biblical times. This is serious."

"I know, Clint. Why do you think I had her stay in the barn?"

"I don't know Alexis, *why* did you have her stay in the barn?"

Suddenly I feel like a teenager answering to a late curfew. "If something happened to me in here, I wanted her to be able to get away."

"Where would she go? There's nobody for miles to help her! And if she is one of them, she shouldn't be trusted alone."

"She comes and goes. It's like there's a faulty wire in her brain. She was okay when I left," I say. Truth is, I'm not sure, but she would've slowed me down and I hoped being in a familiar surrounding would jog her memory. "I let her get out of my sight once before and they almost caught us again. I wouldn't have left her if I thought she'd run off."

"You let her out of your sight?! Talk about faulty wiring. How could you?" He paces the length of the bed. "Don't ever gamble with our children's lives again."

"Clint, you have *no* idea what we've been through. Isn't it better for her to have a chance than to be taken back to *that*?"

"You think I don't know what you've been through? Are you serious?! They were brainwashing people at Camp Mush-For-Brains and you think *I* don't know what you've been through? You're smarter than that."

"You didn't see her, Clint. You don't know."

Feet bounding up the stairs quiets Clint's voice. "We need to get out of here before they find us and turn us into their puppets."

*What do you do with a few thousand puppets?* Ella rushes into the room and leaps onto Clint.

Tanner tugs on my shirt. "Are we really keeping the horse?"

"We are," I say, despite the annoyed look from Clint.

"We need to pack," Clint demands. "Ella and Tanner go grab your backpacks. Ella, you put as much bottled water in yours as you can and fill Tanner's with food."

The kids run off and I turn to Clint as he hands me his hiking pack. "You really think it's a good idea to let a six and eight-year-old pack food?"

"Is everything going to be a fight?" He throws a change of clothes into his pack as I quickly change what I'm wearing, although I'd give anything for a quick shower. "Are you really changing right now?"

"I've been wearing the same clothes for weeks, so yes, I'm *really* changing right now. Be lucky I don't insist on a shower."

"You understand we can't stay here, don't you?"

"They've already checked the house."

"I know—my guns are gone—but that doesn't mean they aren't monitoring the area. Start packing." He jams a few shirts into a hiking bag without bothering to fold them for optimum space. "Make sure you get medical supplies."

Gritting my teeth, I head to our bathroom and empty the medicine cabinet contents into it. I also throw in shampoo, soap, a razor, and every tampon in sight. I almost leave when I spot the empty toilet paper roll. If I know Clint, he's planning on heading deep in the mountains. I pack every roll from under the sink. With the bag now half-full, I toss in my favorite shirt, jeans, a pair of shorts, a handful of underwear and two clean bras. Grabbing my boots on the way out, I head to the kids' rooms to get the same for them. Clint has disappeared to the garage by the time I make it to the kitchen to supervise the packing in there.

Taking the Lucky Charms from Tanner's bag, I start pulling cans from the pantry. "Go change your clothes." Ella pouts as I remove a box of Little Debbie brownies.

Clint enters just in time to see an empty bag and food scattered all over the counter. "What the hell?!"

"Daddy, don't say bad words," Ella scolds. Clearly the switch has been flipped.

"We can't live off sugary snacks," I say in reply to his irritation.

"Hurry up," he booms, opening the junk drawer for a hammer.

I throw cans of Spam, SpaghettiOs, half a bag of potatoes, and various canned goods yanked from the shelf and throw them inside the bag until Tanner and Ella return in fresh clothing and Clint's glare says we've had enough time. Tanner clings to his cereal and Ella to the brownies with pleading eyes. With a deep breath, I cram them both inside the bag and struggle to fasten it.

"Let's go," Clint orders. I almost lock the door behind us but remember the rest of the houses we entered were unlocked. It might be a clue if the place is being monitored.

The horse still grazes near the barn under a gray horizon as I hoist the kids onto her back. Clint drops his pack and races to the barn. He returns with a length of rope and a large case. I can only imagine which weapon he's been hiding from me. After he uses the rope to make saddlebags out of our luggage, we start down the gravel lane leading to the woods on the opposite side of our house.

"Where did you get that?" I growl in as quiet a voice as I can muster.

"It's my birthday present," he says sheepishly and adds, "Aren't you glad I got it early?"

"Your birthday isn't for three months," I say through gritted teeth.

"It was on sale two months ago. And it's going to come in handy."

I guide the horse around a tree and go deeper into the mountains. "How much did you pay for that?"

"It's priceless."

I bite my lip hard enough to draw blood as I try to keep my cool. "Why didn't they take that when they got your guns?"

He shrugs. I want to smack the smirk off his face. "Because I hid it in the hood of the C-10."

I clench my fist around the leather strap in my hand and start to ask what else he's hiding in the gutted engine compartment of his grandpa's truck that's been rotting in the barn for a decade. Instead, I murmur, "If I weren't glad to have a weapon right now, we'd be having words." I shrug, wondering what difference it makes now that he knows our marriage might be over.

"Then you're not mad?" His boyish smile, the one that gets him out of so many fights, once again works its charm.

I smile, wondering if he's giving me a chance to take back my divorce ultimatum. "Oh, believe me, you're going to hear how mad I am—just not while terrorists are running amuck."

"Mommy, are you and Daddy fighting?" Ella asks, looking down from the mare.

I step over a fallen branch and watch as the horse maneuvers over it. "No, I'm just letting Daddy know we're going to have a long talk when we get where we're going." I turn to Clint. "Where *are* we going, by the way?"

"I know a hunting cabin where we'll be safe."

My blood pressure rises as I fear I know the cabin he's referring to.

Coyotes chatter in the distance as our pace slows from walking for hours. Tanner is slumped over the horse's neck and Ella uses Tanner for a pillow. The hairs on the back of my neck stand up as Clint motions for us to stop. Fearing he's heard something, I'm afraid to speak.

He looks around and motions for me to follow. "We should stop here for a bit."

"Do you think it's safe?" I scan our surroundings. Nothing but trees nestled into the mountains.

"I'm sure the terrorists aren't scouring the mountains, Lexi." He takes the reins from my hand and ties the mare to a tree.

I scoop the kids off her back as Clint pulls a blanket from his bag. He unrolls it and makes a bed for the kids, using rolled up shirts for pillows. They are fast asleep by the time we slump against opposite trees. I jump as an owl screeches overhead.

"Get some sleep," Clint says with a smile. For once I'm not going to argue.

# Chapter 7

"We should pick out a name for the horse," I suggest after traversing through the mountains in silence for hours underneath an unrelenting sun.

Clint turns sharply and glares. "We need to stay quiet," he says softly but sternly.

"They are going to burst if they don't say something," I retort, motioning with a nod to Ella and Tanner. Their faces are covered in Lucky Charm dust and they fidget with each other the way they do when they are bored. One of them is bound to burst with a loud noise.

He studies them a minute and scans the looming trees around us. "Whisper," he says, staring at the children.

I stroke the mare's head as I lead her a few feet behind Clint. "So, what are we going to name her?"

"Moana," Ella chimes up.

"Popcorn," Tanner offers.

"Popcorn?" Ella and I say in unison.

Tanner claps his hand over his face. "I was thinking about popcorn."

Even Clint laughs. "How about Seabiscuit?"

"We're not naming her after a racehorse."

"Elsa," Ella suggests.

"We're not naming her after a movie," Clint says adamantly. He catches my smirk. "The movie was made for the horse," he replies sharply.

"Let's rule out movie characters and food," I say, poking Tanner in the ribs.

He laughs. "How about Bumpy?"

Clint turns and walks backward. "Why would we name her that?"

"Because she's bumpy to ride."

We laugh louder than we should, stopping Clint in his tracks. "Shhhh," he scolds. The mare stops abruptly like she's the one in trouble. Clint reaches to stroke her muzzle, but she backs away. The reins tighten in my hand as she rears to her back feet, knocking the kids from her back. Leather burns across my palm as she flees. I have no choice but to let go so I'm not dragged and almost don't get my hand free before she gallops away.

"I've got a few choice names for that horse now," Clint mutters as we each scoop up a child.

"Aw, a baby bear," Ella says, pointing to the trees in the mountain beside us.

Clint almost drops her as he clambers for his bow. "Find the momma," he says through gritted teeth. Placing the kids between us, we turn in the direction we had been walking and see her less than a hundred yards from us, staring.

"Back away slowly. Follow that horse," he instructs.

I grab both packs since they are still tied together and inch the kids up the mountain. With the kids in front of me, I usher them up the side of the mountain and hope there isn't a second cub. The three-hundred-pound black bear shifts her focus from us to her cub as Clint aims his bow at her. She freezes as he makes the initial gesture.

"There are more arrows in the case," he breathes. "Keep moving."

The momma grunts as she moves toward her baby, her eyes keenly focused on Clint. With trembling hands, Ella slowly unzips the bag Clint dropped and pulls out a handful of arrows.

Clint turns his head enough to see the shaking lethal sticks in Ella's small hand.

"If I start shooting, you keep those coming," he orders.

I shuffle the weight of the packs to my right shoulder and take the arrows from Ella. "If he shoots, you drop your bag and run." Ella nods, her eyes filling with tears. "I really need you to not cry right now."

Clint raises the bow, pointing to a distant mountain. He does it so slowly it's barely detectable. "Cabin. Straight shot. That way."

The bear steps toward her cub. Grunting, she stops when she's even with us. We continue up the steep incline, careful to only move when her focus is on her baby. I push the kids up while keeping a close eye on Clint, who continues to walk backwards, never taking his eyes off the dangerous animal.

"Step to the right," I say, guiding Clint away from a large elm tree.

The momma bear calls to her cub and the two are side-by-side in a few short steps. They disappear into the trees and a loud sigh fills the air. The whole family, it seems, had been holding their breath.

"Now that the horse has run off, we should walk higher on the mountain so we don't become dinner," Clint decides.

"She was scared, Daddy," Ella says defensively.

"So was I, but you didn't see me running away."

Tanner reaches for Clint's hand. "You were scared, Daddy?"

Clint unties the packs and holds one in each hand. Passing one to me, he bends to Tanner's level. "I sure was."

"Don't you hunt bears?"

Clint smiles and ruffles the boy's hair. "I was scared the bear was going to hurt one of you."

Tanner's eyes bulge.

"Don't worry, we'd let the bear eat Daddy while we ran away," I say.

Ella laughs while Tanner scrunches his mouth, trying to decide if I'm serious. Clint takes his hand and leads us higher up the mountain. "I wouldn't have it any other way."

*Ugh. Another reason I kept the divorce papers hidden so long. He's a good man who would let a bear kill him to protect us. Not that divorce would change anything, and* that *is why I hang onto the hope that he will make the right decision.*

"I have a name for the horse," Clint says after a long silence, a signal that he believes the danger has passed.

"The horse is gone," I point out.

"What is it, Daddy?" Ella asks, ignoring the obvious.

"Moonshine."

"Pfft," is all I can manage.

"Because I'm gonna need some after that."

"You and me both."

"It was either that or...Poopypants," he says with a glance around.

Tanner and Ella burst into laughter.

"Can I have some Moonshine too?" Tanner asks.

"In about fifteen years," I say, guilt-ridden with his missed birthday.

"Will that be tomorrow?"

I shake my head. "Try six thousand tomorrows, give or take."

Tanner puts up his fingers in an attempt to figure out how many that is.

"Should be just over that mountain," Clint says, interrupting Tanner's difficult math problem.

"How do you know there's a cabin there?" I can almost feel the blood pumping faster through my veins as I prepare to hear a familiar story I don't particularly care for.

"Remember how I told you I went hunting with Richard a few times?" Richard, as in his ex-father-in-law, Richard. The man who manipulated him so much that his relationship with his two oldest kids will never be normal. Richard, the man who robbed us of memories without a second thought. All because of a grudge held against Clint. My rage at the thought of him almost comes out through my mouth, but I hear Tanner's sweet voice as he grabs Clint's hand.

"Jett and Sidney's grandpa has a cabin *here?*"

"Yep." He chuckles to himself. "One time he got lost while we were looking for Old Otis—a black bear he had heard roamed these parts, even though I told him he wasn't out here—and he wouldn't let me guide him back. Richard is not a man you show up, so we circled the same mountain three times because he refused to believe me when I told him it was the next one over."

"How'd you make it back?" Ella asks.

"I made him a bet."

"What did you bet?" I ask out of spite.

His eyes are cold when he looks at me. "It doesn't matter." *And why is that, Clint? I argue to myself. Could it possibly be because he found a way to take it back when you divorced his daughter? I guess the fact that he couldn't buy the husband he wanted for her didn't sit well with him. Yet he continues to control you.* My stomach turns at the thought.

"Then I shot the first turkey and he made me walk home," Clint says, having continued the story about the rest of the weekend while I was stuck in my head.

"And that's when you learned to always let him get the first kill," I say, trying to finish the story faster.

Clint blows what was intended as an insult off and faces Tanner. "Richard couldn't catch dinner if it stopped and held up a sign that said, 'Free supper.'"

Tanner and Ella laugh. I roll my eyes.

Clint points. "And there it is."

# Chapter 8

The cabin looms before us at the top of a mountain. Nestled safely between trees, it appears we've gone back in time. Leaves scatter across the roof and a thick layer of dust coats the windows. Though I've never seen the place, I knew it was a short hike from the old bear hunting trail that serves as a road for this cabin and a few others. Clint had pointed it out the day I took him for a drive to tell him we were pregnant with Ella. I hadn't known how he would take it because of his relationship with his older kids. The mention of his ex-father-in-law killed the mood, and I didn't tell him for another week.

As we walk to the door, hoping we can get inside, Clint tells the same story he told me that delayed the news of Ella's existence.

"Richard won this cabin in a game of poker. The previous owner flopped the winning hand, but Richard was so drunk he kept throwing money into the pot until the other guy folded. Claimed he was going to put the biggest moose head you'd ever seen on the wall."

"Clearly, he didn't know it's illegal to kill moose in New York," I add, thankful he gave the short version of the story.

"Can I see the moose head?" Tanner asks.

"There's no moose," Clint explains. Tanner throws his bottom lip out. "But there is a deer above the fireplace," he adds to console the boy.

Needing to point out the man's flaws, I say, "You know Richard didn't actually shoot the deer, right?"

"I don't care," Tanner says, trying to pull his dad even faster to the door. "I just want to see it."

Clint slips his hand over the sill on the door and produces a key for the padlock dangling from the bolted door.

I inhale the warm, musty air. "So, this is what a cabin looks like when you get drunk and swindle your friends?"

"Look at the buck, Mommy!" Tanner points excitedly to the head above the brick-lined fireplace. The thing has so many cobwebs covering it, it could be a Halloween decoration. "And there's a bear!" He flops onto the rug and spreads his arms and legs trying to fill the large pelt.

"I bet he didn't shoot that either," I say coolly.

Clint's cold stare would've cut through me when we were first married, but now I could care less about whether or not he likes my remarks. "Do you have a better place for us to go?"

He has me there. "Looks like we have some cleaning to do."

"Richard has been busy with the new office in London the last couple of years and hasn't made it up as much," Clint says, pointing to a small closet in the corner next to the open kitchen. "There should be supplies in there."

Ella dances, crossing her legs. "Which door goes to the bathroom?"

The living room we stand in is only slightly bigger than my cell at the storage unit. To the right is a small kitchen, or rather a few cabinets and counterspace which houses a large single sink but no faucet. A wooden table divides the rooms. The closet Clint referenced lies directly behind the table, leaving me to wonder if there's even room to open its door. To our left is a loft with two doors beneath them. I pray one of them is a bathroom, but Clint shoots that down when he answers Ella.

"It's outside, honey."

"Makes sense for someone who has unlimited means," I say with a scowl.

"Richard didn't build it," Clint says defensively. "He won it."

"No wonder Christa never came up here. She couldn't survive without plumbing." I know I sound petty as I say the words, but it's too easy to pass up.

The corners of his mouth rise with a secret he's yet to share. "She's been up here," is all he says.

Ella dances in the corner. "Daddy, I have to pee."

Clint drops his pack and ushers Ella out the door. Tanner scrambles up the ladder to the loft while I dig in the closet for cleaning supplies. The thin curtains need washed, but seeing as there's no machine to do it, I'm going to put that off as long as I can.

"There's a bed up here, Mommy. Can I sleep up here?"

I hang the Swiffer duster I found on the buck's antler's and climb the 'antique' ladder. It may fit the décor, but I know it probably came from IKEA. Two thin mattresses are wrapped in plastic and lying atop two log bed frames. Dead bugs and mouse poop line the baseboards, but none of that takes the smile off Tanner's face.

"You'll have to clean it first."

Tanner points and laughs. "It looks like the deer has a chicken butt on his head."

I can't help but smile as I think how out of place the duster looks even being in this cabin.

Ella and Clint return while Tanner is still laughing.

"What's so funny?" Ella asks.

"The deer has a chicken butt on its head."

Ella looks up and very seriously crosses her arms. "That's a Swiffer," she says.

"Look at it from up here," I say.

She climbs the ladder and bursts into a fit of giggles.

I descend and stand next to Clint. Normally their laughter would be contagious, but we're both too worried about what comes next to find amusement in the situation. Clint faces me and takes my hands.

"We should talk after they go to sleep." For a moment I wonder if he wants to talk about the divorce. "We need to get this place cleaned up," he says, motioning for the kids to come down.

I go to the closet and dig out a broom. "You two unpack our bags while I sweep the loft. Put everything on the table."

"I'm going outside to take inventory," Clint announces.

We're all busy for about ten minutes and seem to finish up at the same time. I'm carrying a dustpan full of dead bugs and rodent poop mixed in dust down the ladder when Clint comes in carrying an assortment of tools. He spreads them out on the counter. I prop the broom against the wall by the door and carefully set the dustpan on the floor beside it.

"Start checking all the storage spaces for things we can use," Clint instructs. An instant game ensues to see who can find the most useful items. When we are done, we form a line along the table facing our loot. Eight rolls of flattened toilet paper, a bottle of shampoo and conditioner, a bar of Irish Spring, a bottle of body wash, my razor minus the shaving cream, about three dozen squished tampons, four toothbrushes and a partial tube of toothpaste, half a box of Band-Aids, burn cream, anti-itch cream, and an assortment of various cold medications along with laxatives and stuff to stop you up lie next to our clothing which amounts to about one change per person, consisting of shorts and jeans, t-shirts, and jackets. Next to the clothes is the food we found in the cabinet—six cans of baked beans, two large cans of chicken and dumplings, and a can of tomato juice—all of which are close to their expiration date. From home we managed to grab five cans of SpaghettiOs, three cans of Spam, half a bag of potatoes, seven cans of vegetables, ten bottles of water, Ella's brownies, and Tanner's Lucky Charms.

On the counter lies a pair of scissors, a small gas cook stove with two cans of fuel, an axe, a hammer, a fillet knife along with a knife block of kitchen knives, a handsaw, a fishing pole and tackle box, rope, and half a roll of duct tape.

"We can survive on this, right?" I put my arm around Clint's waist for physical reassurance only.

He intertwines his fingers in mine. "We probably won't need to stay here long."

"I hope not," I whisper.

Two sets of disappointed eyes stare at us.

"There's enough firewood out back to get us by a few days, but we'd better start working on that tomorrow just in case."

"Can I help?" Tanner asks.

"We're going to need everyone's help if we're going to make it out here," Clint says, picking up a can of dumplings. "Who wants dinner?"

I move to the cabinet and pull out enough bowls for everyone. Not wanting to waste our only source of clean water, I wipe them out with a towel that was probably washed in the lake or creek by a man who didn't think to use soap. Forcing the thought from my mind, I watch Clint work the can opener he found in a drawer. After heating it on the small stove, he glops some into each bowl.

We eat standing around the cluttered table and, in a matter of minutes, Clint is opening the other can. I eat slowly, so I can give the kids what's left in my bowl should they want it. Thankfully, they don't but it doesn't keep my stomach from growling.

We pile the dishes in the sink, and I know I'll have to figure out how to wash them later. I think I saw some Dawn under the sink, but beds need to be made before the kids collapse on the floor. I head up to the loft and remove two sets of sheets from the three-drawer dresser against the wall. The sun is starting to sink, making the lighting dim, and I'm glad I can't tell how badly the linens need washed. I give them a good shake and cover the beds, dusting them with my hand afterward for good measure. I open another drawer and find two thin wool blankets and toss one on each bed. There is an oil lamp fixture on the wall, which I check for fuel before making my descent.

Clint checks the three oil lamps in the kitchen and living room area. "Did you see oil anywhere?"

I shake my head. "It would probably be better if we only light one at a time anyway. We don't want to make the place any more visible than we need to. How much do we have?"

"This one's about empty," he says, pointing to the one in the kitchen. "And the other two have about half."

"The one in the loft is a little more than half full."

Ella yawns and rubs her eyes. "Why don't you two go up to bed," Clint suggests. "Mom and I are going to put things away."

After a quick kiss, they eagerly climb the ladder.

I pick up two cans of baked beans and put them in the cabinet while Clint takes anything that can be used as a weapon and places them throughout the cabin. I take our clothes to the bedroom closest to the door and place them in a dresser matching the one I found in the loft. The room has two twin beds and another identical dresser on the other wall. The walls are bare except for a turkey mounted to the paneling between the beds in the middle of two oil lanterns that match the rest in the cabin. After making the beds with the 800-count white sheets that must've been bought in bulk, I toss the gray wool blankets onto the beds and wonder where the pillows are. I find them under the bed wrapped in plastic. There are even spares which must belong in the loft. I throw them on the dresser and check the oil in the lamps. Moving to the next room, I find a similar setup—two twin beds and matching dressers, two oil lamps above them and a bobcat on a shelf between them. When I am finished, I head back to the main area and take a seat in one of the two large wooden Cracker Barrel-style chairs. Clint moves around like a madman, trying to make sure there is a weapon within every square foot of the place. Shouldn't be hard, considering the place is half the size of our house, but I watch him and wonder...*what if. What if this changes everything? Do we pretend like I hadn't dropped the divorce bomb? What if we never make it out of this cabin? What if we'd never made it out of that prison? Never had the chance to find out if we have a chance? What if we'd never found each other again?*

"Lexi." Clint stands in front of me. "We need to talk." My heart pounds. Had I been talking out loud?

"I agree."

"We should go outside though. I think the kids are asleep, but I don't want them to hear what I have to say."

I rub a hand over my chest, trying to calm my pained, throbbing heart. He grabs his loaded bow and opens the door for me. I step onto the covered wooden porch, which lines the front of the cabin, and take a seat in a smaller wooden rocker. He places the weapon in his lap and stares into the darkness. Coyotes yip in the distance mixing with the crickets' song.

I inhale deeply, preparing to give the speech I've gone over for days—or at least the days before we were taken captive. "I'm glad you want to talk," I say timidly.

"I don't think we have a choice." *At least we're on the same page.*

"I'd appreciate if you'd let me explain before you say anything."

"You have a plan?"

I nod. "I do."

"Let's hear it."

"We can have separate bedrooms if you want, but I think we should act normally. The last thing the kids need right now is to deal with our marital problems." I twist the toe of my boot into the deep red wood of the porch and wait for my heart to decide it wants to stay in my chest.

Clint slaps his hands onto the oak armrests of his seat so hard that I jump. "What *are* you talking about?"

"You said we should talk."

"You said you had a plan."

"I do."

"Then tell me what it is so I can tell you mine and we can see if one idea works better than another." *Now you want to try compromising?*

"I'd like the kids to have a sense of normality."

He grips the edge of the wood and I almost tell him to be careful or he'll leave imprints and owe Richard seven hundred dollars for the damages. "Nothing is normal right now, Lexi.'"

"This is a big change for everyone."

He nods, disgust heavy on his face. "Stop being selfish. You want to divorce me, fine, go find your own cabin. Or maybe think of the kids and realize we need to have a plan on how to survive out here and what to do if we're found."

"Right. Not like there's a lawyer out here to grant a divorce anyway."

"Then tell me what you're thinking so we can compare notes."

I bite my lip, wondering how to make him think I had an actual plan prior to finding him in our house. "Why don't you tell me yours first and I'll add to it if you don't mention what I'm thinking." *That buys me some time.*

"First thing in the morning, I'm going hunting."

"But it isn't hunting season," I interrupt.

He throws his hands up. "Who the hell cares?!" He waves his hand into the vastness of trees as a lone wolf cries. Bringing his tone down, he says, "Maybe that one wolf because I'm going to get his breakfast, but it's not like a ranger is going to come knocking on the door because I shot something out of season. Wake the hell up, Lexi. This is reality now. If there is anyone left out there, they're going to be trying to steal my kill, not turn me in for shooting it out of season."

"I'm sorry. It's been a long couple of days." *Days? Hell, it feels like the longest period of my life, and I don't even know what month it is.*

He reaches over and puts his hand on mine. "It has for us all, but this is not the time to lose your mind. Forget that you hate me for a minute. I know part of you still loves me, right?"

*For days I thought of nothing but you and Tanner. Maybe I'm not ready to give up. Tip the scale one way or the other. I need a sign.*

"It must be that recording. I still can't get it out of my head," I lie, hoping to bring myself out of the mess I've created. Of course this is not the time to talk about a divorce. It's time to unite...finally.

"If you can't, I'm afraid I can't trust you."

Anger burns into my core. "Then you might not want to trust Ella."

"That's got to be the most ludicrous thing you've ever said."

"You didn't *see* her, Clint. It messed her up."

"An eight-year-old isn't going to hurt us."

"They do it all the time in the Middle East. There's no reason to think it can't be done here as well." *There's a thought I never dreamt I'd have.* Children dressed in black with vacant eyes that once showed innocence. All while carrying destructive weapons. In America.

"We have to come up with a plan before it's too late. Are you ready to listen to my idea?"

"I'm all ears," I say, my tone letting him know I'm annoyed.

"Thank you. Now, we'll put what meat we can in the cellar fridge."

"The what?"

He points to the far end of the cabin. "Richard installed a cellar-type cooling box over there."

"I haven't been that far, Clint. I haven't been hunting here, remember?"

"Oh yeah." That's about as much of an apology as I can expect. "There's also a pump that goes to the well so we shouldn't have to worry about water."

I breathe a sigh of relief. "That's good."

"I haven't checked it yet to make sure it's still working."

"We should do that in the morning."

"I'll do that before I go hunting."

"What are you thinking after hunting?"

"I thought you and the kids could clean while I was hunting and afterward, we'll need to start gathering firewood. We don't know how long we'll be out here and could probably use more. Richard usually has a load delivered, because he can afford to do it that way, but it looks like he hadn't planned on coming up this year."

"The kids and I can work on that."

"*You're* going to cut down a tree? You had a chainsaw the last time. This is different. It takes actual work."

"Are you implying I'm incapable of hard work?" I bite my lip, fearing he's again comparing me to his ex-wife.

"How about we fight instead of accomplishing anything?"

"I can cut down a tree, Clint."

"Okay. Just remember not too close to the cabin and make sure the kids aren't—"

"I'm not an idiot." He slaps his hand on his leg as wolf packs talk to each other from opposite mountains. "What's your plan if they find us up here?"

"We stay and fight," he proclaims as if there's no other option.

"How can two people fight off an army?"

"You've seen *The Patriot*."

I roll my eyes. "You can't base your plan on a movie."

"Do you have a better idea?"

"Run and hide?"

"You're a lot of things, Lexi, but a coward is not one of them."

I smile, though I'm unsure of his compliment. "We have a hillbilly's assortment of weapons scattered about the cabin and two kids to think of."

"Ella can shoot."

"You just said our child wouldn't hurt anyone."

He stretches his arms above his head in frustration. "*Us.* I said she wouldn't hurt *us.*"

"We can't ask her to shoot someone. I don't care if they *are* terrorists. That's the sort of thing she'd never get over."

"But if she had to, she could."

"We're talking about an eight-year-old girl. Our girl. And yes, I'd like to think that she could if it came down to it, but let's not use her in our army unless we have to." My voice carries farther than it should, and I pace along the wooden planks to calm myself.

"Do you know nothing about armies?"

"I know they don't involve small children."

"Shhh," he barks, jumping from his seat and sliding his finger across the safety of the bow. "There's a knife over the door frame."

As if we are the couple we once were, I slide to the door as Clint crosses the porch and points his weapon toward the rustling sound I now hear too. The knife is embedded horizontally with only enough room for me to slip my fingers behind the handle and produce the weapon. I take the other end of the porch and turn to wait for Clint's cue to move. He nods, and we step off opposite sides of the porch and begin our sweep of the perimeter. For a moment it feels nice to be one with him again, to know what he's thinking. Whatever is causing the disturbance ceases as if it knows we are on its trail. Clint and I meet at the back of the cabin and he motions for me to follow him. The nearly full moon provides enough light to search for the disturbance. The 'cooling box' he mentioned, which is built into a man-made hill and has a large door covered in grass on one side, is at the corner of the cabin. The only way I can tell it's there is by the large wooden handle protruding from the earth. An old water pump is opposite the door and a wooden bucket hangs from it. There's also a small shed that I wasn't aware of. I have Clint's back as he takes one side of it. We meet behind it and he points to a woodpile between two trees. A tin sheet is nailed to the trees about six feet above it to help keep water off and, though we can see over the stacks of wood, I know Clint wants to check behind it. He trades me weapons and points to the ground, motioning that he's going to go around the left side of it. I nod when I'm ready and he proceeds as if he's going to take down whatever is threatening us, even if it's a squirrel.

The soft whinny of a horse stops us in our tracks. Clint puts the knife to his side, and I slide the safety on but leave my finger on the switch. We tiptoe toward the back of the cabin where the noise had come from. There is no sign of the mare we lost.

"I have an idea," I whisper. "Let's fill the bucket of water and take it to the porch. Maybe she'll come to us."

"Good idea."

"What's in that shed?" I ask after planting the bait and taking my seat.

"A Ranger."

"Great! We can use that if we need to get away."

"Don't you think I would've thought of that? There's no gas in it."

I lean back in my chair, deflated. "Oh."

"Since Richard hasn't made it up here this year, we're kind of stuck with leftovers."

"Okay, so when do you think we should head back home and see if this has all blown over?"

"When we run out of food."

"What if we head to Rockwood and see if we can get help there?"

He shakes his head. "That's too close and too small. If it happened to us, you can bet they suffered the same fate."

"Gloversville?"

"Too risky right now."

I run my fingers through my hair, fighting tangles and tugging slightly on the ends falling past my shoulders. "You're probably right. If we are discovered out here, the kids and I should try to get away. If that's not possible, the kids at least need to know where to go," I say quietly.

"Good thinking. These mountains have cabins scattered all over them. They should know how to get to one and what to do from there."

"That's a good point—what do they do from there?"

Tears well in my eyes as I realize I may never be able to answer that.

Moonshine snorts into the water bucket. I start to walk over to the mare, but Clint holds up a hand to halt me.

"Give her a minute," he says. "She's going to have to stay on her own tonight. I'm not going to tie her up and dangle her in front of the wolves and coyotes. If she's still here tomorrow, I'll turn the shed into a stall, and she can stay there. But now we know we have access to water."

I nod. "Think she'll be okay?"

"I hope so." Clint leans back in his chair. "So, how was your day?"

I'm thrown off guard by his question. He stopped asking about my day shortly after we started dating. I had just started as a surgical nurse and some days were rough, then I switched to hospice and he found I still didn't take death easier, even when I knew it was inevitable. He never knew what the answer would be and sometimes it sent me into a fit of tears, so he finally stopped asking altogether.

# Chapter 9

Clint places a kiss on my cheek before dawn the next morning. He hasn't kissed me goodbye in well over a year and I let him think he hasn't disturbed me despite his inability to quietly do anything except hunt. I try to go back to sleep after he leaves, but the simple act scared the sleep from my system. Crawling out of bed, I go for the coffee pot until I remember there isn't one. I wait for him to get out of sight and take a bottle of water to the porch. The water bucket is empty. I refill it from the spout before settling into the wooden chair to wait for the sunrise. Moving the chair to the end of the porch facing east, I wonder how long I will have to wait. I reach for the back pocket of the jeans I slept in until I remember my phone isn't there to tell the time. My eyelids soon become heavy, sending me into a restless sleep, dreaming of being locked in a tiny room with crazy people climbing the walls. Tanner screams in the background and my eyes bolt open. I jump from the chair, causing a commotion next to me, but I'm to the door before I recognize the silence surrounding me. I run to check on the kids anyway. They still sleep soundly. The water bucket is on its side when I return to the porch. Walking softly, I peer around the corner of the cabin from the edge of the porch. Moonshine stands off to the side, looking at me like I've lost my mind. She comes to me when I hold out my hand.

"Didn't mean to scare you, girl," I say, stroking her neck. "Want to watch the sunrise with me?"

Soft oranges and pinks turn vibrant as I stand, petting the horse as if she were a dog. The light pounding of feet inside the cabin brings me out of my thoughts. If Clint and I can make it through this, we can make it through our issues with his ex and her family, I decide as I listen to Ella climbing the counter for the cereal and Tanner searching for me.

"Moooommmm," comes the cry when he finds me missing. I meet him at the door. "Oh, there you are." He clings to me as if he thought he may never see me again. Of course he would be frightened, and I chastise myself for slipping away.

Stepping inside, I dig bowls from the cabinet and hand them to the kids. After breakfast we'll wash all the dishes, I think as they take their seats.

I open my warm water and take a sip. "How'd you sleep?"

"Can we stay again tonight?" Tanner asks eagerly.

"If you guys want to stay a few more nights, I'll need help cleaning things up."

"Ugh, we did that the last day," he complains.

"I know we did it yesterday, but we have a lot of work to do. We might be staying a few days, so we have to wash all the dishes."

Ella raises her hand. "I can do that."

"Tanner, will you look for cobwebs while I sweep?"

He smiles. "Can I keep the spiders?"

"All pets have to stay outside." He frowns. "Speaking of pets, come here," I say, heading for the door.

Leaving their last breakfast of Lucky Charms, they follow as if they're about to find a puppy wearing a bow. Moonshine grazes near the porch and calmly looks up when Ella stifles a squeal.

Tanner excitedly rubs his hands together. "Poopypants!"

I squeeze him into my side. "Her name is Moonshine."

"But I can't have moonshine for eleven-teen years," he pouts.

"We'll make an exception. Just this once."

Ella's eyes glimmer with happy tears. "We really get to keep her?"

"We really do. When Daddy gets back, we're going to turn that shed into a stall for her to sleep in."

"Yay!"

There is still no sign of Clint after the cabinets are emptied and cleaned so we move on to sweeping and freeing the spiders. I try not to let my worry show as we head outside to examine the shed.

Inside the shed, fishing poles haphazardly gather in a corner and a rusty shovel hangs on the wall, leaving little room to maneuver around the Ranger. Dead leaves from last fall clutter the dirt floor. Putting the machine in neutral, I move behind it and push. It doesn't budge. Going to the front, I squat and yank, but I lack the momentum to make the wheels turn. After a few attempts, I fall into the dirt and wipe my brow. Tanner plops down beside me.

"What's the matter, Mommy?"

I put my arm around him. "I can't move that by myself."

"Why don't you turn it on?"

Smiling, I say, "I didn't think of that."

"Try it."

I brush the dirt from my backside and turn the key in the ignition. It doesn't even pretend to start.

"Better check the gas tank," Tanner suggests, clearly going over things he's seen his dad do countless times.

"I don't see any gas," I announce.

"Want me to get you a flashlight?"

"Can you get me the rope your dad put in the closet?"

"What are we gonna do with *that*?"

"You'll see."

Tanner runs for the porch and emerges less than a minute later with a bundle of rope draped over his arm.

"Don't ru—" I yell, but a strand of rope has already fallen off his shoulder and his leg goes right through it. He hits the porch just before the stairs, his head slamming against the wood. I sprint the short distance to him and scoop him up, rope and all. His whimpers turn into an all-out bawl the second I touch him. Ella rushes out to see the commotion.

"Shhhhhhhh," I coax. "We can't be too loud out here."

He buries his head in my shoulder and quietly sobs. "It hurts."

"Let me see." He rolls over to expose his skinned knees. "That's going to leave some nice scars."

"I need a band aid."

"We have to save those for real injuries."

"This is a real ninjury," he blubbers. I hide a smile at his mispronunciation. "See?" He points for emphasis.

"Be a man, Tanner," Ella says with an eyeroll.

I kiss his head and move him to the side. Leaving him on the porch, I run inside and get the antibiotic cream, a wet rag, and the only two large Band-Aids. When I open the door again, the tears have stopped. Until he hears my footsteps. The sobs return in full force as I quicken my stride to him.

"Don't put on a show for me." Carefully dabbing his knees, I look around. "But the men with guns out there might be interested in it." The moment the words are out, I know I've messed up.

He leaps into my arms. "Are they watching us?"

I pull him away from me so I can look him in the eyes and motion for Ella to sit beside me. "I'm going to be honest with you guys. I don't know what's going on. I don't know where these terrorists are or why they are doing this."

Ella raises her hand. I nod. "What do they want?"

"I don't know."

She scans the trees as if she might spot someone. "How long do we have to stay out here?"

"I don't know."

"What happens if we run out of food?"

"We are going to work very hard to make sure that doesn't happen. Your dad should be back any minute with...something."

"What's going to happen to all our toys?" Tanner asks.

"That's not important, Tanner," Ella says with a twinge of irritation.

"What about Jak?"

"The cat will be fine," I reply.

"What if they find us here?"

"We're trying to come up with a plan for that."

"What if they come before we know what to do?" Ella presses.

I drop my face into my hands and fall against my knees. "We're going to start by finding other safe places nearby. If something should happen, you'll have somewhere to go, and we'll know where to find you."

"You are going to leave us by ourselves?"

"I'm talking about if we should need to fight. We'll want you out of harm's way."

Tanner's eye fill with tears. "What if they kill you?"

"Let's get those legs fixed," I say, waving the bandage in the air.

"Maybe they better share," Tanner says. "That way we don't use all of them too soon."

"Which knee gets the band aid first?"

He points to his left leg as I slather goo on both scrapes. "Right."

"That's the left." He pouts so I give him a quick squeeze.

"You don't think they got Daddy, do you? He's been gone a long time."

Worry crosses their faces as they peer up at me. "Ha. Like they could take *your* daddy. I'd like to see them try."

Ella forms her lips into a tight line. "I wouldn't. That's not nice, Mommy."

"I just meant it wouldn't be an easy thing for them to do. Let's go brush our teeth," I say, running my tongue over grimy teeth. "Then we can get started on Moonshine's stall." I follow as they run in to take care of their teeth. What is usually a task to complete, is suddenly agreeable.

"Let's go," Tanner says, dragging my hand after our teeth are all scrubbed.

"We have to play a game first," I announce, realizing Clint has hidden all the tools but the rake and shovel we found in the shed.

Tanner slaps his hands against his legs. "Can't we play later? I want to work on the shed."

"Even if there's a prize for the winner?"

His eyes light up. "What's the prize?"

Ella takes a stance like she's about to run a track race. "What's the game?"

"The game is called 'I Spy.'"

"I want to go first," Tanner calls.

"I'm going first and whoever wins, gets to take the first swing at the shed."

Ella's posture straightens. "We have to find the axe, don't we?"

"'Fraid so."

"Go," Tanner yells as loud as he can. Before I can scold him for not using his 'indoor voice,' they are gone.

Ella moves straight to the closet while Tanner looks in the fireplace.

I head to the kitchen and open cabinets. "When you find something, call it out so we all know where it is." Climbing onto the counter, I look on top of the dusty cabinets. "Handsaw above the cabinets."

"Knife under the table," Ella chimes.

"Knife under the table?" I get down on all fours and look. Sure enough, Clint has loosely taped a butcher knife to the underside of the table. Ella points to the chairs. There is a small steak knife taped to the leg of each one.

"Saw on the moose," Tanner calls.

"It's still a deer. Keep looking," I urge.

"Screwdriver on table by the big chairs," Ella yells after I disappear to my room.

I'm a little disgusted when I find nothing under my bed or in my dresser. There is not a single weapon in our room.

"I win," Tanner screams.

I run from the room, almost bumping into Ella as we peer into the loft at Tanner holding the axe over his head. "And we have Tanner in the loft with the axe."

"It was under the dresser," he proudly announces.

"We have a winner!"

Tanner dances impatiently as he waits for me to roll a log over for him to stand on so he'll be at the right height. A grin stretches across his face as he raises a wobbly axe above his head. A tiny crack appears in the treated wood from his swing.

"My turn," Ella says, trying to take the axe.

"Whoa!" I grab her hand. "This is not a toy. You have to be careful." Her swing leaves a groove lower than I'd like.

"Okay, my turn. Ella, I'm gonna need the saw. Can you get it for me?"

Tanner laughs. "The moose has it."

"Deer," Ella growls, stomping to the cabin.

I motion for Tanner to move back as I bring the axe over my shoulder. The moment the plank splinters beneath the sharp metal, I realize I've messed up.

"What the hell are you doing?" I turn to see Clint scowling at me. He leans his bow against a tree and walks over to inspect the damage.

"We're making a home for Moonshine," Ella says, proudly handing me the saw.

"That's a hell of a way to do it."

"Clint, language. I just realized a better way to do it."

"I told you I would do it when I got back," he scowls.

"We finished cleaning and thought we would help."

"What happened to getting firewood?"

His tone is gruff and I'm not sure whether to explode into a fit of rage or break out in tears. This is all just too much. It's been a long time since I've cried over Clint, and I know the moment I feel nothing is the moment it's over. The problem now is—am I upset over him treating me like a hindrance or is it because I've been forced from my home to be stuck in the wilderness, dependent on a man whom I fear doesn't love me anymore? His brow furrows as he waits for an answer. "I didn't think we should go into the woods without a weapon that didn't require close proximity for use."

"Look around, Lexi, there are hundreds of trees nearby. All you had to do was cut some branches. Now I have to fix this instead of doing it right the first time. But I can't even do that yet because I still have a deer to go get."

"Why didn't you bring it with you when you came back?"

"Dragging a hundred and eighty-pound deer takes a bit of work. I got it as close as I could. I came back for the horse."

"She's right there." I motion to the side of the cabin and bite my tongue before I spew hateful words.

Clint storms to the porch and begins rewinding the tangled rope. If I hadn't gotten side-tracked, we would have the Ranger out of the shed and Clint would be yelling about that instead. "I'll be back later. Try not to make more work for me while I'm gone."

I let him leave without saying a word. Once he's out of sight on Moonshine, I slam the axe into the plank I splintered as he had walked up. In a matter of minutes, it's in shavings on the ground and I'm working the saw into the hole about waist high.

The kids watch in silence and, as I work, I know something is going to have to change. My relationship with Clint is not healthy for any of us and our innocent children don't deserve to be stuck in a home where their parents have nothing nice to say to each other. There is an obvious strain that needs to be addressed. Maybe out here, we can figure it out.

Stacking the discarded planks next to the shed, I step back to examine my work. Looks good to me, but I'm sure Clint will find fault in it when he returns.

"Let's get lunch," I say, grabbing the tools.

Tanner and Ella opt for SpaghettiOs and I watch as they eat them straight from the can. My appetite is gone, and a knot has developed in my stomach. One I know won't go away until I sort some things out in my head.

Clint opens the door as they are finishing. "Got the deer back, but we'll have to drag the carcass away after I'm done," he says.

"I'm going to get firewood," I announce. He offers the bow he's been carrying around since we got here. "You keep it. The kids are staying with you anyway."

I grab the axe and saw on the way out and head into the cover of the woods. It takes all of twelve steps. I wander through the trees, dismissing the idea of cutting one nearby mainly because I'm angry and need some space to clear my head. I have no idea how to cut down a tree in the middle of the woods and get it to land where I can use it. In this tight space it will most definitely end up in another tree and I'll have more work on my hands. I know I shouldn't go far because Clint will worry, but the longer I walk, the more irate I become.

*I should've run from this situation the moment I found out about it. But I was young and thought that's the way it worked. Then I became pregnant and soon realized it's not the way it* should *work. I thought things would change and get better, but they didn't. For a man of such integrity in so many ways to be weak in just one way—I never thought it could ruin us. And when I try to talk to him about it, he has the audacity to think I am the one with the problem. Why can't he see things the way I do? I let him conform my thoughts so that I believed I was the problem. Our relationship was better when I looked the other way. We even got pregnant with Tanner, but that's when it all went downhill. He chose to be with* them *on Tanner's very first Christmas. I know I shouldn't feel resentment toward his other kids, but he spent Tanner's* first *Christmas with his ex-wife and older children. He missed a milestone he can never get back. The worst part is, I don't even think he cares.*

I snap branches as I pass, as if it will dull the bitterness welling inside me. So much has been building since that Christmas five years ago I snap right there in the middle of the mountains. I drop the saw and swing the axe into the nearest tree, a smaller one, slightly wider than my thigh.

Tears blind my swings. "I can't count the number of times you've dropped what you were doing to drive across the state because she asked you to." I slice into the wood. The marks stagger over a few inches but I don't care. "I don't know another divorced couple who operates the way you two do. I mean, how many times have you spent entire weekends at her house?"

I stop, as if the realization of events never occurred to me before. He's having an affair. With his ex-wife. Surely that can't be so, I think as I swing into the tree again.

*Is that why the kids are only allowed at our house three times a year? They're afraid one of them might spill the beans?*

I swing with a vengeance as I wonder why I can't remember details I should know about my stepchildren.

*How am I supposed to know children I barely see, children who have no interest in me? Is that the teenager in them? Jett is what, seventeen? That would make Sidney fifteen.*

"And that's another thing," I shout into the trees, as I move to swing at a different angle. "You were supposed to make another trip to Middletown next month to be with Sidney when she gets her permit. Why are you so hell-bent on making it to all their 'firsts' and you don't seem to give a damn about our children's? Is it because you've already done this before? That's a load of shit and it sure as hell isn't fair to me to be left wishing you were there. Did you know Tanner rolled over for the first time that Christmas morning?! Maybe it wasn't a big deal to you, but it was to me. I sat on the floor and wept for an hour. Then, two days later when you got home and saw him do it, I pretended like it was the first time. When I quickly excused myself as you got on the floor with him, it was because I was in the shower crying. I may have told you I had been waiting all day for you to come home so I could get my first shower in two days, but it was really to drown out my tears. Bet you didn't know that," I scream into the vastness.

Wiping tears with the back of my hand, I switch to the saw and furiously run the blade across the tree's insides. I know it's too soon, but I need a change in position.

*Maybe that's what this relationship needs. A change in position. How can I see this from Clint's point-of-view? He only sees two of his children once every month or so. That must be rough. He does have a lot to juggle. Maybe I should cut him some slack. But the weekend visits have to stop.*

Wood cracks and the tree crashes into nearby trees. Pausing my thoughts to move toward the wedge where the top branches are caught, I begin chopping away at the spot just above my head.

*Maybe an affair is a little far-fetched, but I'm missing something. All I know is they're complete opposites. She came from money and he came from nothing. When they married, he went to work for her father, but by the time Sidney was only a few years old, his grandfather had gotten sick and he had to come home to run the bait shop. She wouldn't come with him. Did he really choose bait over his children?*

I slide against a tree trunk away from the fallen tree and wish I had brought some water. The tears stop falling, but I still can't help but wonder about Clint's relationship with Christa.

*I don't even know how they met, other than she was drunk and he was young. I don't know why they split, unless it was, in fact, over bait. He always told me his relationships in the past belonged in the past. I offered to tell him about mine, but he never seemed to care. Hell, in the ten years Clint and I have been married, I've only met the woman once. She drove to our house one time when Clint broke his leg in a boating incident and couldn't drive. I had offered to get them but no, I wasn't allowed. So, she brought them, barely said 'hello' to me, spent half an hour talking to Clint as if they were best buddies, and was out the door. Surely, she has to be more than the thin blonde with a flawless fake tan.*

I clamber to my feet and swing the axe into the wood until a log longer than my body plummets to the ground. Making a groove in the side, I nestle the saw in and swing the axe into it next. Wishing I had brought the rope, I lift an end and pull.

I labor beneath its weight a few feet before changing positions. Hoisting the end across my shoulder, I creep forward between a set of pines. The needles tickle my exposed skin as I brush into it, creating a straight path for it to follow. I wipe my brow and let the timber fall. It's too long to keep on like this, the trees too close to carry it straight. I remove my tools and grab the far end. Hoisting it over my head, I topple it over, letting it slam against trees. Retrieving my tools, I knock it to the ground, and repeat the process, following the path it wants to go. My heart beats faster from the excursion and I know, at this rate, it will be tomorrow morning before I make it back to the cabin and that's if I work all night. As I hold a mud-covered end over my head, I realize I didn't pay a bit of attention to the direction I was walking and I'm certainly not particular about where I'm heading now. I know I must get a grip, as I know I was louder than I should've been, too. I stand there holding the timber as I try to remember what direction the cabin faces. The sunrise was to my left, so the door must face south. I search for the sun through the trees and realize how long I've been gone. The temperature is dropping, a sure sign only a few hours of daylight remain. Surprisingly, I'd been moving the log due east, so I pivot slightly and throw my end over the other. If I hadn't inherited my grandfather's stubbornness, I would've left the log to retrieve later, but pride gets the best of me as it seems to do in these situations. I alternate between throwing and dragging the log until I'm huffing and puffing worse than The Big Bad Wolf. Taking a seat on the fallen maple, I catch my breath as I check the position of the slowly lowering sun. I wipe my face on my shirt. It won't be long before I must abort my mission and make a beeline toward where I think the cabin should be. Putting the axe and saw aside, my arms wobble as I lift the heavy trunk over my head. I shove it over, knowing it's the last I'm moving it for the day. I watch as it falls into the crevice of two large branches. I try to budge it from its hold, but with my strength depleted, there's nothing to do but leave it. The last thing in the world I want is to go back empty handed, but it looks like I'll have to swallow my pride and do just that. The moon takes control of the sky before the sun has time to make a complete exit. I grab the tools and begin walking. It doesn't take long for the sun to drop off the horizon and for my mind to play tricks on me. I know I'm bordering on dehydration and the circumstances of our situation don't help the thoughts going through my mind. I jerk around, looking over my shoulder, more times than I can count. Every critter and snapping branch becomes a bear or terrorists anxious to take me back to Zombie Central. I hold the axe in striking position as I hurry along, trying to be as quiet as possible, but I know I need to mark my path, so I can backtrack in the morning to get the wood. Paranoia sets in and I wonder if it's the best idea. Still, Clint may come looking for me, and it may be my only chance to be rescued. The only question is—will he find me before the terrorists?

# Chapter 10

A tiny roof peaks through the trees about ten minutes later. No lights shine inside and I worry that Clint has taken the kids to come find me. I quicken my steps and reach an unfamiliar cabin in a matter of minutes. Well, at least Clint and the kids aren't out looking for me, I think as I cautiously approach. *I hope.* I open the door slowly with the axe ready to strike. Something moves in the corner of the one room cabin and I jump as a tail disappears through a hole in the wall. I shudder as I look around the dark room. An oil lantern and box of matches lie on a small table in the middle of the room as if they were left just for me. My foot stubs against something as I step toward the lantern. Taking the light, I bolt the lock on the door and look around. Metal bowls litter the dirt floor. One of the two windows has a pane busted out. A cot-sized bed in the corner looks as if it were used in prison for a decade. There are at least three holes in the walls, one large enough I could squeeze through if I needed to and the whole place is covered in a layer of dust so thick an asthmatic would go running at first sight. I know it's useless to look for food or water and, after my day, I barely care that there is none. After a quick check for snakes and rats, I flop down onto the musty mattress.

I must have fallen asleep fast because I wake in a jolt to the sound of a leaky faucet. No, that's not right, I tell myself, forcing my brain to focus. My shirt has a damp spot on it. Jumping out of bed, I grab the lantern I left burning on the table. A steady drip falls where I had stood earlier. Grabbing the metal bowl, I place it under the flow. As I spin around, I notice at least five places where water is coming in. I drag the bed into the middle of the room, slipping in a puddle the rain made over the course of time I slept.

Lightning strikes flash through the single-pane windows as I look for something to burn in the fireplace. Shivering at the wind tearing in through the busted-out glass, I drag a large wooden box next to the bed. It had been hiding underneath it and I sit to inspect the contents. My backside absorbs moisture from the mattress, causing me to shake with chills. I put the flickering light on the table. The wick sucks up the last traces of oil, threatening to leave me in the dark. The rusty latch on the box breaks off as my fingers work to pry it free. Throwing the lid back, I remove the first item—a fleece blanket covered with moth-eaten holes. After thoroughly shaking it, I wrap the stale black fabric around my goosebump-covered body. The next thing I pull out is a deck of cards with a mouse-nibbled corner missing. I toss them onto the table and reach back into the crate. A can of tuna is the next item I find. It expired in 2012. Throwing it across the room, I try again. A can of Skoal is on top of a notebook with a pencil sticking out of the spiral. It goes on the table with the cards. There's also a flashlight with dead batteries. Hoping the amount of acid on the contacts is minimal, I place it on the table as well. Aside from a sheathed hunting knife, the box is empty if I don't count the large spider taking residence in the old box.

A streak of light blazes out the window and crackling fills the air in the midst of the rumble of thunder. I jump as a broken tree crashes to the ground so close I imagine I could've seen it if I had known where to look. As the storm rages directly above me, shadows dance between the trees in the streaks of lightning. A monstrous clap of thunder shakes the walls. Large drops of water ping into the big bowls on the floor and create a sharp rhythm with the dripping sequence in the smaller ones. The room goes dark like someone blew out the light. *This is how horror movies start,* I think as I shift awkwardly on the mildewy bed. I try to tell myself it's my imagination playing tricks on me, but I can't help but wonder if there is something out there. And if there is, is it friend, foe, or something else?

Forcing myself to close my eyes, I push the thoughts from my mind. Nothing I can do about it anyway, I tell myself.

My dry mouth wakes me in the early gray of morning. I stare at the bowls of water on the muddy floor. The water in it, though speckled with fragments of shingling, actually looks appetizing. I put a dented bowl to my lips and try to siphon out the particles. Sputtering afterward, I pick a flake off my tongue and try again. I work to pick them out with my finger but it's a futile effort.

After one last sip, I throw the bowls and contents from the table onto the blanket and make a bundle of it.

It isn't hard to find where I left my abandoned firewood. Placing my weakening pack near the tree holding my prized wood hostage, I stand under it and lift with all my might. It doesn't budge. My stomach growls intensely, demanding food before it resorts to eating itself. I ignore it and saw away, saving as much as I can from the length of wood. My arms feel like cooked spaghetti before I reach the halfway mark.

The sun makes its full appearance, announcing a glorious day, in some attempt to make a redemption for what happened on the moon's watch.

I switch to the other side, hoping to split it in the middle when rustling leaves demand my attention. Grabbing the axe, I spin like a madwoman. The perpetrator snaps a branch underfoot and I duck behind the large tree.

"There's another one," comes a tiny voice.

I step away from the tree. Clint lowers the bow he'd been pointing at me. Tanner and Ella race toward me as I drop the axe. I squeeze them until they pant for breath and beg to be let free.

Ella holds out a bottle of water. Clint doesn't wait for me to finish guzzling before squeezing me tightly. He pecks my cheek and holds me at length as if inspecting me.

"Are you okay?"

"It was a rough night," I say, wiping my mouth with the back of my hand.

"You can say that again."

"How did you find me?"

He raises an eyebrow as if confused by my question. "We followed your trail."

"My trail?" I scratch my head. "Oh, yeah. I started doing that after I got this stuck." I point to the problem.

"You didn't snap any branches before you cut the tree?"

"No." Clint points his weapon and searches the trees. "Oh wait, I might have," I admit, vaguely recalling my angry destruction on my way to the tree.

"If you didn't, someone else did." His eyes flicker with anger. "Which is it?"

"I did, but I didn't start when I left the cabin." I bite my tongue to keep from admitting that I'd only broken branches in anger and not to leave a trail.

His eyes soften as he lowers the bow. "I didn't mean to snap. We've been worried sick."

I hang my head. "I'm sorry."

"We need to get this out of here," he says, handing me the bow.

"How did you find me once you got to the tree? I didn't leave a trail while I was moving this thing." I smack the bark as Clint raises the axe above his head.

"We could see where you had dragged it, but then that suddenly ended. Since we didn't see you or the tree we just kept looking until we found large indents in the ground. It took us longer after that."

"That makes sense." Clint frees the lumber in three swings. I pick up the saw and blanket full of loot. "Oh hey, I found a cabin!"

Clint smiles. "I was going to guess that you went begging on the street corner for a room at Lakeside Hideaway."

*And this is why I am so indecisive about the divorce, Clint. You're always good for a laugh.* I bite my lip and return the smile. "Ha. I had a luxurious suite compared to the roach infested rooms at Hideaway. I think my room is available again tonight if you're interested."

Ella and Tanner giggle but their eyes show that they don't understand the joke.

"I've already booked a room at the finest cabin in the resort," he boasts arrogantly, waving his hand across his body.

Anger flickers inside me and I'm not sure whether it's because our cabin *is* the nicest or if it's because of who it belongs to. "And," he pauses for effect, "the best part is we aren't paying the bill!" The jab gives me a tiny bit of satisfaction.

The amusement drains from Clint's face. "Mapping out cabins was on the agenda for today. Now that we're way behind schedule and we have to backtrack, can you please grab an end, so we can get going?"

I hand the blanket and water to Tanner and the bow to Ella. "I moved it all the way here, can't you move it back?" My tone is teasing, but I hope he'll shoulder most of the weight.

He hoists the front over his shoulder and waits for me to follow suit. "I left my Superman cape at home."

"How convenient."

"Guess you should've stuck closer to the cabin."

He turns so that we are backtracking, taking a longer way back, I'm sure.

I shift the weight to my other shoulder as we pivot between the trees. "Why can't we go straight to the cabin?"

Clint turns and glares at the unsteadiness. "We have to cut the branches so it's not so obvious someone is out here."

"Won't it still be an obvious marker?"

"Yes, but not as much as a hanging twig."

Something about his attitude makes my decision to only speak to him when absolutely necessary easier.

My need to speak comes less than five minutes later when a resounding pain throbs across my shoulder and into my back. "I need a break," I whisper.

"Time is of the essence," Clint replies as if he's carrying a toothpick.

"Clint, I'm going to drop it."

He maneuvers around a tree. I stumble and my arm wobbles under the weight. Shifting positions so I can carry it above my head with both arms, I follow him between the trees.

Ella takes her position as weapon carrier seriously. She walks to the side of Clint, her eyes continuously scanning the surroundings. As the terrain shifts and we move uphill, I drop the log to carry it with both hands in front of me, but my arms sag like jelly, and the end drops to the ground. Clint's body squats under the sudden movement and he turns with a glare, but lets the log roll off his shoulder. It rolls down the incline until a tree stops it three feet from us.

"I told you I was going to drop it," I say sheepishly. "I'm not a man."

He takes a seat on the log. "Five minutes. Then we get moving."

The longer we travel, the more breaks we have to take because I lack the endurance to carry that much weight for that long. As we pass the branches I snapped in anger, Clint points them out for Tanner to tear off.

We finally make it back to the cabin sometime after noon I assume, judging by the position of the sun.

With tingling arms, I open a can of Spam and cut it in half. If I couldn't see my arms as I turn the can opener against the can of baked beans, I would've thought they had disappeared. Slapping the cold meal on the table, I vow to have a hot meal for supper.

"Since half the day is gone, I suggest we stay here and cut that wood and tomorrow we go searching for cabins," Clint says, eating his meal in six bites.

Too weak to say anything, I just nod. The effort it takes to eat is unbearable despite the arguing from my stomach. When Tanner looks longingly at my plate, I slide it to him.

"Let's get that wood cut," Clint says the second we finish.

I'll admit his endurance is impressive, but I feel like not moving for the next week.

# Chapter 11

My arms ache when I wake the next morning, but I don't mention it. I know Clint will say it was self-inflicted. The pain takes my mind off the emotions swirling in my head so it's a distraction I welcome. We eat a cold breakfast of peas and baked beans before heading into the woods with the notebook and pencil I found in the abandoned cabin.

"Today we head north. We'll walk until the sun is overhead and turn around. Keep an eye out for anything we can use as a landmark," Clint instructs as he puts the kids on Moonshine's back so we can begin our adventure.

We return late afternoon with nothing to show for our day except an armload of sticks for the fire.

The next day we head west and find a tiny cabin over the next mountain. I open the notebook in the middle and draw a map much like a first grader would. My triangle roof is lopsided on the quickly drawn square cabin, but I label it with a *1* anyway. We raid the cabin and confiscate a wash tub, a length of thin rope perfect for a clothesline, two rusty traps that Clint says should still work, and a Bible.

I wake early on the third morning of cabin searching. I want to say it is Tuesday, but it could be Thursday. Truth is, I've lost complete track of time. Turning to the back of the notebook I create tally marks for the days I know we've been out here. I can't help but think of Tom Hanks in *Castaway*.

"I was thinking I would wash the curtains and blankets before we head out today," I say while we eat deer burgers I cooked over the gas stove. "I don't want them hanging out overnight."

"I'll hang the line," Clint says with his mouth full.

74

The adventure south takes us back to the abandoned cabin where I spent a few nights before. Feeling defeated, I question Clint on his knowledge of the mountains. It turns into a short spat about the last time he had a chance to spend any real time in the woods which was when he and Richard made weekend trips years ago. His tone implies it's my fault he's rusty with the details and I resort to not speaking to him again.

Tanner and Ella cling to their sour expressions from the tension between me and Clint even as I pull them from the mare's back upon our return. "Let's get these curtains off the line," I say, snubbing Clint as he makes an attempt to turn my mood by brushing my hand as he takes the reins from me.

Draping the window coverings over their little heads, I manage a smile from Ella and a giggle from Tanner. A thud against the shed grabs their attention, halting their giddiness. Another blow warrants a glance, even though I'm still angry at Clint and secretly hope Moonshine slammed him against the wall.

"Mom-my," Ella cries as a sharp whack smacks the wood. Probably just the wind beating the door against the side, I tell myself, stepping into the flowing fabric and pretending to fight it.

Ella repeats herself, but Clint's bark overpowers her tiny voice. "Lexi, the bow!"

I untangle the curtain from my body and rush for the bow he left leaning against the porch.

Clint has a man two inches shorter, but stockier than he, pinned to the wall. Tanner and Ella watch in horror as I train the Stinger broadhead between the man's eyes, waiting for Clint's order to fire.

"Don't shoot!"

I whip around, pointing the four-blade arrow directly at a straight-from-the-city blonde. She's almost my height in her two-inch heeled black knee-high leather boots. A tiny red skirt is cut too short over her sculpted tan legs. She crosses her arms over the ruffles on her bodice, showing off a gawdy display of jewelry. Dozens of bangles and dainty chains and charms dangle from her tiny wrists. She takes a powerful step toward Clint until she sees I'm not about to let her pass. Her expensive bracelets clink as she forces her hands into fists at her side. I wonder how she made it this far without being caught. She might as well have put a neon sign above her head. With only a few steps between us, I see her neck is also adorned with multiple necklaces. It's like she had to reminisce one last time of being a kid and playing dress up in her mother's jewelry box before she left the comforts of her penthouse. I'm scared to check out her earrings, but that would be like not checking on the caboose after seeing the wrecked train. I'm sadly disappointed by the simple diamonds hanging from her lobes, barely peeking out from perfectly highlighted curls that cascade over her shoulders. If she lost half the jewelry, she wouldn't look like a hooker who stole from her john on the way out the door. Maybe that's how the rich do it, I think, staring at the slender woman who probably paid to not get stretch marks during pregnancy.

"CJ, he's with me!" Her perfectly painted lips form a thin line. *Why is she calling him CJ? He's never gone by his initials.*

I whip around to focus on the man Clint holds against the wall. He looks past me but keeps his grip firm.

"He's with me." She powers past me, unthreatened, placing her manicured hand on Clint's bicep and pulls him away.

The man, dressed in designer jeans and black polo shirt, slinks to the ground. His dark hair is disheveled, and I can't help but wonder about his ethnicity as I study him. His skin is fair enough to tell one white parent was involved, but the other definitely has darker skin. Mexican maybe? Or Indian? I can never tell. Could be Asian for all I know. Clint reluctantly gives the woman a hug. It lasts only a second as if he's afraid his dirt and stink will rub off. I'm sure she has the same fear as she puts one arm around him, trying to only touch with her bare skin.

Clint's eyes dart across the property and into the woods. "Where are the kids?"

"In the cabin. I sent them in on my way out. I hope that's okay."

Freaked out that our kids obeyed a woman they don't know, I take off for the house, leaving them to their business.

"We're not done talking about what happened in here, Christa," Clint says, joining me in a brisk walk to the cabin.

Jett and Sidney sit at the table, phones in hand, with Tanner and Ella between them. Tanner is mesmerized watching Jett move the device as a controller as he plays whatever game doesn't require internet and Sidney and Ella poke at her screen with wide smiles on their faces. Clint forces hugs from the teens, who immediately return to the electronics when they are released.

Christa drags her man-friend in like the victim she sees him to be. Clint stops trying to pry conversation from his older children and motions for the adults to go outside.

"Who the hell is he?" Clint shoves a finger in the direction of the stranger who lurks a safe distance near the end of the porch.

Christa awkwardly puts her arm around the man's waist. The gesture seems more forced than casual and I wonder if that's because it's the first time he's seen her with another man. "This is Eddie...my boyfriend." Her words come out rehearsed, like she had to work up the nerve to say them.

Clint's muscles tighten underneath his shirt. In the moment, despite our struggles, I'm proud that my husband is the better fit of the two. "Since when?"

Christa bats her fake eyelashes Eddie's direction. "Five, six months?" She runs her left hand over his collar, revealing a large diamond ring.

Clint glances at me and his pecks twitch as he looks back at the couple. "Nice way to tell me about the engagement," he says, almost like it's a struggle to say the words.

Christa's mouth falls as if she hadn't planned to make the revelation just yet. Sure, you probably couldn't wait to flash that around, I think. "I wasn't sure how to tell you," she whispers.

"Moving a little fast, don't ya think?"

Eddie slides his fingers into hers. "When you know, you know, ya know?"

Christa squeezes Eddie's hand and places it to his side. She spins the ring on her finger and gives a stern look to Eddie before turning it on Clint. "How did you get here?"

"We walked. How did *you* get here?"

Christa points to a second Ranger parked next to the useless one we found.

"You drove that thing all the way from Middletown?"

"Yeah, it took forever. Eddie said we should stay off the roads. I wanted to bring the Range Rover, but he thought this would be a better idea. Isn't he smart?" She runs her fingers over his chest as if she's showing off the Queen's jewels, and from the look of her hand, it's clear she's never done a day of work in her entire life.

"How on earth did you have enough gas to make it a hundred and fifty miles?"

"Gas cans. The last of it is in the tank."

"I hope you brought food." He glances longingly at the two suitcases sitting in the middle of the room then frowns, looking at her feet. "And sensible shoes."

"What's wrong with my boots?"

I laugh. "You'll see."

Clint's eyes narrow as if he thinks she needs to be eased into our situation. "The kids will have to sleep in the loft. You two can have the other bedroom."

Christa's eyes dart nervously from Eddie to Clint like she's afraid he'll be upset she's sharing a bed with another man.

"I need to get these curtains hung back up if you wouldn't mind giving me some help," I say, trying to ease out of the weirdness. Christa nudges Eddie who follows me to the scattered drapes on the ground.

"You know there's no electricity here," I say as I slide the rod into the curtain over the sink.

"We brought a solar panel," Jett states without missing a beat on his game.

Clint opens the door for Christa. "Did you hear that, Clint? They brought a solar panel."

"Hmmm. Hey, let me see that," he says to Sidney, taking the phone. "I want to see if I can get any news."

"There's not going to be any service up here," I remind him.

"Shit. Maybe if we go down the ridge we might be able to pick something up. We'll try tomorrow."

"The phone lines were out," I say.

His forehead wrinkles as he looks accusingly at Eddie and Christa. "Do you guys know what the hell is going on?"

Christa shrugs. "We stopped for lunch after a quick shopping trip and all of a sudden there were men in the streets all dressed in black like Ninjas. They were forcing people into those military truck things. Thankfully, I was talking to the owner of the little café when it happened. He led us out the back and gave us the keys to his Maserati. He went back inside, and we left as fast as we could. It was only thanks to Eddie's driving skills that we were able to pass the blockade out of the city and get to my house on the edge of town." She runs her hand over Eddie's cheek. "They had everything blocked, but Eddie made sure we got by them."

Clint nods. "Do you know who they are?"

"I saw a patch on one of their arms. Looked just like the WIN symbol. You know, the one with the two guns crossed over the picture of the globe."

"What would the Worldwide Islamic Nation want with our tiny town?" Clint scratches his thick beard that he's refused to shave since we've been here.

"They're responsible for hundreds of attacks around the world in the last few decades. It only makes sense that they're behind it." Eddie had been quiet up to this point.

"I think we should step back outside," I say, noticing Ella's intent focus on the conversation.

Once we're all a safe distance away from little ears, Clint continues, "They haven't attacked us seriously since they bombed the Seattle Space Needle in 2013."

"I guess taking out their camp in Bum-F—" a sharp glare from Christa stops Eddie's words. "—didn't deter them like we thought," he finishes.

"Whatever they're doing has to be huge," Clint adds. "Did you notice anything else that might be helpful?"

"I think I saw a group of soldiers being put in a separate truck," Eddie offers.

Clint nods. "So they're segregating everyone?"

"Looks that way," he says.

"I wonder why they came *here*." Clint runs a hand through his too-long, too-greasy hair.

Christa jingles her jewelry as she crosses her arms. "Do you think they're doing this anywhere else?" She shudders slightly as Eddie slides his arm over her shoulder.

"If they came to this God-forsaken neck of the woods, no offense," he says, waving a hand at us, "I would assume they're all over the country."

"It makes no sense," Clint says.

"It might if you factor in those prisons they held us in," I add.

Christa's hand flies to her chest. "You were in prison?".

"Not like what you're thinking of," Clint explains. "It was more like a modern-day concentration camp."

Christa stumbles backward. "Were there gas chambers?"

A dull throb pulses in my temples. "It's not being run by Hitler," I say as I try to massage the pain away.

Clint narrows his eyes at me as if I'm a peasant who is offending a member of the royal family. "Actually, it looks like it might be right out of Hitler's playbook."

"I guess Hitler *did* kind of brainwash people," I admit.

"You were brainwashed?" Christa's color pales and she reaches for Eddie's hand like it's the first she's realized how serious this is.

"Thankfully, no. And I can thank you for that," Clint says with a sigh.

Christa's mouth twists to one side. "You can?"

"You remember that Christmas party a few years ago, the one where Drew's friend—uh, the guy who laughed like a dying hyena—"

"Oh yeah—James. That must've been three, four years ago?" She smiles at some shared memory between them.

"Whatever happened to him?"

"He moved to San Fran and opened the largest chain of scrapbook stores on the West Coast."

"Can we get to the point?" My jaw clenches so tightly I barely get the words out.

"Right. That was the year he spilled the cocktail all over your dress and you kept telling people there was a required wardrobe change every three drinks."

Christa laughs, a deep, annoying, belly laugh that echoes into the trees. "Yes! Six women took me seriously. Do you remember that? They had their drivers go get them new dresses. I was so mad though. He ruined my nicest Oscar De La Renta dress."

*Her nicest one? As if we all have at least one,* I scowl to myself as a twinge of jealousy creeps into my bones at the way they're reacting to one another.

"I don't think that's the point," I say bluntly.

"The point is, he was telling me about a friend of his. I thought he was full of shit at the time, but now...now I think he may have been telling the truth."

"Which is?" Anger is evident in my voice, resulting in cold stares from the rest of the party.

"He said he had a friend who was raised in a cult." Christa's eyes bulge. She nervously slides gold and silver bands up and down her arm.

"Everyone can't be born with a silver spoon," I say, getting a sharp look from Clint.

"The guy was so drunk he should've been on his fifth outfit." He exchanges a smirk with Christa. "He went into great detail about how he was brainwashed for years."

I dig my fingers into my pulsating temples. "So?"

"I recognized the signs as they were happening and blocked them out. I never imagined all his ramblings would save my life someday."

Christa nods in amazement like he completed some big feat the rest of us weren't capable of.

I wave my hand to emphasis some urgency. "We need to know if this is something happening locally or how wide-spread it actually is. Ideas?"

"Daddy is in Europe with a major BOS customer. We can find out when he gets back." She turns to me. "Bennett Operating Systems has high maintenance contracts and he has to keep purchasing companies happy," she explains as if I couldn't fathom the responsibility of founding a company capable of being a leader in the cell phone software industry.

"He should be back in a few days. As soon as he sees what's going on, he'll come straight here," she says proudly, as if he will be immune to any roadblocks.

"If they don't capture him," I state coldly.

"He can write a check and they'll leave him alone."

I roll my eyes. "Great. He'll get away and they'll get a nice chunk of change to carry on their mission."

"At least we'll know how big this is," she says like it's worth the price he'll pay.

"Why don't we switch gears," Clint offers. "Let's go inside and take a new inventory to include what you brought."

"This should be fun," I say, eagerly reaching for the door.

"There's no need to be nasty, Lexi," Clint growls, tugging my wrist away from the door. "Spread your things out on the table. We'll be in in a minute." He kicks the door open and waits for them to enter before shutting it behind them.

"I bet she brought a hair dryer."

"Why are you being so cruel to her?"

My breath catches in my throat. "I think you'll understand when you see what she brought. Did you see the amount of jewelry on her? I bet they didn't even think to pack any food."

"She's not that dumb, Lexi. Her background is different than ours. You have to cut her some slack."

"She thinks her daddy can write a check and make this disappear."

He runs his hand through his hair. "You realize she could kick us out at any time, right?"

"I doubt she'd be able to survive without us."

"You're one to talk. Didn't you just get lost and spend the night in a shack because you were mad at me?"

"And I didn't die."

"What if you'd come across a bear? Or a mountain lion? What would you have done?"

I roll my eyes. "It doesn't matter. It didn't happen."

"But it could have. You have to use your head."

"Fine. Next time I'll take you so you can be eaten."

"This is not a time for jokes."

I place my hands on my hips. "I'm not joking."

"You're impossible."

"Let's go see what they brought so we can eat. I'm hungry."

Christa sits at the table cleaning mud off her knee-high boots with the ridiculous heels while Eddie puts the last of their things on the table. It's all I can do not to laugh when I see what's lying there. Clint scratches his head, staring at her lavish belongings. Three hairbrushes of different shapes, makeup tubes, brushes, and sponges surround two large pallets of eye shadow. A dozen bottles of face cream and shampoos, lotions, and soaps, three types of expensive perfumes in fancy bottles, and a laptop lie next to six thick textbooks, a loaf of smashed bread, a tin of cookies, and a box of matches. Fiji water bottles line one edge of the table and in the corner is a cluster of those essential oils everyone goes nuts over.

"These are Jimmy Choos," Christa says when she catches me staring at her rubbing at a scratch on the black leather.

"If those are Jimmy's shoes, I don't want to see the rest of his outfit."

She twists her face up and wipes dirt off the soles with the corner of a shirt—Clint's dirty shirt that I piled in the washtub with the rest of our dirty laundry—and waves her hand. "Jimmy *Choo*...never mind. They're expensive."

"Were you planning on staying at The Five Seasons?"

"No. Eddie said I should wear boots when I suggested we hide out here."

"And you picked thousand-dollar boots?"

"I don't have any like yours," she says, pointing to my Ariat farm boots.

"I hope you like deer," Clint intervenes before I can act on my thoughts of decking her.

"Never had it," she replies with a worried, forced smile.

I smile wickedly at her. "You're about to." I take the matches from the table and take them to the fireplace. "Why don't you kids bring in some kindling and a few pieces of wood."

I catch Christa's face from the corner of my eye. I might as well have asked them to lasso a wild bull. Tanner and Ella jump from their spots next to Jett and Sidney and hurry outside. The teenagers stay engrossed in their devices like the rules don't apply to them. Clint rifles through the cluttered table so he doesn't have to address their laziness.

An hour later I put deer burgers, baked potatoes, and corn on the table. I discretely enjoy the disgust on Christa and her kids' faces as the rest of us enjoy the meal.

Jett shoves his plate away. "Can we have something else?"

"There's a McDonald's on the corner," I offer.

"Is it open?"

"We have baked beans," Clint tells him while silently warning me with his cold blue eyes that I'm on thin ice.

Jett shrugs. "I guess that would be okay."

I point to the cabinet. "They're in there and there's a pan to heat it in the other cabinet." He gives me a puzzled look but gets the can. "Can opener is in the drawer."

Clint gets up to help him when he sees him staring at the device like it came from Mars. Jett returns to his seat and waits for Clint to heat his new dinner.

Sidney takes one bite and turns to her mother. "I'm getting a cookie."

"After dinner," she says.

"I'm done with dinner."

"Okay. But only one."

I stab my fork into my bland potato as Tanner and Ella glare at me with contempt. "You have to clean your plates. We can't afford to waste food," I say.

Sidney returns to the table with two cookies. Christa shakes her head but says nothing.

"Can I have a cookie too? I'm done with my dinner," Jett says after taking three bites of the baked beans.

"If you're done," Christa says.

I clean my plate and take a helping of the baked beans. I've always hated the things, but I'm hungry and don't want anything going to waste.

"I'm going to get Moonshine," I say, tossing my plate into the sink after swallowing the beans almost whole.

Eddie's eyes light up. "You have moonshine?" He follows me outside.

I rub the horse's neck. "This is our Moonshine."

He rolls his eyes. "You named the horse Moonshine?"

"We did."

Disappointed, he retreats to the cabin. I linger outside by myself for a few minutes, inhaling the cool night air before going back inside with an armload of wood.

The kids are back on their phones when I return and Christa and Eddie have taken seats next to the fire, whispering quietly, almost awkwardly in a two-person huddle. I help Clint wash and dry the dishes and wait for the night to end.

# Chapter 12

Christa rubs her eyes as she emerges from her room the next morning. A sleep mask that reads 'Do Not Disturb' rests on her forehead. Her slippers brush against the pine floor as she sways lazily toward us. "Coffee?"

I continue organizing our food, rearranging the items into meals so I have a better idea of how long it will last. "Fresh out."

She wraps her fuzzy pink robe tighter around her waist. "What's for breakfast?"

"I made toast on the fire. There's nothing to go on it though."

"Maybe I'll just take a shower."

"Hope you like them cold."

"What?!"

At her obvious displeasure, I steal a glance in her direction. The jolt seems to have done better than any coffee.

"There's a shower out back or we can heat some water for the tub," Clint says, pointing to the washtub near the door.

"You've got to be kidding me?! Daddy didn't put a bathroom in here? I told him I wasn't coming back until he built one." Her pout resembles that of a toddler's.

Clint coughs into burnt toast. Christa skirts around him to search the cabinets, her cheeks flushed with color. If food weren't so scarce, I might lose my breakfast at the not-so-discrete declaration of their tryst.

"Good thing I just had a blow out," she says into the musty, bare wood. She runs a hand through her untouched hair. I washed my hair the day before yesterday and it still looks stringy and dull compared to hers. Brushing crumbs from the table into my hand, I study her face, desperate to find a flaw. She's seven years my senior and we could pass for the same age. Where I have tiny wrinkles forming around my eyes, she has none. *In another decade, I'll look old enough to be her mother*, I scowl, dumping the crumbs into the sink.

"I can't believe you remembered the way." Clint struggles to wipe the smirk off his face when he catches me glaring at him.

Christa's laugh fills the room. It reminds me of a cartoon rodent's evil squeal. "I could've never gotten here if Daddy hadn't kept a map in his desk."

I want to throw in a jab about how she might've known how to get here if she'd bring the kids once in a while, but Clint speaks before I have the chance.

"Do you want me to heat some water? I was going to take Jett out to teach him to shoot."

She presses her faintly tinted lips firmly together. "You know I don't like guns."

Clint picks up the bow and pats it. "This isn't a gun. Besides, the more people who know how to shoot, the better."

"I don't want him shooting an innocent animal. What if he shoots a mother and leaves her babies orphans?"

"Don't worry, there are plenty of childless criminal deer out here," I say with a smirk.

She crosses her arms and stamps her foot. "I don't like this."

"Do you like to eat?"

She waves her hand. "Go ahead."

"Let's go shoot some stuff, Jett." There's a groan from the large chair a few feet away, but the kid gets up. Wearing a baby blue polo and skinny jeans rolled at the ankles, he looks comical next to Clint in his dirty jeans with a hole in the knee and stained white shirt. They couldn't be more different if they tried, I think, staring from their shoes—Clint's old boots and Jett's white Dockers—to their faces. Clint is beaming, and Jett might as well be heading off to a Shakespeare class.

Christa turns to me when the door closes behind the two. "What is there for us to do while they're out doing boy things?"

"Clean."

"I guess there would be no housekeeper, would there?"

"Not unless you brought one."

"I would have, but she had the afternoon off to take her sick kid to the doctor."

"How unfortunate," I say, wondering if my tone implies how compassionate she is to require the woman to work that day at all.

"Tell me about it."

"I'm going to take the kids out later and teach them to throw a knife."

Her green eyes bulge. "*Why?*"

"They may need to defend themselves."

"How does that make you any better than the terrorists? Teaching children to kill? That's absurd."

I blink in disbelief. "Would you rather they die without a fight?"

"I'm just saying it should be left to adults."

"They didn't leave children out of this and I'm sure as hell not going to leave my kids defenseless should something happen to the rest of us."

"I can't believe this."

"Clint would back me up."

"This is why I didn't want to raise children here," she squeals. "You people are a bunch of heathens." I know she means it as an insult, but I look over at Sidney, her eyes glued to a screen, and my kids who are playing a game on the floor with the deck of cards I found. She doesn't have to approve; I know I'm doing it right.

"Sadly, you're the only one not suffering from your way of thinking." She huffs loudly and picks at a loose string on her robe. "It's not like this is our typical afternoon activity. Under the circumstances, I would like to know that my children could protect themselves if I weren't able to."

She purses her lips and turns away from me. "What do you think, Eddie?"

He studies her for a moment, contemplating what to say. "I don't know if I agree with kids being in on the fight, but I guess I'm not going to complain if a half-pint saves my life or takes out a bad guy."

"Looks like I'm outnumbered then."

"I promise there will be a long speech beforehand."

"I would certainly hope so. If we end up with child soldiers, it will be all your fault." She tosses a nibbled piece of bread on the table and crosses her arms in defiance.

I wonder if this is the best idea for Ella, given her blackouts, but tell myself that she's been her normal self since we found Clint so it's probably safe.

"Eddie, would you mind taking the tub out and filling it with water? I desperately need a clean shirt and I still haven't had a chance to wash the sheets. They smell like 2005." He jumps at my request, and I pretend he's as anxious to get away from Christa as I am.

Christa plops into the chair Jett emptied. "Have fun with that." She pulls a nail file from the pocket of her robe and runs it across the tip of her index finger.

I sniff the shirt I've been wearing for two days as I head to my room for sheets. It smells like a farmer after a long day's work. I consider asking Christa to borrow a shirt, which would barely cover my midriff considering the four inches in height difference, but pride won't let me. "If you want your sheets washed, take them outside," I announce as I roll dirty clothes into our bedding. Tanner and Ella run out with their sheets draped over them like capes as I pour shampoo into the tub. They chase each other around the small yard while I scrub the clothing first. Eddie stares as I am forced to hang my undergarments on the line. Christa emerges from the cabin looking pristine in a black tank top that could've been painted on underneath her jean jacket. Skinny jeans hug her trim waist and I'm relieved that she's found a sensible pair of shoes—sneakers—but she's missing the socks. At least it's an improvement, I tell myself as I prepare to count to ten. Inhaling deeply, I remember the tactic we used at work. I'm thankful her bra isn't hanging next to mine. My basic black cotton would look like rags compared to the fancy lingerie I assume she wears. Eddie stops to gawk at her as she approaches. She places a quick peck on his cheek and glances to the line. I detect a sense of disgust, like she's ashamed to be sharing quarters with someone who dresses like a peasant, but it could be my imagination. I snag the sheet from Ella's head as she rushes by and hurry to distract myself in the tub of suds. It doesn't take long to finish since neither Christa nor Sidney bothered to bring anything out.

"I need something to mark a target," I say, shifting activities before focus can be regained on my boring underwear on the line.

"Nail polish," Ella pipes up.

"We don't have any." I turn to Christa. "Do we?"

"I only brought one bottle."

"Get it."

Christa all but scowls at Ella as she turns to the cabin. "I saw her hide it when she was unpacking," Ella admits.

Christa slaps the bottle in my hand a minute later. Pink. I should've known. I mark a circle in the middle of the wood the size of my fist and hand it back to her.

"Sidney says she doesn't want to do it," Christa says as I pull the knife from the sheath at my hip.

"Fine," I say and begin my spiel to Tanner and Ella before we form a line and I show them how to throw the weapon.

I pierce just outside the circle. Eddie is next and hits the mark on the first try. Tanner's throw isn't hard enough to make it to the wood and Ella's bounces off the edge. I hold it out to Christa. She shakes her head, refusing to take it. When she sees Tanner and Ella getting closer to the circle on their turns, she holds her hand out. I place the handle in her palm. She almost jumps as it makes contact with her skin. Holding it like you would the tail of a snake, she aims and misses the log completely.

# Chapter 13

A brisk wind blows in five days later, bringing with it the imminent threat of an early winter. The thin jacket I'm wearing won't hold up against the frigid New York weather. I pull the axe from the wood I'm splitting as Clint and Eddie approach.

"I'm taking Eddie to check the traps," Clint says. "Won't be gone long."

"I could go if you boys would rather stay here and do manly things like chopping wood."

"Eddie says he's never been trapping, and he might need to know in case something happens to me."

My arms ache, and I take my frustration out on Clint. "That wouldn't make me forget."

"What if we have to split up?"

Hair blows around my face. I tug the hair tie from my ponytail and adjust it, stalling so I don't have to admit he has a point. Without us, he and Christa wouldn't have a clue. "How's Jett doing with the bow?"

"We lost another arrow yesterday, but I'll whip him into shape in the next day or two."

"Do you think it's a good idea to keep at it if he's losing an arrow a day?"

"He's lost two."

"How many can we afford to lose?" The words come out more disrespectful than I mean them.

"We're going to scope out a spot for a deer stand too. I thought we'd take the Ranger to the abandoned cabin and get some planks for it later today."

"I can do that while you're gone."

"I'd rather you stay here."

"You mean you'd rather I babysit instead of doing something useful?"

He lets out a low growl through clinched teeth. "What would be useful is if you'd stop with the attitude."

"I'm not the only one here capable of doing this." I slam the axe into the maple.

"Feel free to teach someone to do it."

"Might as well do it myself. Probably couldn't pull them off their electronics anyway."

He shrugs. "Christa is putting her skills to good use today, so don't go there."

"She's doing manicures?" I wipe my nails on my jeans and admire the dirt beneath them.

"Go in and see for yourself," he says with a furrowed brow. He and Eddie head for the trees.

I wait for them to get out of sight before hurrying inside to see what Christa is up to.

A subtle lavender aroma lingers in the small cabin and I notice Christa has arranged her essential oils next to a dainty diffuser on the counter.

"It's a calming fragrance," she explains, catching me staring at the out-of-place mechanism.

Sewing supplies are strewn about the table. Sidney removes buttons from a dress shirt while Christa drapes Ella in some sort of blanket wrap near the fireplace. Tanner proudly wears his concoction—a makeshift poncho with three uneven buttons down the sides and a crooked seam around the odd shaped hole made for his head. The gray fabric fits snuggly around him, the back side hanging slightly lower than the front, but he proudly shows it off as I stand there trying not to explode at the use of our only blankets. He produces a hood which makes him look slightly like Friar Tuck.

He spins a circle. "How do I look?"

"Like you're ready for the orphan train," I tell him, grabbing one of Christa's expensive water bottles from the counter.

Christa, obviously proud of her garment, focuses intently on the button she's sewing. She sticks her finger with the needle and raises the blood droplet to her mouth. "It's all yours if you can do better."

Water drips down my chin as I guzzle the liquid. "I don't pretend to know how to sew. Besides, we brought jackets."

"At least I'm trying. I thought we might need something warmer to wear later on."

"I like it," Tanner exclaims, spinning around.

"You make it look good."

Christa moves to the floor and cuts into another blanket. "I took a sewing class when Jett was in first grade." She shrugs. "Needed something to do, I guess."

I press my fingers into my forehead. "What are we going to do for blankets?"

"Watch this," Tanner exclaims, his little fingers struggling to undo the small buttons fast enough. I watch with an amused smile as I patiently wait for him to find his way out. He carefully attaches a button from the hood onto the opposite side of the head hole and plops onto the floor, revealing a blanket with a moon shaped hole in it. "See?"

"I don't think we're going to have enough buttons," Sidney says, placing a navy shirt on the table.

"Did you grab the polos?" Sidney nods. "How many do we have?"

"Fifteen."

"That's not nearly enough."

Rolling the water bottle lid in my fingers, I quickly head to my room for the arrow Clint left beside my bed. I pile the shirts into Sidney's arms and shove the arrow tip into the cap.

"Will this work?" I hold the creation out to Christa.

Her smile quickly turns to a frown. "I don't have enough string for that."

For taking a sewing class, she sure didn't pay attention to the terminology, but I don't point that out. "What if we make some?"

"Is there something else we can use for string?"

Sidney quietly pokes holes in two caps before whispering, "We could take them out of some tampons."

"We can't sacrifice those."

"Sidney, go get a pair of your leggings. I can cut the hem off the bottom and use it."

"Why mine?"

Christa separates buttons into two piles. "Because you're going to grow out of them in a year anyway. Just go get them."

I take Sidney's place at the table as Christa snatches the red leggings from the reluctant teenager.

"How many caps do you need?" I ask, more of a way to ignore Sidney's pouting than anything.

Christa's finger hits imaginary points in the air as she counts. "I used nine buttons on Ella's, so...we have fifteen here...like fifty? Can that be right?"

"I don't think we have that many."

"I can cut it down to seven buttons each on the kids and five on the adults."

"I'm still not sure we have enough."

"Eddie and I have belts that we can use to secure ours so that will save us four buttons. Plus, I can probably fashion something from the leggings."

I nod and return to stabbing holes. "What about string?"

"Stupid fish!" Jett draws Tanner's attention by yanking his phone as if it were a pole. "He got away."

"Fishing line!" Christa's eyes connect with mine and we laugh. A deep laugh that feels good in our current situation. How could we have not thought of that?

Sidney snatches her leggings before her mother can destroy them.

An hour later, Christa and the younger kids are waiting anxiously to put on a fashion show for Clint and Eddie.

# Chapter 14

The next week passes slowly with long days full of chopping wood and trapping small game all while keeping watch for any unusual activity in the woods.

"I've been thinking," Clint says as he and I sit shoulder to shoulder on the porch step. "It's time to find out what's going on out there." He motions to the vast spread of trees with his hand.

"Do you think that's really a good idea? No telling what we'll find."

Clint exhales a large sigh. "Christa's eager to know too. She's ready to go home."

"Is she having a hard time out here?" I ask in a mocking tone.

"Don't act like you're happy with our living situation," he replies sternly.

"The only problem I have with being out here is knowing there are terrorists on the loose."

"And dealing with my ex-wife and two teenagers," he bites.

"Do you know how close Christa came to getting kicked in the head by Moonshine yesterday? All because she lost an earring." I laugh sharply. "Why she was looking on the ground under the horse's ass is beyond me. If I hadn't been coming out of the outhouse, she'd be dead by now."

"So I guess she owes you a debt of gratitude now?"

"I'm just saying she's not cut out for this."

"All the more reason to see if it's safe to return. Winter will be here soon, and we're not prepared."

"Don't look at me. I'm doing my part and then some."

"You're expecting too much."

I cross my arms. "My point is, I can only do so much."

"Eddie has been helping. I'll talk to Christa and the kids."

"You do that," I say sarcastically.

"Can we get back to my plan?" I wave my hand for him to go on. "I'm going to go back home to check on things. If I find things as I left them, I'm going to head to Canada."

"Canada? Just you?"

"Yes. It will be too dangerous to take the kids all that way. I'd rather everyone stay here if it comes to that." I raise my eyebrows. "Eddie and I have been talking this over. I'll cross into Vermont to be sure that we do, in fact, need outside help. If so, I'll head to Montreal and get it. He'll stay behind to help here. But I won't leave unless I know your supplies will last. That could take a few weeks."

"You put a lot of faith in a man you didn't know existed until he showed up here with your ex-wife."

"You'll see. We can count on him."

# Chapter 15

Eddie and I spend the morning outside building chairs using slightly bent nails pulled from the discarded slabs of Moonshine's stall door. They're turning out to be slightly lopsided. As we step back to look at our work, a snort echoes through the still mountain air. I rub my aching lower back while waiting for the horse and my rider to appear through the trees. It's been a week since Clint first mentioned going back home, but he only left this morning before dawn. My heart thumps hard against my ribs as I wonder if the short journey is a sign of good or bad news. Eddie runs inside to get the others as Clint emerges into the clearing. Clint looks like a real mountain-man as he guides the horse to a stop near the porch. He has enough coats tied around him with rope that he could be mistaken for a terrorist with a bomb strapped to his chest. Behind him are two bags tied together and thrown over the horse.

He lowers the bags before dismounting and tugs at the ropes, dropping every coat we own. I glance into the bags and see lamp oil, some extra clothes, cans of food and a couple bags of cookies. Well, at least the kids will be happy.

"Doesn't look like it went well," I say, judging the somber expression on his face.

"The town is deserted."

I pick up the reins he dropped and watch as he ushers everyone back inside after they gather on the porch. After a quick cool down and some water, I settle Moonshine into her stall and nervously head for the cabin.

Everyone circles around the table staring at the bags and assorted pile of coats while waiting for me.

"Now that we all know our town is deserted, I think it's time to discuss what to do next. I don't want to scare you," he says, directing his attention to the kids. "All the way back I was thinking about the best course of action. We need outside help. I have a buddy who's a Mountie in Montreal. I will check the towns along the way and gather supplies. Maybe I'll even find somewhere civilized and get help sooner. I'll have to leave soon though."

Eddie runs a hand through his hair, tugging at the ends. "I should go with you."

"I need someone here to protect the family."

"I actually agree with Eddie," I say. "I don't think you should go alone."

"This isn't up for discussion."

Eddie forcefully crosses his arms. "What happened to democracy?"

Clint scowls at Eddie. "Fine. All viable ideas will be taken into consideration and we'll take a vote."

"It will take some time to prepare for the kind of trip you're speaking of," Eddie says. "I say I go to another town and see if similar things have happened there."

"Veto," Clint snaps.

"Democracy," counters Eddie.

"Everyone hold up a hand if you think we should do what Eddie suggests." All hands go up but mine. "Who says I should go to Canada if Eddie finds trouble?"

"I'd like to make a motion that you don't go alone," I say, feeling defeated.

"I second that," Christa agrees.

"I volunteer to go along," Eddie almost demands rather than suggests. The furrow in Clint's brow pushes Eddie to plead his case. "Come on, are you really thinking about taking one of the women?"

"Lexi is staying here." His hand slides over mine. "I know you can handle it. No offense, Christa, but you're not cut out for going."

"You can't seriously be thinking of taking a child." Eddie's words drip with contempt.

"Jett is hardly a child."

"Why don't you just let me go with you? Jett can take care of things here," Eddie argues.

"I think you would be better suited to stay here and watch for trouble." Clint turns to his eldest son. Jett's eyes don't waiver from his phone's screen and I suddenly wish I could smash the solar panel that charges it, but we may need to use it one day. "What do you say, Jett? Will you come with me?"

Jett's eyes flicker up to his father, but his real focus remains on the device. "What?"

"Should've done this when you first arrived." Clint snatches the phone from Jett's long fingers. "Time to turn you into a man."

Christa scowls. "I don't like this."

"Everyone who is against Jett going, raise their hand," Eddie growls.

Christa, Jett, and Eddie raise their hands.

"I won't allow you to take Jett," Christa snarls.

"I'm his father," Clint retorts.

"And I've raised him thus far. I've been there when you weren't."

"Whose fault is that?"

"You were the one who left, Clint."

Clint cracks his knuckles.

"Why don't you let Jett decide," I offer.

Clint glares at me, forces a deep exhale, and turns to Jett. "I suppose Lexi is right. Jett, would you rather stay here and be responsible for all the heavy lifting and other man-chores Lexi needs help with or come with me and follow orders?"

"I kind of like things the way they are," Jett admits.

"If you come with me, you basically just need to make sure I stay alive and know what to do if I don't."

"I don't know."

Clint slides the phone into his pocket. "The phone is coming with me." He shrugs. "Fine. I'll go."

# Chapter 16

Six weeks pass, though it feels like a solid six months, and we have exactly enough food to last two days if we tighten our rations. That includes the few items Clint was able to bring back from town. Hunting hasn't been going well and the traps come up empty more often than not. Clint and Eddie had fashioned a few traps out of sticks, but they keep breaking or malfunctioning, leaving Clint to believe he should give them up. I am certain the worry lines have grown deeper on Clint's face even in the dim light of the full moon as he heads out to hunt. Unable to go back to sleep, I toss and turn until the chatter of birds draws me from bed. I rekindle the fire from the night before and open the last can of Spam and SpaghettiOs for anyone who can stomach it for breakfast.

Tanner and Ella stumble from the loft first. Ella sniffs her shirt as she walks to the table. She wrinkles her nose and I'm not sure if it's because of the way she smells or the breakfast sitting on the table. I give them each a small helping, dividing my share between them. I slip outside with my knife to take my frustrations out on a log with slashes filling a hideous pink circle. Hopefully it will take my mind off my growling stomach. Ella joins me with her own knife before I can work my resentments out. Knowing Clint's impending absence is drawing imminently closer, I want to be as prepared as I can. Christa, having not practiced since our first session, seems to have other concerns.

Ella glances toward the cabin where I'm sure her bowl sits untouched. "Did you eat?"

I fling the knife into the wood, hitting the outside line. "Nah, I had a dream about eating a large pizza and I woke up so stuffed I couldn't eat a bite." The line was stolen from *Cinderella Man*, and even though I altered it, she would never know I was quoting a movie. *Was it ham in the movie? Or was it steak?*

"Jett said he's not eating that again," Tanner announces from the porch.

Sidney lingers in the doorway, a mini version of her mother, clad in Armani or whatever rich people wear. She does have on decent shoes, though socks are still absent. Her shirt is casual, a pretty maroon shade, but it's clear she doesn't have much experience being in the woods. Her jeans, more holes than not, will find every twig and sticker bush in a mile radius.

"Mom has an idea," she says quietly from the edge of the porch.

"What's that?" I prepare to give an explanation why it won't work.

"She says maybe we could find edible plants."

"That's dangerous if you don't know what you're doing."

"She took a class on it. Said she could help identify them."

I sigh. "Bring her out. Let's see what she knows."

She springs into the cabin and returns with Christa, four bowls, and a smile she's been hiding since her arrival. We spend the morning searching for oval shaped Chickweed leaves. Luckily, it grows in clumps and once we spot it, we can pick for a few minutes before moving on. We end up with a bowl and a half before it's time to start lunch.

Jett stares at his phone from the chair with his permanent butt impression in the seat while Eddie snoops in the cabinets. He claps the door shut as if he's been caught snooping in my personal medicine cabinet when I open the door.

"It needs to be washed," I say, grabbing the camp stove from the closet.

"I'll do it," Sidney offers.

"I think you're supposed to cook it like spinach," Christa says.

I remove a skillet and add a touch of water onto the greens Sidney tosses in. "Want to have deer to go with it?"

Sidney chuckles, following me to the fire. "As if we have a choice."

"Bring in enough for supper. I'm going to put it in some tomato juice and we can pretend it's chili."

"Sounds like fun," she says sarcastically and hurries outside.

Tanner and Ella hurry over to Jett and they play a game on his phone while Sidney and I cook. Christa takes a seat at the table and paints the chips on her nails.

I don't have to ask to know how Clint's outing went. The lines furrowing across his forehead when he plops down at the table say it all. No kill.

"I'll go back out this evening," Clint says, staring at the charred green lumps on his plate. "Are you trying to poison me?" He jabs a leaf onto his fork.

"I took a class on edible plants," Christa offers.

He slowly raises the utensil to his mouth and scrapes the leaf off with his teeth. He chews once, twice. "I think our food is supposed to eat this." Clint plops another glob of the green weed into his mouth, quickly following it with a large bite of meat. "Did they teach you how to cook it?"

"I missed that day."

I swallow a chunk of the mushy leaves whole, afraid we're all about to die. "Was there a sale at Nordstrom's?"

Christa stares into her plate, no doubt waiting for Clint to come to her rescue. To my surprise, he doesn't.

"After lunch, I'm going to take Jett out for more practice. If I don't get a deer—or heck—a squirrel tonight, I'll have to venture back to town," Clint says, clearing his plate of the experiment. "That is, if whatever I just ate doesn't kill me first."

I chuckle, nervously swallowing the bite in my mouth. Christa scowls, but I detect a hint of hurt in our reaction to her contribution.

"I thought we agreed I'd go," Eddie says angrily.

He drops his plate into the sink. "Come up with a list of things we may need other than food. Come on, Jett," he orders, ignoring Eddie's stated inquiry.

Jett follows with a groan and soon the dirty plates are the only thing left at the table. Tanner and Ella quickly run back to take theirs to the sink, but I'm left to clean up the rest of the mess. I put the extra meat in a kettle with the tomato juice and hang it over the fire before wiping my hands on my jeans and getting the axe from the loft.

Sidney sits on the porch with her phone connected to the solar panel. I peak over her shoulder with the axe at my side and notice the book is about learning sign language. I'm pretty sure that's the same book she and Ella were studying last night. But I don't have time to ask her about it. I need to get to the task at hand. "I'm going to cut a tree since there's not a man to do it."

"Why don't you ask Eddie?"

"He's busy rubbing your mom's feet. I won't be far. Holler if ya need me."

This time I find a tree the size of my wrist and begin hacking away. The air is cool and heavy, threatening to bring rain, but I am still sweating before the tree falls. By the time I have another one cut, the sweat stains under my arms have reached the middle of my ribs. The smell emanating from my body is so strong I can scarcely stand it. I'll have to suffer a cold shower and try to scrub the days of filth from my skin.

I drag the young trees up the hill on the back side of the cabin, disrupting Tanner and Ella's game of tag in the small yard. Sidney glances up from her phone but doesn't offer any help.

Going inside, I find Christa doing yoga in front of the fireplace and Eddie leaning against the table watching her. I swallow my anger and reach above the cabinet for the handsaw. When I don't find it, I climb onto the counter and look.

"Have you seen a saw?" I ask.

Eddie shakes his head and Christa either ignores me or doesn't hear me. I peek my head out the door. "Have you seen the saw?"

"Isn't it on top of the cabinet?" At least one person was paying attention when we went over the hiding places for the weapons, I think.

"No."

Sidney slips her phone into her pocket. "Want me to help you look?"

I shove my hands through worn back pockets. "If you wouldn't mind. I'm not going to get help from anyone else."

Tanner runs up and tries to swing on my arm. "Are we gonna play 'Tanner in the loft with an axe' again?"

"You wanna play?" He nods eagerly and motions for Ella. "We're looking for a saw this time. You know what that looks like?"

He nods. "It's long and has teeth."

"That's right." Sidney jumps up to help. "Go," I yell when they are poised for attack on the cabin.

The three of them take off in a run, pushing past me. A frantic search ensues. Tanner dives under the table and Sidney rushes up the loft ladder. Ella runs past Christa, tripping over her leg as she balances in a pretzel-like position. The connection sends the two of them to the floor in a heap.

Sidney leaps from the closet with the prized tool and a wide grin. "Do I get a prize?"

I raise an eyebrow. "I wonder how it got there."

"Clint must've moved it," Eddie suggests.

"Where was it in there?"

"Sawed into the wall above the door," Sidney offers.

"Hmm. Sounds like something Clint would do."

"I bet that's what happened," Eddie says, passing it to me.

"Was everything else where it should be?"

"There's a knife missing under the table," Tanner says.

"Keep your eyes out for it. I'm going to get these trees done so I can take a shower."

Eddie smacks Christa's behind as she forms a perfect downward dog. Sidney rolls her eyes and heads back outside with the younger two on her heels.

"Play with us," they call, leaping from the porch. She sails over the steps and chases them. I smile as I put the blade into the fresh wood.

I don't even mind the cold water as it pours over me an hour later after I cut the tiny logs to size and clean up the sticks for kindling. A mess of leaves litter the ground, but the wind will take care of that soon enough. Thick clouds overhead promise a downpour before nightfall.

I shampoo my hair twice, hoping to get the grime from lack of regular bathing out of it. As soap runs down my face, Moonshine makes a noise I haven't heard from her since the day we saw the bear. I fling a towel around my soapy body and peak outside. Eddie crouches near the horse, trying to lift her front leg, but she isn't having any of it. After a couple attempts to get her hoof off the ground, he resorts to stroking her mane. She prances uncomfortably, and I manage to get back inside the privacy of the shower as his head turns slightly in my direction. *What was he doing?* I wonder as I put a moderate amount of conditioner into my soaking hair. Still dripping wet, and covered in goosebumps, I put my clothes on and hurry inside for some answers.

Eddie rises from the table when I enter. "I was trying to help, but I startled the horse."

"I thought I heard a commotion." I say coyly.

"I thought I should check her shoes since she may need to go to town. I still think I should go. I'm going to talk to Clint about it again when he gets back."

I wring my hair over the sink. "Clint's planning on going."

"It makes the most sense for me to go. He knows how to shoot and would be here to protect you if something happened." Apparently, he doesn't know that I can also shoot. I retreat to my room for a brush and wonder whether to mention it.

The door slams and I rush from the room in time to see Jett stomping across the floor to the large wooden chair. Without a word, he picks up his phone and stares into it.

Christa comes out of her room, holding her sleep mask against her forehead. She looks around as if we're under attack. "What's going on?"

Clint swings the door open. "Jett lost another arrow."

"Don't you have like ten more?"

"I haven't even gotten to the best part! He bent one! Now we're down to nine arrows. Nine!"

Eddie slaps a hand on Clint's shoulder. "Calm down, Clint. It's not like he meant to. He's just learning. I'm sure he'll get the hang of it."

Clint steps back, scowling at Eddie and his gesture. "I sure hope so, because if he doesn't, we'll all be out hunting arrows instead of food!"

I step toward the fire. "Speaking of food..."

Clint turns on his heel. "I'm going out hunting—Now!"

He burst back out the door, not even trying to shut it behind him. As if the weather wants to match Clint's mood, the clouds unleash pent up water in giant droplets. He throws his hand in the air as I watch him walk away. Christa rushes to put an arm around Jett. His face stares blankly into the screen.

Clint returns to a cold dinner and his youngest children in bed. Disrupting Christa's nail painting, Eddie's gawking, and Jett's screen time, Clint motions for us to come outside.

"I was done cleaning anyway," I mumble, tossing a rag onto the counter.

It's been raining steadily since he left, and he's soaked to the core, leaving a puddle forming at his feet on the porch. The pounding on the tin roof echoes over our heads and we huddle together to avoid shouting.

"I've got bad news, and well, bad news," Clint begins.

"Tell us the bad news first," I say in an attempt to lighten the mood.

Clint frowns. "I took a shot, but...I don't know...it was like the arrow was bent or something. I got her in the thigh, but it was too dark to chase her even if the rain didn't wash away the blood trail."

Christa places her manicured hands on her hips. "What's the rest of the bad news?"

"I need to make a trip to town."

"We still have food for one more day, two or three if we ration correctly," I offer.

"I'm going to provide for my family one way or another."

Christa looks past us. "Do you think it's safe?"

"There's only one way to find out."

Eddie stares at a spot on the porch for a long minute before looking at me, then at Clint. "Let me go. You can stay and protect your family and I can get what we need. That way, if something were to happen in town, those kids in there wouldn't be without a father." He waves his hands toward the cabin. "I couldn't live with myself if I didn't step up."

Clint runs his hand through shaggy hair, water dripping from the ends. His gaze turns to Christa. "This is a decision you should make."

She takes a step backward, throwing her heavily ringed hand to her chest. "Me?"

"You know who's better suited for what roles here. You choose."

Eddie steps beside her and slyly slips his hand over hers. "I can do this. Let me help."

She nods.

"Get the list," Clint whispers to me. I slip past the awkwardness into the cabin and produce the notebook a minute later. Clint inspects the list, draws an X over Christa's added beauty supplies, and scribbles a map on the back while giving Eddie instructions as he goes. The paper is soggy from Clint's sleeves when he shoves it in Eddie's hand. "You should be able to make the trip and be back before dawn."

"I have to go tonight? I thought this would be a day trip."

"I'm already wet. I could go instead," Clint offers.

"You'll catch Pneumonia and won't do anyone any good," Christa says, stepping between the men.

Clint raises an eyebrow to Eddie. "Less chance of being caught at night." Eddie shoves the paper into his pocket. "Remember, if you run into trouble, get out. We can survive a few more days if we have to."

"Got it."

Moonshine's reaction to Eddie reminds me of my own—disgusted. She dances around the yard while he works to gain control. She submits after a few strokes down her neck and they race off into the darkness. Christa immediately retreats to her room. Knowing Clint had a rough day, I leave him to his thoughts on the porch and go to my room and pick up the Bible we found.

# Chapter 17

Nobody gets much sleep knowing the door is unlocked. Nobody but the kids, anyway. Clint and I drag ourselves from bed well before daylight. We know there's no use just lying there. I urge him to go hunting, but he's reluctant to leave until Eddie returns. Christa joins us before long, and I'm relieved to see her hair a mess, like she's spent most of the night tossing and turning. Near daybreak, Clint resorts to a nervous pacing, and Christa soon becomes as frazzled as he. In the dim light from the oil lamp, I quietly line the countertop with our remaining food—two cans of baked beans and one can of peas. I know we have enough meat to make two meager meals if mixed with the canned goods. I sort them around and around until the pacing of Clint and Christa drives me to my breaking point.

"Clint, go hunting. We are alone here without a weapon every time you do. This will be no different. Christa, go do yoga or something."

Clint stops, pulls at his long hair, and looks at Christa for approval.

She reaches over, tenderly brushing a long section off his forehead. "Why don't we cut your hair?"

I want to scream and throw a big fit over her even being in the room, spill my outrage over terrorists holding us hostage together, but instead, I raise my arms and lock my hands over my head. "This is hardly the time for that. Hunting is better during early morning or evening hours. His hair can be cut any time."

Clint puts both hands in his hair and pulls it away from his scalp. "I would feel better without all this. Let's do it."

Christa smiles and prances to her room. She returns with a blanket and takes the scissors from Clint's hand. She eyes them, seeing they're just regular scissors used to cut paper. "I guess these will do." She positions him at the table and drapes the blanket over him. Might as well let a blind-folded toddler do it, I muse as she slides the faint light closer. Christa's hands run through his hair, gently lingering over the nape of his neck as she cuts. For an instant, I want to take the scissors and stab them both, but the divorce papers flash to mind and I know I'd better get used to seeing this type of behavior. Unlike Christa, I won't be living so far away that we never run into each other. The sting of jealousy lingers as I take my notebook to the table. Clint and Christa whisper giddily to one another across from me. Instead of flipping to the middle where I put the maps, I open to the first page. Out of respect for the rightful owner, I had not looked at anything written in the beginning of the notebook until now. Must be the surge of anger welling up in me, at least that's what I tell myself. That only something new and possibly interesting can calm the rage growing inside me.

"Guys, look at this," I almost yell, sliding the book to them.

Clint bows his head over the book and Christa doesn't miss a beat, making me even angrier. *How can those two be so in-tune while he and I are so...not?* Two solid inches of hair fall onto the paper with the scribbles and sketches. Clint swiftly brushes them away.

"It's a trail map!"

"Like a hiking trail?" Christa asks enthusiastically.

"Even better." Clint's voice raises and, from the loft, Jett grumbles for five more minutes. We share a smile as Clint points to the different lines on the paper, all marked with distinguished dots, dashes, or a combination of both. "Animal trails. Each one of these lines shows the paths different animals take. See the key here? Dash-dash-dot is a raccoon trail while dot-dot-dash is rabbit." Christa pulls the blanket carefully from Clint with a blank look.

"I don't understand the point. Where does it go?"

"Wherever the animals go." The news breathes new life into Clint. His eyes dance across the paper. "Do you remember where you found this?"

I slide the book back to my side of the table and flip through the pages to the maps I've been working on. Curved lines outline the ups and downs of mountains while my trees look like lollipops with uneven circles resting on straight lines. The one exception to my forest of suckers is the giant tree with the large knot on the side. On paper it looks like a cinnamon roll clinging to the side of the sucker stick, but in reality, the knot is large enough to sit on. The cabins, on paper, are squares with a sloppy triangle on top. I added lopsided windows and a number to each one. On the next page I listed the supplies taken from each cabin according to number. I point to the correct cabin on the map and slide it back to Clint.

"I'm going to check this out as soon as Eddie is back."

"You can go now. We'll be okay," I urge. Anything to get Christa's fingers out of his hair.

"I want to be here when he gets back." He holds up the mirror inside Christa's compact, checking her progress. "What did you have planned for the day?"

"Thought I'd sit around eating bon-bons and catch up on the soaps I don't watch, why?" His frown deepens. "I was thinking about putting another window in the loft."

He jerks against Christa's grasp. "What the hell for?"

"I thought it might be nice for the kids to have a second way out if we are attacked. We could use some of the rope to make a ladder."

"Oh," he says like air whooshing out of his arrogance balloon. "That's a good idea, but you'd better let me handle that so it doesn't turn out like the shed."

Christa watches our exchange as if we've morphed into one of the reality shows I'm sure she watches. I turn so neither of them see the tears threatening to spill. Even here I'm a prisoner.

"There are some small logs from the last batch of wood I cut that would be perfect for the ladder," I say.

"Food comes first. Can't escape if we're dead or weak. If you're okay by yourselves, I'll go scout those trails, maybe set some of the traps we have left"

"It's still dark," I argue.

"It's almost light. I'll check my normal hunting areas first."

I nod. "Go. We'll be fine."

I retreat to the bedroom and dress in a stiff pair of jeans and a shirt that still smells of sweat, despite having been washed several times. After hearing the heavy thud of the thick door closing my room, I fall onto the bed and let the tears flow until there are no more before brushing my hair and returning to the kitchen. Christa has also changed, into yet another outfit I haven't seen, a black pair of tights with an oversized green shirt that hangs off her shoulders, revealing the thin straps of a tank top underneath. Her hair is brushed to perfection and her makeup is subtle, but her long lashes and dark lipstick prove it's there. I hope she doesn't notice my red, puffy eyes, or the shirt she's seen me in sixteen times.

"This will need to be washed," she says, thrusting the blanket containing the cuttings from Clint's hair into my arms. Though I want to shove it back and tell her I'm not her maid, I take the blanket outside to shake, eager to be alone.

With it on my lap, I sit on the porch and stare at the fading sliver of moon. The sun threatens to break over the horizon with the first hints of gray changing the sky above me. I wipe my nose with my hand. A shadowy figure moves in the tree line about fifty yards away. Slowly putting the blanket down, I inch toward the door and look for whatever weapon Clint hid there. The crevice is bare.

I crack the door. "Find a weapon and be ready." Getting down on all fours, I creep to the steps, knowing there should be a knife or something embedded above the first step. My hand touches cold metal and I feel around until I find the handle and pull the large kitchen knife from its concealed place. *Now what? There's no place to hide unless I put the door between me and the lurking figure. Maybe this is all my imagination.* I squint into the pale light, searching for the threat. *Should I go inside and lock the door? We might have a better chance as a group, but if I can stop him before he gets inside, the kids won't be so traumatized. Unless I'm dead. Hopefully it's Eddie and I'm freaking out for no reason. But what if it's not? If there's more than one, I'm doomed. At least I can get a warning to the others.* I move quickly around the back side of the cabin and circle around to the trees. Rustling comes from the spot I saw the figure. It stops when I step on a twig as I try to get closer, but I hear it again as I move behind a large oak tree. My heartbeat rings in my ears as I stand motionless, wishing Clint were here. The silhouette slinks away from a cluster of trees and heads for the cabin door. I rush for him in slasher movie fashion, knife held straight out, seeing red. I have only one goal—to get to him before he gets to the door. Eddie wouldn't have been acting like a stalker, I tell myself as I find a hole with the toe of my boot and end up falling with a thud to the ground. The knife goes flying. The impact takes my breath away and I pant helplessly as the intruder hits the first step to the porch. He stops and turns at the noise as I scan the grass for a reflection of light off the metal. One hand is at the small of his back underneath a large hiking pack. He turns and takes long strides toward me. Time stalls as I crawl toward the knife several feet away. As my hand touches the handle, his foot clamps down over it. I roll over and cover my face with my free hand like I'm some sort of child who believes protection lies in not being able to see.

"Lexi?"

Slowly removing my arm, I look up to see Eddie standing over me. He releases my hand and I clamber to a sitting position. "You scared the hell out of me!" I grab the knife and hold it close. "What were you doing?!"

"I was going to wait until daylight so I didn't scare anyone, but I heard a noise and thought maybe it was a bear. I got spooked and took off for the cabin. I guess it was you." He helps me to my feet. "What are you doing out here anyway?"

"None of us could sleep. I came outside to think. I thought you were a terrorist." He chokes on a cough and laughs like I'm being preposterous. "Don't laugh at me. It's very probable at some point for them to invade the mountains."

"I'm not laughing at you, but do you really think they'd go looking for a dozen people that *may* be living in the mountains like primitives when they have thousands, maybe millions in captivity?"

"Why leave loose ends? Maybe all of us who have escaped will band together and form a revolution."

"Have you seen anyone else out here? Where are all these people going to come from?"

"Appalachia." I mean it as a joke, but I suddenly can't wait to get Clint alone.

"Never mind all that." He takes my hand like an old friend. "Come on, I've got news."

As we hit the steps to the porch, I remember my warning to Christa. Before I can utter a word, Eddie flings the door open. I break free from his hold and lurch backward, dropping the knife as the ball of my foot slips over the side of the porch. My ankle twists, sending me down the three steps. I catch myself with my left wrist, landing with a thud on the wet grass. My painful cry is matched by a deeper one a few feet away. Eddie clutches his right arm and curses. Christa yells at someone to put the axe down as chaos takes over inside. The crying of a child has me hobbling up the steps as fast as I can. Eddie stands in the doorway with blood dripping onto the oak floor. Jett resembles a statue in the corner, eyes frozen on the scene. Tanner stares at the gash like it's the coolest thing he's ever laid eyes on. He inches closer, eager to inspect every inch of gore. I wrap my arms around Ella, thinking she's having a meltdown, only to find her mouth closed and eyes dry. Screams continue to pound our eardrums as if someone needs rescuing. Sidney scatters the medical supplies onto the table, no doubt trying to decide what to use first. Christa holds the knife like she's prepared to use it again while wailing at the top of her lungs. Eddie's fluent curses nearly drown her out.

"Stop!" I grab hold of Christa's hands and take the knife from her. She stops mid scream, her eyes bugging from her head. Her breathing becomes difficult and forced.

Eddie pulls his hand from the wound and looks at the glove of red ooze covering it. "Are you crazy?!"

Christa gasps for air as I try to gauge the severity of the laceration. I shove her into a chair and guide her head between her knees. "Breathe," I instruct.

"If anyone has a shirt they haven't worn, I need it," I say, looking at Jett and Sidney. Jett darts up the ladder and tosses a red V-neck over the edge to Sidney.

Taking the shirt, I wrap it around Eddie's arm. "Did you think I wasn't coming back?" His tone is light, but I ignore it.

"Apply pressure. Christa, I need your sewing kit!" I sort through the contents of the table, sending half of them flying to the floor. "Where is the needle? I need everyone looking for a needle!"

The children drop to the floor on all fours, frantically searching for a sliver in the crack of the boards. Christa remains motionless, her head between her knees. I glance at Eddie, wondering if he can be of any help. Blood covers both sides of the shirt. He angrily opens cabinet doors and throws drawers back against their stops, searching in vain for a needle we all know we aren't going to find. Sidney rushes to the closet, handing things to Ella as she pulls them out. I rush to Eddie as he slams doors against hinges.

"Hold still." I wrap a dish towel around the shirt and reach for the duct tape that rolled into the wall during my sweep of the table. He slams his free fist into the table as I wrap tape tightly across the three-inch gash and secure it near his wrist. "We have to get the bleeding stopped before I can do anything."

"What are you planning on doing if we can't find the needle?"

"Christa, I need that needle!" I look to the fire. "I'll have to cauterize it. Christa, the needle!" She is all but comatose.

Eddie's eyes are cold and steely as he shifts his focus to Christa. He flexes his hand into a fist, causing blood to ooze from the edges of the tape onto the towel. The sound of metal hitting the floor draws our attention to the closet. Sidney scoops Ella up and places her inside the closet to avoid the mess she created. She bends down and triumphantly holds up a fishing hook.

"Will this work? Mom's kit is gone. I can't find it anywhere."

"It's gonna have to do," I say, limping across the distance between us. Hooks and lures are strewn about the tiny area and I carefully avoid stepping on them.

"I don't think so," Eddie bellows. "That thing has got to be about six inches long and two inches thick." Christa lifts her head for the first time since I placed her in the chair. She stares at the hook in my hand as if it were a grenade.

"Don't be such a man," I say, holding the tiny hook in front of his face. "It's about two inches long and the same thickness of a needle."

"A knitting needle."

"How can I help?" Sidney asks, having released Ella from the closet by scooping up all the lures.

"I'll need some boiling water to sterilize this and a hammer or some pliers to remove this barb. Was there fishing line in there?" She nods.

Eddie squeezes his fingers. "My hand is tingling. There's vodka in my bag and some pliers too."

I help him remove the load from his back and dump everything onto the floor. Reaching in the mess for the only tool inside, I take it to the counter and try to make the hole on the end of the hook smaller. Jett jumps in when I stop to rub my wrist at the slightest amount of pressure.

"I need a hammer," he demands.

"I don't remember where it is. Tanner, go outside and find the biggest rock you can," I say after glancing out the window and seeing it's now well past daybreak.

Tanner goes to the fireplace instead, climbing onto the bricks near the coals that still burn red underneath a thin layer of gray ash. "Hammer on the fireplace, Mom."

"Right," I say, passing it to Jett.

Jett bangs onto the table. "Are you hurt?"

"I think I sprained my wrist when I fell down the steps."

"Are you sure it's not broken?"

"No way to tell without an x-ray."

"I thought I saw you limping." He reaches for another hook.

"Twisted my ankle."

"I keep breaking the holes."

"My hand is really numb over here," Eddie says from the seat he's taken next to Christa. I unwrap the towel.

"That's better," he says, flexing his fist.

Fresh blood seeps onto the saturated shirt. "Stop that."

Sidney hands Jett another hook.

"See if you can pull the barb off," I tell him after the third break.

"The what?"

I point and wait for him to crush the tiny hook from the side.

"Looks like this will have to do," I say, inspecting it.

Eddie reaches for the vodka. Taking a swig, he watches as I attach a length of line, cutting it with the bloody knife. "Wait." He takes a long drink from the bottle. "If you can't make the eye smaller, you should leave the barb on to make room for the eye."

"Good idea." I pick a fresh hook from the box and string the line to it. "This is going to hurt."

He chugs a good three shots of the cheap vodka and pours some in the cap for me to use on the hook.

I unwrap the soggy shirt from his arm and place it on the table. "Are you ready?"

He takes a long draw, grits his teeth, and nods. A low groan escapes as the alcohol trickles over his arm. My eyes meet his and I put the tip of the hook to his skin. He takes one last drink from the bottle before I pierce his skin. A blood-curdling scream comes from the grown man as the eye rips through his flesh. His breathing turns to heavy panting with the second entrance of the hook. Sidney takes Ella and Tanner into her mother's bedroom when Eddie begins violently cursing during the next stitch. I wait for him to move the bottle from his lips. Sweat beads across his forehead. He slams his free fist onto the table as the needle slides through. I give him a minute to empty the vodka and continue the sutures until I've completed the first inch. His screams have made me almost deaf and I'm sure if there were a threat nearby, they would certainly have our location narrowed down by the time I finish. He sweats profusely, a large portion of his polo with missing buttons sticks to his chest, but he doesn't seem to run out of curse words. I stop with the hook inside his flesh, just before pulling the eye through, and look into his eyes. He clings to the edge of his chair but looks as if he may lose his balance at any moment.

"I'm going to pull this one through then you're going to need to lie down. I can't have you passing out in this chair." He takes a deep, shaky breath. "On three...One...two..." I pull the hook into his flesh without further warning. He screams and clutches the side of the table. I grab his shoulders as the color drains from his face. With a swift sweep of my arm, I clear the table and help him to his feet. He wobbles and falls into me, knocking me backward against the cabinets.

"Don't shoot!" The words stop my heart. Jett is behind me in an instant, blocking us from Clint standing in the doorway with his finger on the trigger.

"Put that down and help me," I demand. His finger slides to the safety and he slowly puts the bow down. "I need him on the table."

For once he does what he's told before asking questions. "It sounded like someone was being tortured. What the hell happened?"

I work quickly while the man is unconscious. "Christa cut him." His gaze turns to his ex-wife who has taken to pacing the twelve feet of living room area. "I was outside on the porch when I saw someone acting shady in the distance. I told her to grab a weapon and watch the door. I guess he startled her so much she spooked and cut him."

"Where were you?"

"It all happened so fast. One minute I was talking to Eddie and the next I was on the ground and he was screaming."

"Walk me through it, Lexi." I recount the events as best I can as I finish the next inch of stitches. "You could have been killed. What were you thinking?"

"I was thinking it would be better to stop an intruder before he got to the cabin with everyone else. Even if it meant sacrificing myself."

Clint picks the supplies off the floor and stacks them on the counter. "Do you have any idea how lucky you are? This could've turned out so much worse."

"I realize it wasn't the best course of action, but at the time, I thought it was the best thing to do. And I'd do it all over again if I had to."

"Why didn't you use the knife?"

"There was a chance it might be Eddie."

"We can't afford these types of mistakes."

"I know that." I slither the words off my tongue. "What if I hadn't investigated and it turned out to be an actual threat? Did you consider that?"

He scratches his jaws, leaving his beard shaggy. "Did he say how it went? Where's the food?"

I point to the opposite side of the table. "He didn't give me any details."

"Why didn't you ask him? It's not like you didn't have time while you were playing doctor."

"First of all, I do have *some* medical experience, in case you have forgotten. But I thought his well-being was more important than how things went in town."

"I want you to show me where you found him." He scans the items spilled from Eddie's pack. "Two towels, a bag of flour, and some oil? Didn't he take our list?"

"He took it, but I don't know what happened."

"Take me to where you saw him." I check on Eddie before leading Clint to the general area where I saw the dark figure hours before.

It's easy to spot the exact location because two five-gallon gas cans sit by the tree where he had been. Clint nudges them with his foot. "Where's Moonshine?"

"He didn't say, but I haven't seen her."

"Dammit. Why didn't you ask?"

"It didn't cross my mind."

A small smile crosses his face as if he's sharing an inside joke with himself. His shoulders are broad, proud, as he carries the fuel toward the shed. Even the back of his head gives away the punchline I was missing. He got a deer.

"I'll be back with dinner," he says, pouring the gas into the Ranger Eddie and Christa had used to get here. He throws his hands in the air and starts the engine.

# Chapter 18

Our stomachs growl as if they are talking to each other as I cook the meat Clint brought back. Eddie has moved to the bedroom and is still resting. Christa checks on him more than a new mother with a sleeping infant. Jett returns to his phone and Tanner and Ella play with acorns they found early that afternoon while Christa and I were looking for plants she couldn't seem to identify. Sidney stirs a gravy of water and flour over the camp stove while I cook on the fire.

Clint paces nervously and I imagine this is what life may have been like for him and Christa right after Sidney was born. "When will he be awake?"

"There's no set time. It could be minutes. It could be hours," I explain.

"But he's going to be okay?" Christa asks, emerging from their room.

"As long as there's no infection."

"What are the chances of that?"

"I sewed him up in the middle of the woods with a fishing hook and vodka. I'd be more surprised if there weren't."

While we eat a meal of unseasoned meat and tasteless gravy, Christa twists her head around like an owl between bites, hoping for signs of life from her room. Jett is lost in his phone and everyone else is exceptionally quiet. Again, I am left to clean the mess our rich hosts leave on the table. Clint heads outside the minute he's finished. I wash the dishes with shampoo, irritated that Eddie didn't bring back Dawn like I asked, and head out to tell Clint my idea I'd been holding in all day. As I pass the first bedroom, I see Christa sitting on the edge of her bed watching Eddie sleep. Their beds aren't pushed together like I would have assumed, but maybe she moved them after the incident. I shrug it off, having more important things on my mind. Mainly I'm hoping Clint will hear me out before it turns into a fight. We've all been on edge lately, and though I have little hope of saving our marriage, this is bigger than that. I need him to consider my thoughts before dismissing them. He's looking in the engine compartment of the Ranger when I find him.

"Clint," I whisper, not wanting to anger him by making him lose his train of thought.

"Hmm," he responds, pouring gas into the second Ranger.

"I've been thinking."

"Hmm." He goes back to the engine on the first vehicle and touches some wires.

"I bet we're not the only ones out here."

That gets his attention. "Have you seen someone?"

I shake my head and tenderly kick the tire next to him. "If we were able to escape, maybe others were too."

"I haven't seen signs of anyone, but there could be."

"I'd almost bet there are people crawling all over the Appalachians. If we could get to them..."

"That's an awful big *if.*" He turns the key in the Ranger that was left up here. With some work, it purrs to life.

"Yes, but you know how those people are. We could have a small militia and take back our towns one by one."

"Whoever these terrorists are, WIN, I'm assuming, they have to be all over the country. Who knows how large this is? If I thought they were just taking over the state, I'd say the Appalachians were a good answer, but why would they pick New York? Why not D.C.? My guess is that this is happening on a much larger scale than we could have imagined. Our military should've been enacted by now and we've seen no sign of them. Our only hope now is outside help."

"How do you plan on getting it? It's not like you can go across the border and demand help."

"Why not?"

"Well, for starters, how would you even get there? This thing can't get you that far. And if it does, do you think you can just walk across the border? If things are as bad as you fear, wouldn't they be guarded?"

He slams the hood. "I don't know, Lexi. Obviously, there's a lot that has to be figured out before I go and you're disrupting my train of thought."

"Do you plan to take Jett?"

"And take him away from his phone? He's not cut out for it."

"I'd feel better if you didn't go alone."

"I don't have a choice now that Eddie's injured."

"I could go," I offer, but the thought worries me even more than sending him alone.

"And leave them here to die? They won't survive without one of us."

"Jett—"

"Jett couldn't catch dinner if it were sitting on his feet."

"Why don't we all go?"

He shakes his head. "It would slow me down. It will be better if I go alone."

"What if—"

"Stop with your *what ifs*. If you'd stop hounding me, I'd be able to come up with a plan."

"I couldn't help but overhear," Christa says, suddenly standing next to me like she was dropped from the sky.

"How long have you been here?"

"Long enough." *Isn't that what they all say?* I don't even feel badly about what she may have overheard concerning Jett. Maybe it's good for her to know her son needs to step up. "Are you really going to Canada?"

Clint turns the engine off and nods. "I have a few things to take care of here first, but yes."

"When?"

"In a few days, maybe a week."

"Can you get there in this?" She points to the Ranger.

"Not unless I can pick up gas on the way. Wish I knew where that horse was."

"Eddie's still not awake to tell us what happened." She nervously coils blonde strands around her long index finger. "What will you do when you run out of gas?"

"Walk, I guess."

"How far do you think you can get before that happens?"

"That's what I'm trying to figure out," Clint's tone takes a comforting note as he explains each step to her one at a time.

"Will you take the bow?"

"No. The plan is to get enough meat to last you a month before I go."

"You'll be gone that long?"

"Maybe. I'm just hoping I can get to Mitch in time. He's the Mountie I mentioned. The one in Montreal. He'll know what to do."

"How can you be so sure?"

"I've known him for years. He comes down a couple times each summer. We can trust him."

She places her hand on his shoulder. "Will you teach me to shoot?"

I walk away wondering if they even notice I've left. After checking on the kids who are doing the usual—Jett on the phone, Ella and Tanner playing a made-up card game, and Sidney, having tired of her phone, reads that same book on sign language while sitting by Eddie's bedside—I flop down on my bed and punch the pillow a few times. Tears that would've welled up a year ago under the same circumstances never hint at making an appearance. Instead, anger takes its place, but lasts only through those few punches before calmness sweeps over me. It's an odd sense of calm, like I'm finally letting our relationship go. It no longer has power over me. There's nothing more I can do if he won't meet me halfway.

# Chapter 19

Tanner and Ella throw their growing collection of acorns in the air like confetti near the fireplace, creating plunking noises on the hardwood. The wood crackles in the night air and I throw another log into the flames. Groans seep through the closed bedroom door where Eddie rests. Christa rushes inside as he mumbles unfamiliar words before finally forming Christa's name. Clint and I stand behind her as he groggily opens his eyes.

"It's...fine," he breathes.

Christa lurches for his side, resting her hand on his. "You're going to be fine," she nods.

He slowly moves his head to the side. "Normal."

Sidney brings him the last bottled water and Christa helps him drink. I wish she would've brought him some from the well, but it's hard to argue with an injured man.

"The town is fine," he whispers as Christa helps him sit.

"Describe what you saw in detail," Clint orders.

"It's like none of this even happened. We can go home," he says, letting his head drop against one of the wooden rails of the headboard.

Sidney bolts from the room. Her feet are heavy on the ladder to the loft and drawers squeak open before we can stop her from packing.

Clint scratches the beard I wish he'd shave. "Are you sure?"

Eddie lifts his head as if to nod but doesn't complete the motion, just leaves his chin raised. "I brought gas so we can leave."

"Where's the horse?"

His eyelids droop and he forces them open. "She bucked...ran off. Don't know what spooked her," he whispers. With that, his eyes close and remain that way.

Christa ushers us from the room like she's protecting a delicate creature who may break if disturbed.

"I wonder why he didn't just tell me that when he first saw me," I say as we gather around the table.

"Maybe he didn't get the chance," Christa defends.

"I'm going to check this out before we all go," Clint says. "If everything is as he says, I can take the Ranger and be back in a few hours."

"We should all go," Christa says, placing her hands flat on the table.

"He could be delusional," I say. "He may have dreamt all of it."

"Wouldn't he be more confused if he had?"

"He could be mixing reality with what he wishes were true."

"I believe him. He knows how important this is." Christa's defensiveness leaves me wondering if she's reacting to her feelings for Eddie or if she's anxious to get out of this place and back to her cushy life.

"The mind works in funny ways. He suffered a great trauma today. If he had been in a hospital and the procedure had been done properly, it would've been a minor inconvenience, but out here it's a bigger deal. He had a fish hook pierce him thirty-six times. The recovery time on that is going to be significantly longer. I'm not even sure he should travel for a few days."

"We can take both Rangers and put him in the back of one," she argues.

"I'm not risking everyone's safety until I know his words hold truth," Clint says sternly.

"He wouldn't put me—us—in danger."

"And neither will I. End of discussion."

Sidney drops a bag over the side of the loft and hurries down. "When do we leave?"

"I'll go in the morning and make sure we can trust Eddie like your mother says we can then I'll come back for you."

"What happens if he is delusional?"

Christa's eyes dart to Sidney. "I'm sure he's not," she says.

"I'm working on a plan. Right now, I want everyone to pack a bag." He looks directly at Christa. "I want only the essentials packed. If I don't return by lunch tomorrow, you'll have to move."

"Why?" The whine comes from Christa.

"If I don't return it means something terrible has happened and they might come looking for you."

"You'd tell them where we were?"

Clint cracks his knuckles, the first time he's shown a sign of being irritated with his ex. "I'd rather die."

"Then why would we have to move?"

"Where you find one, there's likely to be more," I offer in explanation.

She nods. "Will you help me pack?"

"You're a grown ass woman, Christa."

She looks as if she may cry.

"You'll want to pack light," I say. "And for god's sakes, leave Jimmy's shoes here."

After throwing one change of clothes for everyone in a bag, I put it by the front door, waiting to put the weapons and other survival items in until morning. Christa brings her stuffed bag out and watches as Clint throws makeup and those ridiculous high-heeled boots out. She stops him when he tries to toss the oils and he decides to let her keep them. Half of the belongings lie in a heap on the floor, but he motions for her to leave them and follow him to the porch. I kiss the kids, who have settled into the loft next to Sidney to listen to her tell a story and meet them outside. I take a seat on the railing across from them in the rockers.

Clint looks at me, knowing I'll be the one to execute the orders he's about to give. "I'll leave at daybreak. If I'm not back before noon, I want you to head north. Stay in the mountains as long as you can. Once you reach the end of the range, leave the kids with Christa and scout out the land." He turns to Christa. "She may need to be gone for a day but trust her judgement. She won't leave you in a place that isn't safe. If she isn't back when she says, head back into the mountains."

"What will I do then?"

"Lexi will give you instructions when the time comes." I nod to her, feeling the pressure already. "A lot of this you'll have to play by ear. You've got to get into Canada however you can. It will probably be easiest to find a river and follow it, but keep a sharp eye out because the terrorists may be doing the same. I'm going to write down the name of my buddy in Montreal, but once you get across the border you should be able to look him up and get a call in. Use my name and tell him it's an emergency." Clint studies my reaction. "Any questions?"

Christa blinks, taking in the details. She shifts her gaze from Clint to the porch and back again. "How will we find you again?"

"You're to stay in Canada until Mitch gives the all-clear to come home. I'll find you if I can."

I take her arm, suddenly feeling sorry for her. "Let's go see what we can pack for Clint to eat tomorrow."

The thin, itchy blanket scratches my chin and, if it weren't for my uncontrollable shivering, I wouldn't think I could move. Though Clint and I are in separate beds, I know he's staring at the ceiling too. He's running every scenario through his head and channeling his inner Rambo while I picture the outcome of the ones playing in my own mind. Somewhere in the middle of the imagined chaos, I realize deep down I will always love him. I still want our relationship to work, despite my inklings that it's truly over, and now I'm afraid I'll never get the chance. The thought of four kids without their dad cripples me, but nothing paralyzes me like Clint's last words as he leans over to kiss me.

"If I'm not back by dark, kill Eddie."

# Chapter 20

Armed with Sidney's cell phone, I head up the mountain in the opposite direction Clint had gone. Unable to get his words out of my head, I claim I need some time to myself. I didn't tell anyone what he said and, as I walk, I contemplated how I'd do it. How I'd lure him away and shoot him. I'd have to shoot him. I couldn't bear to be any more brutal than I had to, but how many shots would I need to get the job done? How quickly can I reload the arrows and make the shots? It's not like he would accept his fate. Of course, he's not in a position to fight at the moment. I could always slit his throat while he sleeps and say he tried to attack me but that's a little more hands-on than I'm comfortable with. Plus, there's not much chance of getting him alone while he's laid up in bed. If he's that much of a threat, why did I just leave him there with my kids? Benefit of the doubt. My biggest weakness. That's the reason I didn't leave Clint sooner. I'm not certain he's having an affair with Christa, or anyone else for that matter, and all the problems we have because of his previous marriage can be explained away if I choose to believe Clint. My thoughts shift to my marriage as I pant up the side of the mountain. When will he choose *me*? Maybe he never will but that's not important right now. I check the phone for signal at the peak. Nothing. There's a clearing a few feet away and, as I approach, I see the groundwork for a new cabin that was started—and abandoned, presumably from the invasion. Two-by-fours are stacked neatly next to a half dozen or so tresses, and two stacks of shingles piled six high are another six feet away. Normally I'd be irritated by the land being invaded by all the cabins I never really knew existed, but today I'm thankful for visible sky without trees blocking the view. I run back and forth across the area, waving the phone in the air as I desperately search for signal. The low growl of an engine disrupts my search. Could Clint be back already? I start to run back to the cabin when I realize the noise comes from overhead. The hum of engines loom closer. I stand next to the shingles, wondering if I should run for cover or try to flag them down. It all boils down to how much trust can be put in Eddie.

Would I bet my life—and my family's—on his word alone? No. I make the split-second decision too late. The single-propeller plane crosses the clearing at an elevation only crop dusters use. I drop to the ground as it passes directly over the clearing. I can't risk waiting around to find out if I'd been spotted. Crawling to the nearest tree line, I check to see if it circled around. The faint hum in the distance does nothing to assure me it won't be coming back. I have to get back to the others. Smoke wafts past the treetops from the cabin in the side of the nearest mountain. A clear sign leading the enemy straight to us if they are looking. Wasting no time, I slide down the steep slope, leading the way with one leg outstretched. I have to get there in time. I could yell a warning, but if they're looking for us in the air, would they also be looking on foot? Better not risk it. Twelve-hour shifts have passed in shorter amounts of time than it takes to coast down the side of that mountain. My descent is sketched with leaves scattered to the side and in piles. Fresh dirt shows, leaving telltale signs of movement in its wake. My heart races, adrenaline pumping like it used to when I was a surgical nurse and the patient on the table was lingering between life and death. With each boot that hits the soft earth I can almost hear the doctor yell, "Clear!" The drone of the plane is once again audible, though some distance away. I replay my last time in the operating room. Blood is hooked to an IV. The lines on the monitor flatline. Orders are shouted and metal clings against metal, but the smell of death leaks into the room. My colleagues thought I was nuts when I admitted to them that I could always sense it coming, like there was a visible sign only I could see before anyone else realized the inevitable. My mouth would go dry after the first five minutes of blood leaking out of the patient as they tried futilely to save him. As I run, I try to wet my mouth with saliva to keep the sensation from happening. The doctor had tried to revive that last patient—an eleven-year-old girl—for only a few minutes before calling time of death. It was at that exact moment—11:24 p.m.—that I knew my time in the operating room was over. It was the first time I hadn't smelled 'death' or whatever it was that gave me the inclination that all was hopeless. Even though it was later explained to me that the girl's parents and younger brother had also died, I still felt she was done an injustice. I knew I couldn't witness that again. It was ironic that I turned to hospice, but now most of my patients are elderly and have accepted their fate as if they welcome death. I force myself to remember the few times where I had given up and a miracle happened. The cabin is over a football field away and my mind works quickly. A young boy is on the table, a new heart refusing to pump blood into his veins. I can almost hear the seconds ticking away on the digital clock, though I know they aren't there. Tick. Tock. Tick. Tock. Fifty feet to go and no pulse. Twenty. Ten. Too many minutes pass. The doctor looks at the clock and calls the time. I hit the porch as instruments cling onto trays in my head. The monitor springs to life as I touch the door.

"Put...out...fire," I pant.

Christa puts down her nail polish bottle and blows on her nails as if my urgency is for effect only. Jett drops his phone, springing to action, grabbing bottles of well water from the counter and emptying them into the fireplace.

I point to the fireplace. "Out," I wheeze, placing my hands on my thighs to catch my breath.

Sidney leaps from the seat where she's braiding Ella's hair. "Fill this with water," she says, shoving a bowl to Ella. I barely miss being hit as she runs out the door. Sidney takes the half-full pail and douses the flames. Ashes fly into the air as the wood fizzles down. Ella rushes back in, water sloshing over the sides as she does. A tiny stream of water covers an area already extinguished. Sidney darts out the door as I lurch for Christa's Fiji bottle on the table.

"Hey," she protests as I pour it onto the mess of smoldering flames.

Sidney races in and dumps another load, sending tiny particles of ash over us and dusting the hearth.

All eyes turn to me, waiting for an explanation. "There's a plane."

"So?" Christa twists the cap back on the bottle of polish with her thumb and index finger, a look of indifference covering her smug face.

"It could be terrorists." Tanner and Ella cling to me, their little eyes wide with terror. Jett lays an armload of various tools onto the table.

"Eddie said everything was back to normal. It could be rescuers looking for us," Christa says, rubbing a smudge from the cuticle of her pinky.

"Then go out there and flag them down. They can take you back with them, but I'm not trusting them. It was an unmarked plane. Rescuer don't fly unmarked planes."

She pushes her chair away from the table and tucks her pink bottle of polish into her large makeup case. "You wouldn't even be here if it weren't for me."

"*You* wouldn't be here if it weren't for your father. Clint and I would be somewhere in these woods, and we'd be just fine."

"This isn't helping," Sidney chimes in.

The airplane soars low, muffling my insults. "I have to find Clint. He may be walking into a trap."

"Eddie said everything was fine," Christa whines, looking into the open bedroom door where Eddie appears to be sleeping.

"You'd better hope we can trust him like you say." Christa's eyes dart to the bow. "I need to get to Clint."

Sidney opens her arms for Tanner and Ella. "What can I do?"

"Get this place looking like nobody has been here. Throw everything that would give us away into the outhouse." I pull Sidney to the side, but make sure my voice is barely audible to her mother. "Be prepared to run."

"If you won't take my word on Eddie, shouldn't you stay here with him and have me go after Clint?" Christa adds a dramatic eye roll to her suggestion.

"You couldn't find your way out of a paper bag, let alone find one man in the woods." I pick up the bow and point to the safety, showing it to Sidney. "Flip this, aim, and pull the trigger. Don't ask questions, just aim for the chest and shoot first."

"You're going to get us all killed," Christa growls.

"Eddie's telling the truth, remember?" I open the door and glance at Sidney. "I'm taking the Ranger. There's a map in the notebook. Once you have things cleaned up here, move to Cabin One. Hurry up!"

Sidney springs to life, shouting orders that disappear as the Ranger purrs to life. Weaving in and out of the thick trees, searching for the safest path, I unbutton the knife from its holster. Saplings fall beneath the machine as I press it to full speed. Clint's tracks faintly mark his path on the fallen leaves and I pray I reach him in time, but he should've already made it to town.

Ten minutes pass and I swear I hear every beat of my heart as I dive into the valley between the mountains. Twenty minutes, then thirty without a sign. Maybe I'll meet Clint on his way back. I press on, ramping over a large decaying limb. The jolt sends me out of my seat and I'm sure my white-knuckled clench on the steering wheel is the only thing keeping me from ejecting.

The smell of death infiltrates my lungs. Or does it? It could be my imagination at this point. Up ahead, before even getting into town, I spot the familiar black and green metal of a matching Ranger, but no sign of Clint. My heart could explode in my chest as hard as it's working. Should I turn around or keep going? I let off the gas as I struggle to make the right decision. Clint's head pops up from the passenger side's front tire. Gunning the gas, I power forward until I have to lock the brakes to stop. The machine skids and jolts to a stop, inches from the back of Clint's ride.

"What the hell?" Our voices match in pitch and urgency.

"There's a plane," I say as he says, "Tire fell off."

"What?" We ask in unison.

"Tire's off," he explains as I again say, "There's a plane."

He points to me. "You go."

"A plane flew over. It looked like a crop duster. I don't know if it's friend or foe."

"I thought I heard it come by an hour ago."

"It's circled around a few times. Could it be a rescue plane?"

He scans the sky. "We'd better not trust it if we aren't sure."

"My thoughts exactly. What happened here?"

"The tire fell off."

I get out and go to the passenger side. The wheel lies on the ground. "Fell off?"

He scratches his head. "Looks like the lug nuts were loose."

"Can you fix it?"

"Sure, if I had the parts and tools."

"How long have you been here?"

"Long enough to try to fix it with sticks." A smile tugs at the corner of his lips. "I was going to give it one more go before heading back. I was just about to give up so you didn't make a huge mistake."

"I had everyone leave the cabin. They're using the map to get to another cabin. That one where we found the Bible."

"We'd better get back just in case. I can come for this tomorrow."

"Will there be enough gas?"

"Should be enough to get back to town anyway." He tosses everything that isn't bolted to the Ranger, including the wheel, into the back of the working vehicle.

I slide over so he can drive. "Christa and I had a bit of a disagreement before I left." My voice barely carries over the sound of the motor and the cracking branches.

Clint nods, staring straight ahead. "About?"

"Eddie."

He whips the machine around a large pine and scoots toward me as the branches push inside. "I've been thinking about it and Christa has been seeing him for months. I'm telling you she wouldn't bring anyone around that she didn't trust. Especially in these circumstances. I'll admit I had my doubts at first, but he's been pulling his weight"

"Has he?"

"Keeping Christa out of the way is the best thing he can do sometimes."

"Just seems like, aside from your short-lived bromance, that he's been pretty lax."

"I'm vouching for Christa on this one." He offers a smile that doesn't hold any weight as far as I'm concerned. "We should trust her."

"Is that why you insisted on checking out the town before taking us all home?"

He raises his arm to block a branch. "If he had told us everything before he was injured, I wouldn't have questioned him."

"I'm still going to keep an eye on him."

"I'm not saying I believe his claims that everything is back to normal, but I don't think he's a direct threat to us."

"Why on earth would you tell me to kill him then?"

Pine needles push inside the Ranger as he whips between trees. "I was thinking worst case scenario I guess."

I brush fallen needles from my leg. "You broke down out here and if you hadn't returned, I would've killed him—all because you were paranoid?"

"I have a right to be a little on edge," he growls. "There could be terrorists *anywhere* and Christa's still adjusting to life without snapping her fingers and getting what she wants."

"But you just said you don't think he's a threat to us and we should trust Christa's judgement. Seems to me you still want things both ways."

"Now we're just going to fight about everything?"

The tires pop twigs as he accelerates up the winding mountain. He waits a few minutes and slides his hand over to mine where I'm gripping the edge of the seat. "Look, if I still need to go to Canada, I don't want to leave with things the way they are between us." I swallow hard, wondering if he's finally ready to admit our problems. "I know you've been unhappy lately and you've tried to talk to me about it. I haven't exactly been open to hearing what you have to say. I'm sorry for that."

"Does that mean we can talk about it without you getting defensive?"

"I'll try."

"That's all I can ask."

He massages the back of his neck and slides his arm over my shoulder. "So, where do we start?"

"I don't know if we'll have enough time before we get back."

"If you'd stop talking about talking about it, we'd have time." His tone is gruff, but realizing it, he takes my hand again and softens his pitch. "I promise not to leave for Canada until you're comfortable."

"Thank you."

"What would you like to start with?"

I stare out the side, afraid to face him. "How did you meet Christa?" He silently contemplates his answer, a controlled exhale escaping his lips. "I mean, she's so different than us. I just wonder how you ended up married to her."

"This is something I should've told you long ago." I turn to face him as he takes a deep breath. "I was seventeen and my mom had just shown up for one of her visits." That much I knew about. His mom struggled with heroin addiction from the time she was a teenager. She stayed clean during her pregnancy—at an early age—and managed to maintain it until Clint was five. She insisted she didn't know who his father was. On Clint's fifth birthday, she relapsed, supposedly because of a split with the only father-figure Clint knew. The man wanted to take Clint in, but his mother kept coming around when she was low on cash. Everything fell apart the last time. She took Clint away because she didn't get the cash she was looking for. A car accident followed and she was arrested for OWI. His grandfather later explained that the man had wanted to get custody of Clint but knew he couldn't handle his mother's violent outbursts while high. The boyfriend moved away while she was in jail and Clint's grandfather had taken him in. Clint always thought his grandfather regretted the decision, but he assured him—and me—that he was grateful to them both. His mother got out of jail when he was twelve and came looking for him. He had a normal relationship with her for about two years until she started using again. After that he wrote her off, saying she'd used up her first and last chance with him. For the next three years she only came around when she needed money. She'd even broken into the bait shop a few times, stealing anything she thought she could sell. He pleaded with his grandfather to write her off and not give in, but he always did. He claimed he'd rather she get money from him than do the unthinkable for it. She died when Clint was seventeen.

"I argued with my grandfather for the millionth time to not give her money as he pulled out his wallet. The look on her face as she took it—I can still see it. She was mocking me. Like she had won the battle and knew she always would. It was a game to her. I can still remember what she was wearing—jeans with holes in them, and not the stylish kind, her hair looked as if it hadn't been brushed in weeks, and she smelled of vomit." He dips his head at the confession.

I link my fingers into his. "I'm sorry you had to go through that."

"It was the last time I ever saw her." My heart aches for him. "I don't know why I left to go after her. I was so angry. She was getting into a car that looked as if it had been in a demolition derby. The guy driving had rotting teeth. I'll never forget that either. He smiled at me with a cigarette hanging out of his mouth. When he told her to get in, he had the butt lodged between the gap in his lower teeth. Weird how those details stick out."

"That's an awful memory. Addiction is worse for the family and friends of the addict, in my opinion anyway."

"Why couldn't she see what she was doing to me?" His voice almost cracks. This is painful for him to talk about and I'm curious as to how this involves Christa, but I give him time.

"It's the drug."

"That's such a lame excuse." He pounds the steering wheel and I come off the seat as we hit a bump. "Anyway, I peeled out behind her and followed them as they swerved along the highway. At first it was to keep an eye on her, you know, to make sure she was safe, but somewhere along the way I got even angrier. I drove on their bumper as they went through town and followed them down a side road. At some point, the man started throwing stuff out the window at me. She was holding the wheel, I could tell, while he chucked beer cans toward my truck. I finally skidded to a turn down the next road. It was at that moment I knew I was done with her. I was going to make her regret choosing drugs over me."

"I just started driving around, trying to figure out how I could move out of my grandfather's house so I didn't have to see her again." Did he marry Christa as a way to escape, I wonder. "No, I didn't use Christa to get away," he says, reading my mind.

"Then how did it happen?"

"I was weaving through the mountains, no real destination. Just driving around. It was almost two in the morning when I came across a limo stopped on the side of the road."

"That's something you don't see every day."

He laughs. "It certainly was out of place on the one-lane road. There was a man dressed in a black suit that probably cost more than my beat-up truck standing outside talking on a phone. I may have been angry at the world, but my grandfather had raised me right. I pulled up behind him and got out. Inside the limo, girls shrieked. I tried to ask the man what the problem was, but the girls had rolled down the windows and kept sticking their heads out. One of them handed me some concoction in a cup. Being seventeen, I took it. As the man explained they were lost, I chugged the drink. In a matter of minutes, a gaggle of girls paraded around me in the dirt road. They were dressed as if ready for a night of drinking in the city. Clearly they were out of their element."

"A little."

"The driver finally calmed." He laughs. "His face was so red when I first showed up, but I charmed him into living in the moment. He refused the drinks the girls kept shoving in his face. I'm still not sure how he managed that. They were all persistent."

He lets off the gas as we descend the side of the mountain. "An hour passed as we laughed and drank in the middle of that road. It wasn't hard for Christa to charm me that night. Any other night and I would've seen how ridiculous we were together. We were both pretty drunk, though I hid it well, when she convinced the driver to let us leave together. I practically had to sign over my first-born to make it happen. He made us promise to be back in an hour. She wanted to see her father's cabin and there was no way the limo was making it there."

"I see," I say, finally understanding their inside joke about the place.

"You should've seen the panic on that driver's face when we showed up three hours later. The other girls didn't seem to mind though."

"That's lovely." I don't try to hide my displeasure to his story. "What happened after that?"

"I showed them the way to the main road and thought I'd never see her again."

"Obviously that didn't happen."

"Three months later I was working in the shop when the same limo pulled up. Thankfully Granddad had an appointment and was gone for the afternoon. He wouldn't have liked the scene that day. The driver came in with a giant of a man. They both wore expensive suits and everyone parted the aisle as they passed. I knew immediately who the second man was."

"Christa's father?"

"Bingo."

"I'm guessing he didn't come to buy bait?"

Clint shakes his head dramatically. "He was the one with bait that day. And I took it."

"I always knew you were part fish." I jab him playfully, trying to lift my spirits for what I know is coming.

"He knew virtually everything about me when he walked in. He knew I wouldn't be able to say no."

"To what?"

"A job, a fancy house, and...a wife."

"What?" My eyes bulge.

"When you knock someone up at seventeen the last thing you expect from the girl's father is for him to fast-track you to success." I nod in understanding, careful to hide my shock. This must be the way the rich do shot-gun weddings. "He explained that there would not be a Bennett girl having a baby out of wedlock. By the time he was done listing the benefits, I couldn't say no. He knew we were barely keeping our head above water at the store and had already arranged to buy the building from the man we were leasing it from. If I didn't agree to his terms, he would bulldoze the store. I had no choice. I went to work that day wondering if we were going to make the overhead for the month and left with an office job in the city, a sixteen-thousand square-foot house, a yearly salary of more than I had made in my entire life, a trust fund for my unborn child, and a fiancé."

"I bet that was mind-blowing."

"You could say that. We were married a month later and I moved to the city."

"What was your job like?" I ask, happy he is finally giving me a glimpse into his past.

"Awful. I am not cut out to wear Armani suits and sit behind a desk all day."

I laugh. "No, you're not."

"I hated it. He put me as head of advertising, which I guess could have been worse. He could have had me designing his software systems, but he thought I wasn't smart enough for that, he said. He thought I'd be better at bossing people around. Basically, the people below me brought me ideas and I either approved or rejected them. I think he made the whole gig up. Plus, they hated reporting to a kid who had yet to finish high school."

"I thought you graduated."

"Thanks to a private tutor Richard hired."

The cabin looms into view now and our conversation will soon screech to a halt. "And that's all the time we have for this episode," I say in a journalistic manner.

"More on next week's show titled 'Living the High Life with Christa."

I smile and squeeze his hand.

# Chapter 21

Taking the oil lamp from my room to Eddie's, I tiptoe to his bedside to check his wound. Underneath the bandage oozes yellow puss. I rest my finger gently on the swollen, reddened area. Christa stirs in the bed next to him and flips her eye mask to her forehead. "He needs an antibiotic," I tell her. "This is infected and the cream I brought is next to useless for something of this magnitude."

"I have some oils that could help."

"He needs actual medicine," I reply sharply.

"What if we try the cream and the oils together?"

"Maybe we can go to town and get what he needs," I say more to be nice than out of actual concern. "Or maybe we could find some maggots. That's what they used way back in the day, right?"

As if the prospect of hunting maggots is a serious option, she leaps from bed to retrieve a bottle from her dresser. A rich lavender scent fills the room as she smears an oily substance onto Eddie's arm before rebandaging it. "This will do just fine." As she plops his arm back to the mattress, Eddie pops an eye open. I almost jump.

He slowly lifts his head. "Did Clint make it to town?"

"There was a problem with the tire," I say.

"Really?" He closes his eyes. "Maybe he could take me with him and I could get something for this throbbing arm," he suggests.

"Christa has oils."

Clint raps lightly on the slightly opened door. "You ready?"

I turn to Christa. "Clint is going to show me where the deer stand is and go over some trapping stuff. We're going to prepare for him to go to Canada if the trip to town doesn't go well. Think you can manage things here?"

"Of course. I'll make breakfast," she replies as if she does it every day.

138

The deer stand Clint and Eddie built looks like something a child tried to replicate with scrap pieces of wood. Four planks nailed to the tree serve as a ladder to an uneven platform, held up by more used planks. I climb up after Clint, handing him the bow after he's settled. The contraption would fail to meet safety standards, but Clint is trusting.

"Is this safe for two people?"

"Eddie and I tested it. It'll hold."

"I sure hope so. Where'd you get the nails?"

"We found a few stray ones and salvaged the rest." He leans against a large sycamore. "Try to stop picking fights with Christa. She could kick us out if she wanted to."

*So that's why you invited me along? You wanted to tell me to play nice with your ex.* I exaggerate a yawn. *Not this song and dance again.*

"You're going to scare every deer from here to Canada," he says with a frown.

"She couldn't survive without us and we all know it. That's probably why she didn't move everyone like I told her to do."

"It's lucky she didn't. She probably would've gotten lost." He smiles and reaches for my hand. "And if you repeat that, I'll have to cut your tongue out."

I run my hand across my mouth like it has a zipper. "If you have to go to Canada, she'd better learn to follow my orders."

"You both need to learn how to deal with each other if that happens."

"I'll try to do better."

"Thank you."

"You're welcome." I slather sarcasm on my words.

The sky lightens but the sun sticks behind a mass of clouds so thick it may never break free. I scratch the bite on my hand, swelling the bump three times larger.

Clint yawns. "How about the next episode of 'Life with Christa?'"

I lean into him. "I could go for that."

"I was such a mess when I met Christa. I was busy trying to make sure my grandpa didn't lose the store and I had the whole 'mom' thing to deal with. Then there was school, which took the back burner. I was barely passing and missed a lot. It was easy to take Richard's offer. I didn't have to worry about anything. As an added bonus, I knew my mom wouldn't show up on the doorstep."

"There's always a silver lining."

The boards squeak and shift as he stretches his legs. "That's the way I looked at it."

"What was it like, the drastic change in lifestyle??"

"Suffocating. She demanded I attend a charity event at least once a month. Then there were the galas and rubbing necks with the elitists.

"For the first few years I felt like I was trapped. Her family had so much power and money, I didn't think I could leave."

"Did you love her?"

His eyes meet mine then drop in shame. "I do now. As a friend. As the woman who gave me two of the greatest gifts I could ever wish for."

I blink incredulously. "If she ever loved you or the kids, she wouldn't hold them hostage."

"Let's not get ahead of ourselves. That's a different episode. I was all set to leave her when I found out she was pregnant with Sidney. Looking back, I think she planned it."

"Why would she do that?"

"I confessed my feelings to her—told her I wasn't happy with the lifestyle and wanted to raise Jett somewhere a little less public. He was in tabloids before he could walk."

I slip my hand onto his thigh. "I can't imagine what that was like."

"I hated it. After the quick wedding, there were all sorts of stories about how he wasn't mine and how the family had recruited a 'nobody' to mold into their likeness so the baby had a respectable father. It was ridiculous. And, sadly, mostly true."

"Don't sell yourself short. You've never been a 'nobody' in my book."

"But I was in theirs. I let them mold me until I didn't recognize myself anymore."

"But you got out."

He hangs his head, adjusting the bow on his lap. "I left. There's a difference."

"What does that mean?"

"Again, that's another episode."

*How deep does this story go?* "What was your actual relationship with Christa like?"

"It was great in the beginning. Her pregnancy hormones gave her the desires every teenage boy dreams of."

"Gross." I furrow my brow. "That was *not* what I meant."

His shoulder raises against mine as he shrugs. "Sorry. Once Jett was born, we realized we had nothing in common."

"Shocking."

He closes his eyes. "We fought all the time. About work, about galas, about the nanny...about how her father arranged our lives."

"Nanny?"

He stares into the distance, squinting as if a deer will come along and save him from this conversation. "Of course. I didn't want one and she insisted. Then she accused me of having an affair with the first three."

"Did you?"

"I'm not the cheating type if you haven't figured that out." His tone makes me wonder if I'm crazy or if he's covering his tracks with the statement. "She also thought I had the hots for one of the maids—which I did, but I never acted on it."

"So, you had lots of sex, fought, and found out she was pregnant again—how did that turn out?"

A quiet laugh escapes his lips. "Well, we had Sidney."

"Obviously." I roll my eyes.

"We learned to get along. By Sidney's second birthday we had come to some sort of agreement."

"Which was?"

"I slept in my bedroom, and she slept in hers. We lived separate lives. I managed to appear at the required functions, and we learned to be friends. That's about as simple as I can put it."

"Clint, I don't want simple. This part of you has made you who you are today. Sometimes I feel like it's holding us back from being the couple we could be if you'd just let me in. I sometimes wonder if I hadn't gotten pregnant if we'd still be together. In all this time you've never told me any of this and I was too stupid to demand answers before we were connected for life."

The boards beneath us creak as he props the bow against the tree and takes both my hands. "I've always been afraid I'd lose you if I told you about my past."

A tear trickles down my cheek. "Let me in. That's all I ever wanted."

He awkwardly brushes the tear with his thumb. "If you'll let me, I will try."

I stiffen, my index finger trembling as it points. The floorboards threaten to spill us, I fear, as they wobble with my shaking body.

"Stay still. Maybe it will go away." Clint's barely whispering as he helps me to my feet, crowding our shoulders side by side, his body beside mine. He's using an old trick to make us appear larger to the cougar staring at us from the ground. Its attention focuses on us as if deciding whether breakfast is worth climbing for. Clint stoops for the bow as the creature steps toward the trunk and sniffs the air. An arrow points at the beast's head and, just as suddenly as he appeared, he leaves. We watch as he darts into the trees, wondering if he was spooked or found an easier meal.

"Please don't leave me," Clint whispers, dropping the weapon and taking me in his arms.

"Do you hear that?" A low whirring grows louder as my heart races inside my body.

Clint presses against me, flattening me against the bark. His head spins as he searches for the source. He raises the bow and swings around when a drone dips under the canopy. He fires a shot and quickly reloads when the arrow glides just under the device. The second shot makes contact, wavering the projectile slightly. The boards beneath us groan as he pulls another arrow from the holster. I can almost feel the eyes on us as he takes the shot. This time he makes direct contact and the tiny machine falls to the earth. Clint almost leaps off the stand. I stagger down the ladder behind him.

Picking up a nearby rock, he bashes the main components. "Get the arrows," he shouts. "We have to get this thing out of here."

"I don't see them," I yell, frantically searching the earth around us.

"Forget it. We need to get out of here. Who knows how close they are."

He takes off at a run with the bow in one hand and the battered drone in the other. I quickly match his stride.

I pant as I follow his lead to the cabin "Why are we going this way?"

He doesn't answer me until the cabin is in sight. "Get everyone out of here. Go straight to Cabin Four."

I'm pretty sure he doesn't know which one I'd labeled as that, because I don't remember, but I nod as he jumps into the Ranger and purrs the engine to life.

I swing the door hard against its hinges as I burst into the cabin. Christa jumps from the table, spilling a plate of what looks like pancakes. All eyes stare at me. Even Jett looks up from the phone still glued to his hand. I am surprised to see Eddie sitting there but pay him no attention.

"Jett, can you track a drone if it's been destroyed?" I shout the question and wave my hand impatiently when he doesn't respond immediately.

"It depends."

"On what?"

"What type. What kind of system it's running. That sort of thing."

"Why?" The question comes from Eddie, not Christa like I would expect.

"I was thinking of getting one." I grab a bag from the corner and throw everything nearby into it. "Because Clint just shot one down. We have to get out of here."

Jett flies into motion, gathering the weapons that haven't disappeared from hiding and placing them on the counter next to the door. I can't figure the kid out, I think as I watch him. He's so self-absorbed in his electronics, but the moment disaster strikes, he's the first to take action when given an order.

I sling the bags we previously packed for our escape—or trip home—over my shoulder. I give thought to the coats Clint brought, but it's still slightly too warm for them yet, and I figure we won't be gone long enough to warrant the extra baggage of grabbing them. "What about the camera system on it? Do the images go through immediately or do you have to have the device to get it?"

"It depends. If I had to guess, I would say whoever was manning that camera was watching a live feed."

"I thought you said everything was back to normal?" Christa shouts the question at Eddie.

"It was...is."

"Then why is there a drone out here?"

"Maybe it was a photographer," he suggests.

"Are you sure? Lexi said there's a chance you might have dreamt the whole scenario about things being back to normal."

His icy eyes dart to mine as I literally turn the kids toward the door. "You guys go ahead to the cabin and I'll stay behind. If I'm right, which I am, I'll come get you before dark."

"And if you're not?" Christa's voice is as shaky as her body as she glances to her room.

"Then I'll be the one captured and you can get away safely." Christa nods, the answer clearly suiting her, but Eddie rushes to her side. "If it turns out I was delusional, you won't be harmed. I couldn't bear the thought of anything happening to you." He plants a kiss on her cheek and gives her a nudge toward the door. She breaks free and rushes to her room, returning with a handful of jewelry she hurriedly works to fasten to her limbs.

"Oh no," I yell, stopping her. "You're not wearing dinner bells out there."

"But—" she protests.

Eddie holds his hand out. "I'll keep it safe for you." She reluctantly drops the assortment in his lap. "How will I find you?"

"Leave him the map," Christa says.

My lips form a tight line as I pull the notebook from the bag. "This is where we're going." I slap the page on the table and point to the cabin labeled with a *4*. He reaches for the paper. "No. We can't let this get into the wrong hands. You'll have to remember it." I yank the page back to my chest, clutching it firmly.

He nods. "I would never give it up," he says sullenly.

"Don't run with a knife, Mommy," Tanner calls as we dart into the trees, each carrying the weapons Jett gathered and passed out. I'm worried about how Clint will find us and he has to repeat himself before I turn to him.

"Smart thinking." I slow to encase it in the sheath at my waist.

I lead the way with Christa bringing up the rear. When I turn to look, she's trying to stay out of the mud left from the peaceful rain the night before. Her precious loafers don brown splatters. I would smile if the situation were less critical.

Shrugging off my pack, I hand it to Sidney. "I'll buy you a new pair of shoes if you hurry up," I tell Christa as I fling Tanner onto my back.

"You can't afford these," she says, turning up her nose.

I quietly urge everyone on, falling to the rear of the group. We look like a band of misfits I think as I watch Jett take the lead with his axe held high. Ella trails behind him carrying a hammer, followed by Christa with her knife shaking in her hand. Jett weaves through the trees like a skilled hunter following some invisible curved path.

"Hold up. I need to check the map. None of this looks familiar."

Everyone gathers around me, looking over my shoulder. I point to the box on the map that marks our destination. "We need to look for this tree," I say, pointing to the one with the giant knot on the side. All eyes scan the nearby trunks. Heads shake.

"We haven't gotten to the next mountain yet, see?" Tanner points to my squiggly line marking the dip of the mountain.

"Good eye. Forward march!" I imitate a Sergeant's command.

Suddenly I have an overwhelming urge to watch *Jungle Book*. The way my line is moving reminds me of Colonel Hathi trying to keep his pachyderms in order. How I wish we could go back in time a few months when Tanner became obsessed with jungle animals. We had watched the video dozens of times. It seems like so long ago.

My troop marches tirelessly for a good half an hour, always on the lookout for a metaphorical Shere Khan. Defeating our tiger won't be as easy for us as it was for Mowgli.

I stop again to check the map, wishing I had put more detail into it. The knotted tree is still nowhere in sight. I urge everyone higher up the mountain. The last thing we need is to be caught in the valley. Another ten minutes of walking takes Ella to her breaking point. She finds a fallen tree and sits.

"I'm tired of walking," she pouts.

I nudge her with my knee, hoping to get moving again, but Jett takes a seat next to her.

"We could use a break," he says.

Christa sits and removes her ruined Sperry's. Defeated, I plop onto the bark facing the opposite direction and watch her rub dirt smudges from her shoes.

"Keep your eyes open," I order, pulling a lone bottle of water from the pack. I pass it around and gulp the last ounce after it's handed back to me. I shove the empty bottle into the bag, careful to avoid crinkling the plastic. A glimpse of black flashes in the corner of my eye. If I didn't know better, I'd think it were a ninja. I nudge Sidney and discretely point, whispering in her ear. She passes the message down the line and we rise to our feet in an instant. I wedge Tanner between me and Sidney. Down the line Christa shakes and tears well in Ella's eyes. Jett scans the trees, weapon poised.

"We have a better chance if we split up," I whisper.

"We fight them together," Jett says.

"This isn't *Call of Duty*," I respond sharply.

"They won't hurt a child," Jett retorts.

"Are you willing to bet your brother's life on that? Terrorists don't care."

"If we split up there's a better chance we'll be forced to surrender. They outgun us."

A swift movement from our other side draws all eyes to it. "Keep moving," I order.

The group hesitantly moves upward as the figure in black multiplies and closes in. We position ourselves around Tanner and Ella for the impending battle. I unsheathe my knife from my waist and hand it to Ella. The dominant man, less than fifty feet from us, lurks behind the trees as he inches toward us. I wish I had taken the bow from Clint, I fume as I study the guy to my left. He also lingers in the safety of the trees, moving slowly, calculating each step.

"We've got company behind us," Jett whispers. *How does he know?* With a quick backward glance, a streak of black darts behind a tree. A looming six-foot man dressed in black garb from head to toe fills the final position encircling us. Gun barrels threaten us, freezing our positions. Only the whites of their eyes show from beneath their headwraps, giving no clue about nationality or gender. Being so ill-equipped, attacking wouldn't be the best decision. The tension palpable, I fear they'll shoot when a handful of leaves fall from a nearby maple.

"Can you hit your marks?" Jett asks, as we form a protective square around the little two.

"I can't," Christa whimpers.

"Then we're all dead." His voice is cold, devoid of any emotion.

Static comes from a radio worn by the guy facing me. "*`Iihbat almuhimati. 'Akrir, 'iihbat almuhimati.*"

Ella drops to her knees, crying loudly. I spin around to check her condition, catching the drop of a masked man in my peripheral. A long groan escapes the fallen man's lips. I lunge to cover Tanner and Ella from the spray of gunfire sure to come. Christa is as stiff as if she had looked into Medusa's eyes. I slowly reach out and tug on the thin fabric of her skinny jeans. I'm pretty sure a strike from a rattlesnake wouldn't have gotten her attention.

"*Obtener las armas!*" The slender man from the front yells to the bulky one behind us. The barrel of an M4 points at Jett and Christa as the larger man darts toward the fallen comrade to our right. Seeing they are about to retreat, I make a move to stand, but a warning shot from a semi-automatic halts me. I slink back down and watch the skinny one check the pulse from the second fallen man. He must not have felt any because he grabs the AK-47 strap and yanks it over his head. The body plops back to the ground, causing Christa to shriek.

"*Prisa!*" One of them yells, slipping into the thick cover of trees.

The air rushes from my lungs, releasing the breath I didn't realize I'd been holding. I pull myself to a sitting position and grab Tanner and Ella into a bear hug.

I reach for my knife when I hear a voice ask if everyone is ok. Clint appears from behind the corpse of the first fallen terrorist and I feel myself breathe again. He kicks the body with his boot and, when it doesn't move, carefully checks for a pulse. He plants his foot between the man's shoulder blades and pulls the arrow from his back. After quickly wiping the blood on the black garb, he passes his loaded weapon to Jett and comes to us. Tanner and Ella cling to his legs while Christa remains statue-still.

A tear slips down her cheek and she suddenly comes back to life. "Oh CJ," she sobs.

Clint steps around her, curiously inspecting the blade protruding from the second fallen terrorist. He turns to me. "Nice work."

I shake my head. "Not my work." I jerk my head toward Jett.

"Well done." Clint states as he shakes Jett's hand. Jett doesn't beam like a child with the compliment, instead he receives it like a man who did the job that had to be done.

"Let's go over here," I say, ushering Christa and the kids away from the scene about to unfold. "Stay right here until we come back," I order.

"Momma," Ella whimpers, clinging to my leg.

"I won't be long." I pull her from me and plant her firmly next to a tree. "You can watch me from here."

Tanner takes her hand and I glance at Christa. Her eyes meet mine and she seems to understand the events taking place. She bends to their level, encircling them with her arms.

"Want to hear a story about your daddy?"

I slip away as she begins.

Clint and Jett frantically search pockets on the man struck by the arrow. His head covering has been removed, revealing a lock of jet-black hair atop a squared face. Brown eyes stare into oblivion and I can't help but focus on his skin. It's the golden brown most women dream of in summer and here it is the middle of fall. Either he was born with it or he went to a tanning bed regularly. My bet is on the former. He doesn't look like the terrorists normally portrayed on television. He looks more like an immigrant, though I'm not good at guessing where people are from.

I force my gaze from the man's lifeless face. "Find anything?"

"Nothing more than a snack," Jett says, holding up a blue Quest bar.

Clint makes his way to the other fallen man. He nods for Jett to remove the weapon from the bloody chest. Without flinching the boy-turned-man pulls the axe from the corpse. Setting it aside, he carefully removes the headwrap with the utmost respect. I gasp when the face is revealed. Clint straightens, placing his hands on his hips, his eyes darting from the body on the ground to me. He's at my side, steadying me in an instant.

"It's a woman," Jett whispers. "A *White* woman."

My lip quivers. Her freckled face with a hint of laugh lines and red hair burns an image into my brain that will haunt me forever. Clint slips his arms around my waist, squeezing me against him.

"That's Ella's teacher," I whimper. "Mrs. Connelly." Clint swings me away from the sight, leaving Jett to finish.

"You can't go back to Ella this way," he says, brushing a tear from my cheek.

"How could she?"

"I guess you never know what people are hiding."

I cover my mouth with my hand. "How are we going to tell Ella?"

"We aren't."

"Do you think it had anything to do with the recording?"

He embraces me, disguising the gesture to whisper in my ear. "I think that's the only explanation. They're brainwashing people to turn them in to soldiers."

"I think I'm going to be sick." With that, I pull away from Clint and hurry to a nearby oak to lose what little my stomach contains. Clint pulls my hair back and gently rubs my back as dry heaves wrack my body. When I finally stand, he moves us away from the mess I created and runs a rough finger over my lips.

"I need you to pull yourself together." His thumbs brush across my cheekbones, smearing salty tears into my damp skin. Sharp breaths take me to the edge of hyperventilation. Clint cups my face with one hand and takes my hand with his other, placing it on his heart. "Be the strong woman I fell in love with."

"I...don't...know...who she is...anymore," I gasp.

"Alexis JoAnne Jennings, if you can hide behind a façade to the point of divorce, you can certainly hide this from Ella." I shake my head in his hands. "I'm starting to see how awful I was to you—how awful I've been this entire time—and I'm going to work the rest of my life to make it up to you, if you'll let me. I'm so sorry I've never told you the things you deserve to know, but right now I need you to hide behind that wall you worked so hard to build. Ella can't know about this yet."

With my hand already on his chest, he places my other hand on my own chest where the pounding matches that of a runner mid-marathon. His is calm, steady. Keeping his calloused palm over mine, he locks his blue eyes on me. His mouth mimics the breathing techniques used for mothers in labor. I find myself copying his moves, drawing peace from him and, in a few minutes, I regain my composure. He draws his hands away from our bodies, sweeping his arms around my waist and pressing us flat against each other. His eyes don't waiver as his lips meet mine and he kisses me in the way he had when we first started dating. Desire stirs inside me and I fall for him all over again. Maybe we really will be ok. We need to move, but it's more important for me to be okay because he's going to ask me to do something he wouldn't trust Tim, his best friend of thirty years, to do. And I trust him enough to agree without knowing the terms. I had done it when we said our vows and I'll do it again now.

Jett coughs, bringing me—and I'll bet Clint—out of the memory of our first hunting trip together. Clint pulls away, leaving me longing for the privacy of the duck blind we had shared many years ago.

"You good?" Clint takes my hand, moving me beside him, and turns to Jett.

I run a finger under each eye, wiping away remnants of my tears. "I've got this."

"What'd you find?" Clint asks Jett.

Jett stands tall, his shoulders broader than they appeared a few hours before. "Just this." He conveys a calm, collected tone, a walkie talkie in his hand.

"Maybe we can get some answers with this."

"They aren't speaking English."

Clint clips the device to his waistband. "We need to keep moving."

"What about the bodies?" My voice sounds unfamiliar, even to me.

Clint brings my hand to his mouth as we walk toward Christa and the kids. His lips brush over my sweaty skin. "They'll serve as a warning not to mess with us."

"That will only prove we are still out here," I argue.

"And they'll know not to come around."

I don't like his answer, but don't have a better solution to offer.

Ella rushes to me and would've knocked me over if Clint hadn't been there to steady me. I avoid eye contact with her as she blabs the story Christa has just told her about her dad. I barely register the words she's saying. Clint must pick up on my quickening pulse because he shifts his hand to the back of my neck. Running small circles over my clammy skin, he moves through my greasy hair. *At least I still have a hairbrush,* I think as the urge for a shower surges through me. I can't wash away the grime I feel from what just happened, so I focus on the silver lining. Something changed in Jett. He left the cabin as a spoiled teenage brat and now, now he's a man. Even his walk is different. He doesn't do the lanky skater-boy strut that he used to; his posture is erect, and his head held high. I guess that's what responsibility will do.

Ella pushes her way between me and Clint as we continue the search for the lost cabin, but he still manages to hold my hand as if we're teenagers on a leisurely stroll. Tanner takes the lead with Jett, clearly wanting to be just like his older brother. He copies his movements, looking to the side when Jett does and holding a rock the size of his fist in the same way Jett carries the axe. Clint is being extra cautious also, looking behind us every few steps. Christa finally stops worrying about her shoes and Sidney pulls out her phone to draw a map as we walk.

Thick clouds roll over the horizon as the sun sinks to the west.

"Looks like we might be in for some rain," Clint comments, blowing a faint puff of air over his head.

"We should pick up the pace," Jett suggests.

"I'm tired of walking," Ella complains.

Clint removes his hand from mine, giving it a brutal taste of the chill in the air after being warmed by his heat for so long. "Here," he says, handing me the bow and hoisting her onto his back.

"I wanna ride too," Tanner whines.

Jett bends without a second thought and Tanner's smile couldn't be wider as he climbs on.

Giant droplets pelt us like water balloons dropped from the sky. I take my free hand to pull Tanner and Ella's uneven poncho hoods over their heads. They bury their faces into our backs and we press on.

"Double check that we're heading north, Sidney," Clint says before the last trace of light vanishes.

She whips out her device and swipes a few times. "We should veer this way slightly." She points with a finger. "I'm down to thirty percent. Jett, did you happen to grab the solar panel and charging cords?"

Jett shakes his head. "There wasn't time."

"We have a decision to make," Clint announces as our visibility diminishes. Christa turns to him with a fragile expression. She, too, knows what he's going to say.

"I'm not spending the night out here," she objects.

"Then we press on. We'll eventually come to a town."

"I'm tired, Daddy," Ella whines.

He tickles her side with a twist of his arm. She squeals. "I'm doing all the work," he says light-heartedly.

We trudge up the side of another mountain. They might as well be closing in on us, I think of the vastness of trees and peaks, but they also provide safety I'd rather not give up. I try to visualize where we may be or may come out but am so lost by our journey that I have no intelligent answer.

Jett maintains the lead, carefully watching for signs of danger from the front while Clint does the same from the back.

Tanner still rides on Jett's back so I instinctively go to check on him as we pause underneath a tall hemlock. "He's asleep."

"So is she," Clint says, motioning with his head to Ella.

Jett points. "Did you see that?"

"What?" Clint is at his side almost instantly.

"A light." He points to the mountain off to our right. We stop and squint in the darkness. "It was just there."

"I don't see anything," Clint says, both relieved and frustrated. I point the scope toward the location, suddenly wishing Clint had opted for one with night vision. "Keep on, soldier," he orders.

We lumber along until Jett stops so suddenly, I almost run into the back of him, the arrow less than an inch from his back when I gather the traction to stop.

"There it is again," he says.

This time we all see it. A faint light blinks in the distance.

The four of us stare at each other. Christa places her trust solely in Clint, her eyes fixed on him. I watch the two men share an understanding nod. We turn our course toward the light.

# Chapter 22

A looming mansion sits on the hillside before us. The light had come on exactly three more times as we cautiously approached. We stand in a line, staring, anticipating our next move. The chilled water continues to bombard us from the sky. Tanner, having woken up when Jett slipped, now waves his hand across his face like a windshield wiper as beads trickle down his face. My soaked hair lays heavily on my neck and back. We are all drenched to the core, the girls shivering from the dampness.

Christa shifts, either out of discomfort or in an effort to keep warm. "What if they're bad guys too?"

Jett runs a hand through hair that now reaches past his pierced ears, sending tiny streams down his cheeks and over his forehead. "Why would they hide their light?"

"I think we should knock," I suggest with a shiver.

"We already know there are terrorists out here," Clint says. "What if they're disguising themselves?"

Jett steps forward. "I'd like to volunteer to find out."

"No!" Christa slaps her hand over her mouth at her sudden shriek.

"If they are terrorists then they only get one of us, but if they aren't, I think they'd be less threatened by a teenage boy."

Clint nods. "He has a point."

"I will not let you put our son in any more danger," Christa retorts.

"He's in just as much danger as the rest of us. Would you like to go instead? I'm sure they'll be as welcoming to a woman." Clint's tone reveals annoyance, sending Christa into submission.

Sidney twists a lock of drenched golden hair. "I should be the one to go." Her voice is barely a whisper, but it's enough to draw Clint's attention and bug out Christa's eyes.

"No," Clint snaps. The light dots the darkness three times then a brief pause followed by more blinks, some a fraction of a second longer than the previous.

"Actually, I agree with Sidney," I say. "And I think she should take Tanner with her."

Clint's eyes burn into me even in the pitch black. "No way."

"If they aren't terrorists, they can't refuse a teenage girl with her young brother."

"And if they are?" His tone is as cold as the night air and I shudder at the thought.

"We'll be right outside to rescue them," I argue.

"We don't know how many are in there."

"It's our only chance."

Clint looks to Christa, no doubt wanting to gain her approval. The clouds abruptly stop pouring their heavy load on us like they, too, are waiting for her answer. A harsh exhale escapes her lips and the reprieve we gained from the sky is over. I can't help but feel like a drenched rat while she still looks stunning despite her soaked and muddy pants. Her hair falls neatly as if it were made for this look. Mine falls in tangled tendrils like usual. I wonder if that is part of my resentment toward her. *She does make me feel inadequate, inferior,* I admit as I channel my hostility to warm me. My socks squish in my boots, further irritating me. It's time to make a decision, I scowl through gritted teeth. Christa's arms cross over her chest. She bows her head and, as she lifts her long, thick lashes to look at Clint, I can tell she's used the move before to get exactly what she wants.

"There has to be another way," she whispers, rocking back on her locked knees.

I almost wish she'd pass out from the gesture so we could do what needs to be done. She doesn't. Instead, she takes a tentative step forward, closer to Clint. Pain radiates along my jaw as I press my teeth tightly together. A cold chill jerks my body as I watch their exchange. Christa starts to shake—a ploy to get her way with Clint? If she wins this battle, I think the answer will be very clear. With great effort, I pry my teeth open enough to put a stop to her objections.

"Look, Christa, we have two choices—stay out here and freeze or hope these people will help us. They can do this."

Christa's thin frame trembles as her eyes meet mine. "I'm scared."

I take her hand with my icicle fingers. "Me too. But Sidney went from doing nothing but staring at her phone and reading textbooks while expecting to be waited on to actually learning to be a productive member of this family and Jett, Jett saved us back there." I point a rigid finger in her direction. "He became a man back there. I don't know if you noticed that or not, but he did. Sidney is offering to risk herself for the rest of us. I have no doubt that she will protect Tanner while she's in there. She can do this. Look deep inside yourself and see that you have amazing children who have adapted to this awful situation and let them do what they can to help. We are a team." As I finish my speech, I vow to make good on my last words. It's time to start treating Christa with more respect.

She nods, so slowly I fear I may have imagined it.

"Once inside, you have five minutes to send us a sign that all is well," Clint tells Sidney. "How's your phone battery?"

She pulls the phone from a protective inner pocket. "Eleven percent."

Christa gives a small nod in agreement of the plan.

Pulling Sidney in for a hug, I slip my knife into the waistband of her jeans. "Don't be afraid to use this," I whisper, the gesture having gone unnoticed by her mother.

"Listen to Sidney," Clint orders Tanner as the boy takes his sister's hand.

"Wait!" Christa's voice produces a tiny echo, gaining her glares from our irritated party. "You can do this," she says, going to Sidney for an awkward hug. "I know you can."

After watching Sidney take Tanner's hand and go the short distance, Clint glances at the watch I gave him for Christmas the moment the double door is cracked. They slip inside a moment later and the longest five minutes of our lives begin.

We spread out, positioning ourselves behind trees to watch for the sign. Milliseconds tick by in slow motion. Jett's movements around the trees are like that of a stealth fighter, like he was born knowing exactly what to do in these situations. It's as if something unlocked inside him, revealing a totally different person. Clint's eyes bore into the mansion as well, his gaze only wavering to look at his Rolex knock-off. I'm almost certain half an hour has passed when a flickering light in the window closest to us reveals a faint image of a looming figure holding a long weapon over the two children.

They are placed directly in front of the window where we had seen the light. The thumping of my heart pounds so strong it could beat the elephant off my chest. I watch as Clint and Jett remain calm as if they were watching a movie. The weapon, I assume a machete, pulls back into a striking position. I gasp as it lurches forward, spraying blood over the clear windowpane that spans two stories. Clint and Jett sprint into action as screams echo off the mountains. My legs are suddenly made of something other than flesh and bones. They wobble beneath me and my world turns black. Voices call to me from the distance. I can't make out the words, but I recognize the sounds. They comfort me as I slip completely away.

# Chapter 23

My eyes flutter open and my first conscious thought is that my toes don't squish. I wiggle them to be sure. I must be dead, is my next thought as I struggle to focus on my surroundings. A thick fleece and fur blanket gloriously cover my near bare skin. The crackling of a fire draws my attention to the smooth rock surrounding it. My eyes scan the mantle, complete with pictures of a family, each with their own fish. I study them a minute, a young blonde boy standing on a dock with a Northern Pike the length of his tiny chest, a woman dressed in blue plaid cleaning a large Muskie, a tall man with a ballcap proudly displaying another Pike, and a teenage girl with the same blonde hair as the woman struggling to hold a Walleye in a net. My gaze moves up to the rafters, large wooden beams that seam nicely into the wooden walls. The only light comes from the fire but the room is so large most of it is cast in shadows. I pull the blanket tighter and move to a sitting position. The couch is high-backed, with wooden trim, the kind that is uncomfortable to sit on, much less sleep on. A low groan escapes as I massage stiff muscles in my back. I jump at the movement next to me.

"Hey," Clint whispers, straightening from his slumped condition in a chair that matches the couch. It looks more like a throne than a chair and I imagine he's stiffer than I am if he's been sitting there long.

"Where are the kids?!" I stumble to my feet, the events from earlier suddenly coming back to me.

Clint leaps to his feet, circling me with his arms before I can react further. "They're fine. They're asleep."

"But I saw—"

A woman slips through the doorway, a dainty tea cup in her hand. Her soft green pantsuit clings to her curves as if it were designed just for her. Her hair rests heavily in a thick bun at the nape of her neck. I immediately recognize her from the picture on the mantle, though her blonde hair has been lost to gray. Her gray eyes smile at me, along with her soft pink lips.

"You're up," she says, eyes beaming in delight. My foggy brain refuses to place her accent. "The boys carried you in and we've been worried sick."

Clint helps me sit and takes the cup, complete with saucer, from her and places it in my hands. He tucks the blankets snuggly around me and turns to the woman. "Could you give us a minute, Mrs. Watson?"

"Sure thing, doll. Probably need some time to fill in some blanks, eh?" With a curt nod, she turns to leave.

"You passed out," Clint explains, moving the frail cup toward my lips.

The hot liquid, a weak tea, warms my insides. I savor it as I study Clint's fresh appearance. His beard has been trimmed and he wears a matching green flannel pajama set with moose on them. The soap he'd used lingers in my nostrils as he cups my chin. I want to get up and find Ella and Sidney, make sure they're okay, but my legs still tingle.

"There was so much blood." The cup clinks against the matching plate and I'm embarrassed to have faltered when I saw blood every day for six years before I changed to hospice care.

Clint takes the chattering dishes from me, placing them on the glass top of an antler end table. It's between the couch, which I now see is covered in a bear scheme, and the chair Clint had slept in, only it's not where it can be reached from either piece of furniture without stretching. Why wouldn't they move the three pieces closer for better comfort, I wonder as Clint runs a finger over my hand before clasping it.

"There was no blood," he says. I tilt my head, and for a second wonder if I'm losing my mind. "Sidney gave the sign just as you fell. Jett was focused on the window as I ran to catch you and he saw it."

"There was no sign. They were taken to the window and slaughtered."

"No. Sidney explained our situation to the Watsons and we were eagerly welcomed. Everyone is fine. I think your nerves got to you."

"I want to see them."

He helps me to my feet and guides me down a hallway lined with pine paneling. Lit candle sconces reveal five doorways down the lengthy hall.

"Christa is in there," he says, pointing to the first door on the left. "Jett and Sidney are in these rooms." He points to two rooms across the hall from each other. "The bathroom is here." He motions to a cracked door next to Jett's room. "And the rest of us will sleep in here, though the kids could've had a separate room. I told Mrs. Watson you'd want us all together after you woke."

I nod as he turns an antique knob. A soft glow flickers from an oil lamp on the wall. Something tells me it was supposed to be for decoration only, but circumstances made it otherwise. A queen bed is opposite a large dresser with a mirrored backing. The room is larger than our living room at home and our children look even smaller nestled under a turkey-covered comforter. Tanner wiggles in his sleep, making me catch my breath. I inch toward the bedside, afraid at any moment this dream could end. Slowly I bend and graze each of their cheeks, reveling in the reality of their warm bodies.

Clint stands beside me, allowing my need to watch them sleep. Several minutes pass before I'm satisfied that I won't wake up. I nod my content and Clint presses his smile into the nape of my neck. Wrapping his arms around me, he guides me from behind back down the hall and across the living room into an expansive dining room. I'm sure this is the kind of room Christa is used to. A picture comes to mind of a part of a kitchen where her servants eat. The sixteen-foot ceiling is high and decked with two chandeliers crusted with crystals that drip from them in elegant teardrops. They are off, of course, and the room is lit by three half-burned candles along a glass table with a delicately embroidered cream runner down the middle. Mrs. Watson sits at the end of the table as if she's waiting to be served.

"Lexi, please sit," she says.

As if on cue, a man, dressed in jeans and a navy dress shirt, enters the room with a silver tray from the swinging doors behind the woman. His full head of gray hair pins him as a businessman with a slightly rebellious side, judging by his tie covered in tiny fishing lures. I'll almost bet he was made to 'clean up' and the tie is his way of keeping things casual. He places the tray in front of me. It's heaped full of eggs, a slice of ham, and a stack of pancakes. A tiny tin holds syrup next to a thin sliver of butter.

"I'm afraid we're down to slim pickings," he says, looking embarrassed.

"It looks delicious," I admit, scooping some onto a plate. "I'm Lexi, by the way."

He extends a hand, not waiting for me to stand to shake it. "Albert Watson."

"Mr. Watson, I'd like to thank you for opening your home to us."

He waves his arm across his broad chest as if he's done nothing out of the ordinary. "Please, call me Ab, and eat."

I slide the tray over to Clint. "We ate earlier," he says.

"Clint, you go ahead and get yourself some more," Mrs. Watson orders. He takes a plate and pulls two pancakes from the stack.

"It's been so long since we've had eggs," I say, trying not to talk with my mouth full.

Mrs. Watson's laugh matches her style. Light and airy, friendly. "We have good neighbors." To the look of confusion on my face, she explains. "They have chickens. We take care of each other. Always have."

"How long have you lived here?"

"Oh, about ten years, eh?" Mr. Watson says more to his wife than us.

She reaches across the table for his hand, squeezing it gently. "Will be twelve this summer."

"That's right. Time gets away from me since I retired."

Mrs. Watson laughs again, this time with hidden meaning behind it. "If you'd get yourself a hobby like I said, you wouldn't have that problem."

Ab looks at her, the love radiating out of his green eyes and I can't help but want Clint and I to have a similar exchange someday—without all the ritzy stuff surrounding us now.

"I do things," he says.

Her eyes hold the same affection as she smooths a stray wisp of hair back into her bun. "Hanging out with Ralph Reynolds is not 'doing things.'" She uses air quotes that seem unnatural to her.

"We do all sorts of things," he responds playfully. "We shoot chickens with slingshots when they get to fighting and catch fish with our bare hands."

Mrs. Watson's focus turns to us with an amused grin. "It's more like two old men wallerin' around in the water. They look like schoolboys itching for an excuse to get wet."

"It's better than embroidering with Betty," he shoots back in jest.

I laugh at their banter. "How did you know about what was happening?"

Ab points to a small radio that has obviously found a new home on the ornate table. My guess is Mrs. Watson only tolerates it because she has no choice.

"Ralph and I were listening to the radio. We like to do that sometimes while we're waiting for a co...chicken fight." Mrs. Watson's thin lips purse at his almost use of a word she doesn't find appropriate. "Right in the middle of the news broadcast we were listening to, they came across with a warning. We had gotten distracted by Clancy, the big co...rooster, and thought they were talking about foreign affairs, but it turned to static right after."

I lean forward. "What kind of warning?"

"It wasn't the voice of Hal Rutherford, the normal broadcaster." He shudders. "I can still hear the rasp in his voice as he sternly warned people to arm themselves and to fight—this is an invasion, he said. Still thinking we had misunderstood, we ran over here and turned on the television, only to find it fuzzy with static too. We only get three channels anyhow, but none of them would focus."

Having cleaned my plate, I put my fork beside it. "What did you do next?"

"Waited on our porches with our guns. Like they do in the old movies, you know? Three days later Ralph got antsy. You'd have to know Ralph." He laughs like he's got an inside joke. "Let's just say he's a Vietnam Vet who doesn't take kindly to a threat."

Clint places his hand over mine. The tenderness in his action makes the hairs stand on the back of my neck. He holds his hand up to Ab, telling him he'd like to speak even though Ab's mouth gapes open.

"Lexi, you're probably not going to like what you're about to hear, but I want you to listen. I'm truly sorry we made decisions without you, but time is running out. I hope you understand that." He waits for my nod and continues. "I'm going to let Ab start at the beginning and, once you're caught up, I'll finish by telling you what happens next."

Ab clears his throat in the gravelly way old men have. "Ralph isn't the kind to get stir-crazy. I mean, he's lived up here since he was shipped home. Said he's better off up here with Betty and God than in a town full of people. He rarely even goes into town, usually sends me or Betty. Anyway, about a week after we heard the warning, he decided he had to check it out. Said he'd be damned if he was going to let another country ruin us. Once a soldier, always a soldier, I guess." He chuckles and pauses. "So, he goes out scouting.

There's a campground not too far that way." He points with a thick, crooked finger.

I sip a fresh cup of tea, painfully enduring his dramatic pause.

"There were five men camping up there. All in their forties. They had come to fish, leaving behind wives and children. Apparently two days after we heard the warning, they had decided to head up the mountain to—" he leans closer as if he's about to reveal a secret, but he's still two chairs away. "—go bird watching, but if you tell their wives, they'll cut out your tongue." He chuckles again.

"That's what saved them. Ralph thinks the camp was invaded and somehow the captors miscounted or something because they never came back. The men didn't know what had happened, just that the place had been ransacked. They searched the woods for two days, thinking a bear had torn into the place." He laughs deep in his belly. "Like bears had learned to use zippers. Anyway, long story short, they headed into town where they didn't find a soul. They agreed it was safer at camp, so they headed back. A few days later, two of the men agreed to go to Rockwood. The deal was, if they didn't return, the three remaining would expect the worst and plan accordingly. Ralph showed up just after that first week. They had no idea what was going on. Thought it was the Apocalypse." He laughs again, but I remember thinking the same thing.

"Ralph explained what we knew and has been checking in on them ever since. I could see the wheels turning in Ralph's head when he returned from finding them. We offered them shelter here, but they seemed to think whatever was happening would end soon. The only reason he hasn't gone all Rambo with them is that very reason. Last week when he came back from checking on them, he had a wicked smile on his face. We had been talking about heading down through the Catskills to the Appalachians to form a small militia—you know there've got to be people crawling in those mountains."

Now it's my turn to laugh. "That's what I said."

"Ralph has a whole notebook dedicated to different scenarios on how to handle this." He laughs again, a belly laugh I'm afraid will wake the kids. "Some of them—possibly most of them—would never work due to our resources."

"I'm guessing he got the men to go along with a plan. What is it?"

Ab nods to Clint. He takes both my hands, placing them in his lap. "We're going to Canada." I almost drop the fragile cup in my hands. I had been mentally preparing myself for this and now it's real.

"Ralph will be on board." Ab chimes in with a chuckle. "He's itching to do *something* and I've been telling him Canada was the best option for weeks now."

"That will give us six guys," Clint says. "It betters our chances. And doubles our weapons. I'll be able to leave you the bow."

"Make that eleven," Ab corrects. Clint counts on his fingers, checking his math. "The two men who went to Rockwood came back with a couple strays that were hiding out in Rockwood State Forest. Almost had a shootout before they came to an understanding."

"You didn't mention that earlier," Clint says.

"Didn't I?" Ab scratches his head. "Must've slipped my mind. They found these guys who managed to escape when the towns were raided. What better place to for them to hide?" He beams with pride as if it were his idea.

I mentally count the men planning to embark. "You're including Jett?" I swallow hard.

Clint nods. "He's proven himself. And he wants to go."

"Christa will never agree," I argue.

"She already has."

Mrs. Watson places her hand on Ab's shoulder. "Come dear, they have a lot to talk about, eh?" She hands the tray to him, following him through the double doors with the dirty dishes.

"Ralph has it all planned out," Clint says. "He has three ideas on how to cross the border."

I can't help but laugh nervously. "And we're so worried about people coming *into* our country illegally. Now you're going to *leave* illegally."

"I don't want you to worry." He brushes my hair off my shoulder.

"How can I not?"

"They have running water here."

I lay my head on his chest. "Are you trying to console me with a shower?"

"I am." He places a soft kiss on my forehead. "The Watsons insist you, Christa, and the kids stay here while we're gone."

"They can't possibly feed four extra people."

"Did you see the food she brought out for just you? You'll be fine."

"Where does it come from?"

"Apparently Ralph knows where there's a small pig farm. He walks three miles each day to feed them and when they need meat, he shoots one. Ralph has the chickens so they're good there."

"All they need is a cow."

"Ralph has a goat."

"Of course he does." The chair legs screech against the wooden floor as I scoot it closer to his. "When will you leave?"

"Within a week I imagine. Maybe sooner."

I place my head on his shoulder. "I'll want a detailed plan."

"I know." He brushes his hand over my tangled hair. "I don't want to leave things undone between us when I go. There's something I need to tell you."

I place my finger over his lips. "Shh. There's nothing I need besides this right now." I lift my mouth to his and kiss him. Nothing else matters.

# Chapter 24

My eyes are still heavy when Clint nudges me. "I'm too tired," I moan, keeping my eyes closed. The rich aroma of coffee fills my nostrils and I open one eye. Darkness lingers through the off-white curtains. Clint's body presses into mine as he wraps a strong arm around me.

"I was hoping we could talk," he whispers. I groan lightly as to not wake the kids and roll onto my back.

"I need a nap," I groan.

His lips meet mine, his passion confirming that he, too, is thinking about our tryst in the empty room only hours ago before we moved to sleep near the kids.

"Round two isn't until later," he whispers, leaving a trail of kisses to my ear.

"You're lucky you brought coffee," I say, playfully sticking my tongue out at him.

He pouts. "I'm not worth getting up early for?"

"Your stock is going up after its recent plummet."

I reach for the mug as my feet slide over the edge of the bed. He produces a pair of slippers which are too small for my size ten feet, but I slip them on after one foot touches the cold oak flooring.

The house is dark and quiet as he leads me through the dining room doors where we talked with the Watsons last night. He guides me into the kitchen and out a matching set of swinging doors to the other side. We step into a thin hallway where he makes a sharp left and heads up the stairs with me tagging along, attached to him by our linked hands. At the top he stops at a small table and motions for me to sit next to the railing in a white upholstered chair with a tall back.

"I wanted a little time with you before the kids wake," he says as he takes a seat across from me.

I rub sleep from my eyes and take the first sip of coffee in months. Even without cream or sugar, it tastes like what I imagine a sip of whiskey would taste like to a recovering alcoholic. We sit silently for several minutes, our eyes adjusting to the darkness. Across from the railing I admire the floor-to-ceiling windows and wonder what the view is like.

Clint's heavy sigh breaks my interest. "I haven't been the best husband, but from here on out, I'm going to do better." I slide my arm past our cups and reach for his hand. "I know there are still things to get out in the open, but for now I was hoping to focus on us."

"I think we can both agree there are more important issues at stake than your affairs with Christa."

"I never cheated on you." Even in the dark, his pain is obvious. "I'm sorry if it ever appeared that way."

I warm my hands on my mug, taking a long sip. "The thought crossed my mind."

"If it were up to me, things would've been different. Once this is all over, I'm going to make sure changes are made."

"Clint, I'm eager to give you the chance, but you have to be sincere about it." He nods, the weight on his shoulders evident. "I was ready to throw our marriage away and you're pulling me back in. I'd be lying if I said I wasn't concerned."

"Please give me the chance."

"I want to know about your past. But I don't want you to tell me just because of our current situation."

"I wanted to tell you, but I was afraid you'd leave me—still am."

"You're not giving me much credit. How bad is it?"

He hangs his head. "I wouldn't have stuck around if the roles were reversed."

"Wow." I busy myself by savoring the last of my weak coffee. He slides his cup to me with the hand that isn't nervously squeezing mine.

"It's not that our love isn't worth it, but it's a lot to ask of someone. If it were you coming to me with this, I'd feel like I'd have to walk away even though it would kill me."

"Is that what I should do?"

His eyes burn into the carpet. I slide a slipper off and run my feet over its softness, appreciating the luxury I once took for granted. "I hope you don't."

"If it's what you would do, maybe I should feel the same way."

He rubs his fingers over his jaw. "You're a better person than me."

"Clinton Michael, you aren't a bad person."

"I've treated you in a way that I wouldn't tolerate. And you've stuck by me. Why?"

I clasp my hand over his. "We're a team," I say, though I feel like a fraud uttering the words when I had divorce papers drawn up.

He smiles, his eyes meeting mine. "Maybe we should talk about something else. I don't want this to be the last memory you have if I don't make it back."

"Don't talk like that," I order sternly.

"It's possible."

"It's not going to happen." I slide onto his lap. "Besides, if it won't matter if you don't make it back—which you will—why does it matter at all?"

"You'll probably find out anyway. I just won't be around to see the disappointment on your face."

The words sting, but I know what he needs right now is one last memory to take with him—to keep him going while he's away. "Do you know what I miss?" He inquires with a glance. "I miss when we'd all wake up in the same bed on Saturday mornings."

"And we'd make breakfast together at lunch time." He nuzzles into my hair.

"I'll cherish those moments long after the kids are grown."

"I wish Jett and Sidney could've been there for some of those."

"It's never too late, Clint. Sure, it might be a little weird for teenage kids to be in the same bed, but you can still make lasting memories. You should see the way Sidney looks at you when you aren't watching. You're her hero."

Clint moves his arm around my waist. "You're beautiful."

"And Jett desperately wants your approval. Clearly, he had some anger issues where you're concerned, but he's come around."

He points over the railing where the first hints of color tint the sky. The lake looms in all directions, narrowing off toward the back of the house.

We sit there, wrapped in each other's arms, as gorgeous pinks and oranges paint a backdrop before us.

Clint kisses my cheek, letting his lips linger against my skin. "Let's go back to bed and wait for the kids to jump on us."

With one last glance at the sparkling water, he hoists me into his arms and carries me down the steps. "Please don't divorce me," he whispers at the bottom.

"I'd battle an entire fleet of terrorists with you. Trust me enough to give me the chance."

He pauses for a lingering kiss before taking us back to bed to wait for our children to 'wake' us.

# Chapter 25

A gusty wind blows a rich campfire aroma across the cove as Ab points out his neighbor's tiny shack. From across the lake it must look like a mansion sitting next to the local dump. The cabin is small, one or two rooms with a tin roof and a tiny porch that might collapse at any given moment. A bathtub peeks out on the far side next to a fenced area filled with clucking chickens. As the rooster crows, I can't help but wonder how they've survived this long. Between the two fires and the chickens, anyone in a mile radius should be able to track them.

Clint drags three canoes to a long wooden dock. Mrs. Watson had provided us all with warmer jackets from the closets belonging to her children and grandchildren and I pull the thick purple fleece tighter around me as we make our way to the freshly painted boat landing. The sleeves are two inches too short, leaving my wrists wishing for the extra inches on Tanner's aqua jacket. Christa, of course, lucked out and is the same size as the daughter, but the rest of us are dealing with clothing that is either too big or small. Nobody complains at being able to ditch Christa's homemade ponchos.

As we sink the oars into the chilly water, Ab explains how they couldn't see their neighbor's cabin when they bought the land and wanted to sell after realizing the eyesore next door, but once they met the Reynolds family, they knew they were in the right place. The story comes to an end as quickly as our journey. A gray pony-tail dangles past the shoulders of the mammoth of a man chopping logs near the ramshackle cabin. His beard is as untamed as his hair and a pipe hangs out of his mouth. He wears a thick plaid jacket with patches covering the elbows. A ruckus from the chickens draws my attention to Betty. With one hand holding her apron and the other throwing food, she curses at the fowl. She's as round as she is tall, but it's obvious by her demeanor that she doesn't take any crap—at least from chickens. Her hair is as long as Ralph's but is pulled into a loose braid with wisps flying about in the cold breeze that blows off the lake. Her shirt is thin, and she wraps her arms around herself, shivering after shaking her apron out. She kicks at a chicken who follows her when she turns. He runs circles around her, stopping in front of her, forcing her to sidestep him. She finally tires of his game, picks him up, and places him on her shoulder.

"Come on in," she orders, heading for the tiny porch.

I think we all share the same thought as we watch her stomp her boots, complete with Tinker Bell pom-poms dangling from the sides—how are the Watsons friends with these people who are obviously so different?

"Better get on in before you make her mad," Ab says, scooting us along.

Christa stops at the stairs as if it's a death trap waiting to swallow her up. Clint softly urges her up the creaky steps and over the weathered hole at the top. The thin windows on each side of the porch remind me of the ones in old westerns. I imagine Ralph pointing his rifle through one and shooting anyone who threatens his homestead.

The kitchen and living room is one big space with a door at the back wall. Ralph pushes past us to throw some logs on the fire as Betty slaps a dead bird onto a thick table that looks like someone cut a tree down, sawed it in half, and slapped some legs onto the trunk. Knicks cover it and knives rest in grooves on one side. She pulls one and begins sawing away, skillfully carving around the bones with the chicken still perched on her shoulder.

"Does that bird want to become dinner?" Clint asks, his tone bordering confusion and disgust.

Betty waves the knife toward her shoulder. "This is Kitty. Closest thing I can have to a cat...Ralph won't let me bring home a mountain lion."

Christa's eyes double in size. "Why would you do *that*?"

She laughs. "Well, I wouldn't. Didn't even want a cat, but this stupid chicken thinks she is one."

Christa raises an eyebrow. "I've never seen a cat perch on a shoulder."

"I'd have eaten her long ago," Clint says.

"Psst. She's too much fun to watch when she's not being a pain in the ass."

Ab strokes the chicken's back. "Don't mind these old hens. Betty here was a pirate in a past life and poor old Kitty was a parrot. Only logic I have on the matter."

Betty shoos Ab from her kitchen with the tip of her knife. "Selling that story again doesn't make it any more true."

Ralph takes a stack of crinkled papers from the counter, clearly annoyed by the chicken distraction. "Operation Takeback begins tomorrow at Zero Four Hundred." He scoffs at Betty's use of the table and motions for us to move so he can place them on the floor. There is barely room for us to stand along the walls when he's done scattering maps and plans on the dirty floor. It also looks like it was made with simple methods, one board sticking up slightly higher in the middle. Ralph scrambles for a torn page in the middle, a map with routes outlined in three separate colors as angry clucking ensues outside. Ab nods to Ralph, picking up a slingshot and a couple pebbles from a bucket on the small countertop next to the door. Clint catches my eye in the moment before Ralph demands his attention. I can tell he'd rather the kids not be present for this, but I don't know what to do with them aside from sending them out to watch a chicken get pelted with rocks.

Ralph shoves a notebook paper into Clint's hand. I can't make out the writing but can see it has instructions scribbled on it. "We'll split into three groups once we meet the others. You'll need to memorize the routes. This one's yours." He yanks the map from Clint and points to the one on the left. Bob and Joe will lead the group on the right and I'll take the middle. I assume your boy will be the one going with us?"

"Yessir." Jett steps forward, extending a hand.

"How old are you, son?"

"Seventeen."

Ralph nods, a knowing smile coming over him. "I was barely older than you when they dropped us in 'Nam."

"I've already made my first kill," Jett offers as qualification.

Christa's eyes burn into him and I'm increasingly aware of the heat in the room. I can't be sure whether it's from the fire, our extra clothing, or the conversation.

Ralph slaps the boy on the back, knocking him onto one of the papers. "There are thousands more terrorists out there."

"I'm ready to do my part."

Ab returns from his mission triumphantly. "Ole Bill was after Tommy again."

The color fades from Christa's face. "You name your chickens?"

Betty looks up from her chunk of meat. "'Course. That way we know who we're eating." She laughs, a hearty laugh with a hint of evil amusement. "Becky is for lunch if y'all are stayin.'"

Christa pales. I scoot beside her as Ralph corners the men. They pass papers around and Ralph covers all scenarios, which he has written on various papers.

We head back across the cove before lunch and Christa is so eager, she almost tips the boat. The rest of the day is spent in a mad dash to pack supplies. It reminds me of the McCallisters in *Home Alone* when they realize they've overslept. Mrs. Watson moves about the kitchen with the zest of someone half her age. Sidney takes to being her assistant while Christa and I take the younger ones to help pack. Ella and I search drawers, looking for clothes that might fit Clint and Jett. Tanner catches the socks we toss to him and stacks them on the bed. I find jeans a size too big for Clint in the room we are staying in. Thankfully there are a few belts in the closet because Jett will have to wear the same size. I roll everything as tightly as possible and have the duffel bag Mr. Watson dropped in the hall stuffed with several pairs of long underwear and thermal shirts when I notice Clint out the window. He circles a pair of sawhorses. Grabbing my jacket, I head outside. The sound of metal pinging metal fills the air as I approach.

"What are you doing?" I ask, watching him spray white paint strategically on a set of overalls. A thick coat is on the ground waiting for its turn.

"Creating camouflage," he says, his eyes never moving from the task. "Going to start snowing while we're gone." He stands back so I can see his creation. The pants and coat that used to be black are now mostly white with specks of black.

"You're a genius."

He pauses for a quick kiss then turns when Jett puts the next set on the board.

Mr. Watson drags a wooden sled across grass that had been green not long ago. It's piled with a dozen skis, poles, and snowshoes. A small chest wobbles atop it all.

"This is all the ammo I have," he says, tapping the chest. "Ralph will have more. I just hope it's enough."

Clint stares at the ripples floating across the cove. "We'll have to make more than one trip."

I glance toward the open shed doors. "Are those paddle boards?" Ab nods. "Can we tie them together and float it across?"

"I'll get rope," he says and hurries away.

We drop into bed, exhausted, but fully packed, shortly after midnight.

"You're amazing," Clint whispers in my ear.

"I'm not the one going out to fight bad guys."

"You're the one protecting our kids...and dealing with my ex-wife."

I almost laugh out loud. "That's going to be the biggest job."

"You can handle her." His arm slips around my waist. "There's something I need to tell you before I go."

I take his hand. "Clint, I promise you, this can wait. You need your rest."

"I can't leave with this on my chest. All day I've been thinking about what you deserve. And it's so much more than what I've been giving you." He leads me out to the fireplace to avoid waking the kids.

"What you're about to embark upon tomorrow is so much bigger than our issues," I say once we are settled on the uncomfortable couch.

"When I come back, I want you to be proud of me."

"You're going to come back a hero. Hell, you already are."

"You should look up the definition of 'hero.' With what I've done, I shouldn't even be considered a man."

"Clint, you're the most hard-working man I know. You're loyal and honest—"

He stops me there with a squeeze to my thigh. I know the words aren't the truest, but I know the potential is there. It's why I married him. "I was young when I left Christa and I did something so stupid it's still haunting me to this day. It's the cause of so many of our problems. I'm completely responsible for those divorce papers you handed me."

"We all do stupid things when we're young."

"I should've fixed it by now."

"We can fix it together."

He shakes his head. "I have to do this on my own."

"Then I'll have your back. I only got the divorce papers to scare you into facing our problems." I move the thin diamond on my left hand. His gaze follows. "I hoped it wouldn't come to that, but, yes, I was prepared to follow through. See? I was honest. You go."

He takes a deep breath and exhales slowly. "Christa's dad used his money to push me around." Pain fills his eyes when they meet mine. "He made me sign an agreement that would ensure financial security for Jett and Sidney. I was too stupid to realize he would've done that anyway."

"What was in the agreement?"

"I only agreed to sign it because it guaranteed that Boats 'N Bait would stay in the family. If I signed his agreement, there were stipulations that kept me from worrying about money ever again. We're not broke," he says with downcast eyes.

My blood pressure spikes, knowing I've taken on extra shifts to help cover the overhead of a small business that barely keeps afloat. "What?"

"He's allotted me ten grand a month and has trust funds set up for all the kids."

I figured Jett and Sidney had one, but the news that our kids had one as well has me baffled. "What's the catch?"

"Basically, Christa calls the shots. He didn't want to hurt Christa's reputation by me leaving her. I had no idea it would turn out to be like this."

"So, she's allowed to be engaged to another man and you're still supposed to be at her beck and call?"

"Pretty much. It didn't go over well when I told them we were getting married. I told them you were pregnant."

"Is that why you wanted a baby so quickly?" He can't face me as he nods shamefully. "How do we fix this?"

"I have to stand up to him."

"Let's assume he makes it through this," I motion with my hand. "How do you do that?"

"Have the agreement revised. We haven't used any of the money he's provided us. I'll give it back and he'll agree to give me my freedom."

"You think that will work?"

"If it doesn't, I have another plan."

"Which is?"

"Trust me, I'll get it done." He fingers the diamond on my hand. "Still love me?"

I wrap my arms around him. "You've taken the first step."

"I'll make it right. I promise."

"I know you will." Laying my head on his shoulder so we don't have to face each other when he answers, I ask, "How do you not hate her?"

His lips brush my forehead. "What good would that do?" I shrug into him. "Don't get me wrong, I was bitter for a long time. Then I realized I didn't want to be like them. I didn't see any way out of it, so I made the best of it."

I softly kiss his neck. "You're a good man, Clint."

He tousles my hair playfully. "Let's go back to bed."

He leads me back to the vacant room where we spend our last few hours alone tangled in moose covered sheets.

# Chapter 26

The flickering light from the oil lamp casts an eerie shadow between the beds in our room. Tanner and Ella are still sleeping soundly while Clint dresses. I sit on the edge of the bed we slept in, watching the three of them. Clint pauses as he pulls his jeans up. His gaze lingers on the children a moment before he layers shirts over his muscled chest. I soak in the view, wanting to bottle it for the weeks he'll be away.

"How long do you think you'll be gone?" I ask, breaking the silence.

"Depends a lot on the weather. Crossing the border could take some time too. I'm guessing about two months. And that's if we come straight back."

A lump forms in my throat, despite the news not being an entire surprise. "By your tone, it doesn't sound like you plan to do that."

He shakes his head. "This isn't going to end overnight."

"Do you think the President is trying to do anything?"

"His hands are most likely tied. I would be surprised if he's still alive."

"Why do you say that?"

He leaves his boots next to the bed and takes a seat beside me. "These guys are going for total control. They've taken over most of the country, if not all of it. I don't know why, but it doesn't make any sense for them to take over a small area, especially here. It has to be bigger than what we're seeing. It's the way war works. Take as much control over the enemy as you can. On the scale they're working on, I'd expect they've taken over D.C. I don't know how, but it would have to have been done for it to still be going on. Troops should've been sent out by now." I lean into him, taking his hand as a shiver crawls down my spine. "We would know by now if they had. They must've gotten this done quickly, so we should assume we're alone."

Clint wraps his arm around my shaking body. "We can't be. There *has* to be others," I whisper as a tear falls down my cheek.

He wipes the salty drop with his thumb and kisses my forehead. "We may not be as bad ass as Seal Team Six, but I think we can get the job done." He lifts my chin and kisses me so deeply my bones tingle. "It's time to roll these kids out of bed so they can send their old man off properly. If I'm not ready in ten, Ralph will shoot the place up."

Exactly ten minutes later Clint dons full gear—including the coat and overalls it will be too warm for by noon—and we step into the cold night air. Jett meets us on the porch, his mother next to him looking as if she got up extra early to dress up for the event. She wears designer jeans, UGG boots, and a sleek gray coat, all belonging to someone else. How fitting, I scowl, that she hit the jackpot and the rest of us are forced to make-do. Sidney chose to wear her own clothing, probably out of lack of options rather than desire to wear the same outfit *again*. Standing next to them, Tanner and Ella look as if they came straight from an orphanage. Hair stands up in every direction and their eyes contain the last remnants of sleep they struggle to hang on to. My hair and teeth have been brushed, but I didn't dress more than a layer of long underwear underneath too-short pajama pants and the purple fleece.

We step off the porch as a unit, and round the house. A light flashes intermittently in our direction. The raft with a loaded sled waits at the dock to depart. Ab glances briefly at us from the dock, his attention focused on the blinking from the opposite shore.

"'Morning," he says, pulling a flashlight from his side. He returns a sequence of flashes and turns his focus to us.

"Morse code? So that's your secret?" Clint shakes his hand. "And here I thought you were a spy."

Ab chuckles softly. Mrs. Watson scurries down the path with a large picnic basket, the flashes hitting our side again.

"Your cover is blown," she says, placing a peck on her husband's cheek. She holds the basket out to Clint. "He was going to tell you he was a prophet."

"It would be easy to believe in a time like this," Clint says, securing the extra luggage on the raft.

"I've been waiting for someone to ask how Ralph knew help had arrived, but nobody did." He pretends to pout, earning him another peck from his wife. He rubs his hands together. "Ralph says to get the show on the road."

Ella lurches for Clint's leg.

"I'd like to thank you for the hospitality you're showing my family," Clint tells the Watsons. He shakes Ab's hand with a kid wrapped around each leg.

"We owe you so much more than we can ever repay," Ab responds.

With Ab and Jett in one canoe and Clint and I in the other, we take the first step to reclaiming our freedom. Chaos ensues as the bow of the first canoe touches the dock beneath Ralph's flashlight beacon. Jett and Ab scurry to wind the ropes that Clint drapes on the ground in heaps. Betty runs over with one chicken under each arm. Kitty plays her game of trying to trip the woman as she yells and kicks her away. Her large breasts flop around with each waddled step, contained only by the chickens on the side. I can't help but stare at the sight of her awkward sway, wondering what on earth she is doing. Dropping the birds into a canoe, she turns and runs back for more, swooping Kitty up on the way and placing her on her shoulder. Pretty soon the bottom of the boat is filled with smelly birds.

Clint startles me when he takes my hand. "Above all else, take care of the kids," he says. "I'll find you when this is all over."

"We're going to have to leave, aren't we?"

"I'd be more surprised if you didn't."

"How will I know where to go?"

He kisses my forehead, his lips lingering warmth on my skin. "You'll know."

"I'll leave you clues."

"We're late, boys," Ralph calls.

Clint swoops me into his arms, kissing me passionately. "Love you, baby."

Jett surprises me by a quick embrace after Clint pulls away.

"Take care of your old man," I instruct, holding him tightly.

"Will do."

Ab, Betty, and I watch them leave as everyone else waves from the opposite bank.

"Let's get these pesky birds out of my boat," Ab says, as the men reach the corner of the cabin. He motions for us to get in. I wade past the birds to the front of the boat, taking a seat as a chicken pecks my boot. Betty and Kitty take the seat in the middle and Ab pushes us into the water.

"We'll get the goat after the water freezes," Betty says as we row.

"Ralph and I decided Betty should stay with us while he's gone," Ab explains.

"Probably a good idea," I admit.

# Chapter 27

The month after Clint leaves is a struggle. It reminds me of a circus side show where Ab plays the ring master and the rest of us are different acts struggling to know our parts. Mrs. Watson plays the host well and we soon settle into a routine. Betty is clearly the loose cannon, running amuck trying to keep the dwindling chickens in check. Christa settles back into her old lifestyle, trying to take advantage of the catering Mrs. Watson offers. I am left to find useful things to do while Sidney is stuck somewhere in between.

I'll admit the hot showers provided by the generator are a luxury I enjoy, but I try to insist we be frugal about them. Christa ignores me, taking lavish baths and doing laundry even when Mrs. Watson explains we must conserve. Not that there isn't a full closet of clothing at her disposal.

"Why don't I take the kids around the cove to get the goat?" I offer as we're washing breakfast dishes one morning.

"That's a long trek," Mrs. Watson comments, looking at Betty.

"The air will do us good," I argue, knowing that pent-up energy from the kids has taken its toll on the two elderly women. "I'll even take Christa. Give you two some alone time."

"Bring back some more chickens," Betty says without looking up from the china plate she is drying. Kitty perches on her shoulder and Mrs. Watson keeps a careful eye on the bird, clearly not wanting it in her kitchen.

"I'll go get everyone ready."

"Make sure to hold them like footballs," Betty calls after me as I scramble to find everyone.

"Why do we have to do this?" Christa grumbles as we head to the round of the cove. "I just found a great book to read."

I sling the bow over my shoulder and adjust the strap. "We've forced ourselves on these people and I think the least we can do is help two little old ladies out. Besides, we're out of milk."

"What I wouldn't give for a ShopRite," she sighs. "Why aren't we taking the boat?"

"Do you want to put a goat in a canoe?"

"Why not?"

"You've never been around a goat."

She turns up her nose. "Thank God."

"You'll understand soon enough."

Tanner and Ella race Sidney up and down tiny inclines. A heavy dusting of snow came overnight, and they are having a ball making snowballs to toss at each other.

"Christa, I think we need to have a talk."

"About?"

"Our situation."

"I think we all know what that's like."

"I'm talking about our family dynamic."

"Oh." She slips in the snow, and I reach out to steady her. She waves my hand away.

"We should be raising our kids together."

"Jett is practically grown, and Sidney is a few years from it. I think that shipped has sailed."

"I know. And that's unfortunate, but with what time we have left, I think the kids should be allowed to build relationships. Aside from the last few months, they barely know one another."

She shrugs the shoulder of the designer coat she lucked into. "They're spending a lot of time together now."

"It's not by choice."

"They're still doing it."

"What I'm trying to say is that I want things to be different when this is all over."

"We don't know how this is going to end," she says curtly. "Maybe we should have this discussion after we know how it turns out."

We round the bend and trudge toward the rickety cabin. "I'm just saying we should try to figure out how to blend our families in a better way."

Our eyes meet, and I know she knows Clint has told me things she wished he hadn't.

"Where does that leave Eddie?" Her tone is clipped, giving me the feeling that it's the first she's thought of him maybe since we left him.

"I wasn't excluding Eddie," I say, though I'm not sure he's going to be around for it to matter.

"I should go back and check on him. See if he's still there," she says.

"You can't go alone."

She pulls at a wisp of hair flying in the slight breeze. "Why not?"

"Are you being serious right now?"

"He was willing to stay behind to protect us and we've left him to die alone."

"We don't know that he's dead."

"Well he could be, and nobody cares." The sob that escapes sounds fake, forced, at least to me.

I reach out for her hand, stopping her. "How long have you really known him?"

"Long enough." She breaks free and quickens her step.

I hurry to catch up. "I have a feeling your father doesn't approve of your relationship."

"That's none of your business," she snaps.

"Christa, I'm going to be honest with you. When Clint and I first started dating and he told me about you and the kids, I was worried about how it would affect me. Then I realized it wasn't going to be something I dealt with every other weekend, so I relaxed. Little did I know I would end up alone at cookouts and holiday dinners because you called him away. I told myself any chance he got to see his kids was worth dealing with the questions I got about it. I let it go."

"Where is this going?"

"Everything changed when we had Ella. I suddenly saw what he was missing. When I pushed for him to have a greater part in Jett and Sidney's lives, we started fighting more. I thought having another baby would fix it—would make us have a greater pull—but it didn't. Somewhere in there he started leaving for longer periods of time to be with you. I actually thought he was having an affair."

"With me?" She scoffs but amusement lurks in her eyes.

"I can count the number of times Jett and Sidney have been to our house." The corner of her mouth twitches up. "I know our house isn't as elaborate as yours, but Clint deserves the freedom to have all his kids under the same roof, even if only for a few days at a time."

"He made his choice."

Chickens squawk loudly from the Watsons. I pull my gaze away from Sidney gently lobbing a snowball at Tanner when voices mingle with the clucking behind us. I can't make out what is being said, but I'm almost certain there's an unfamiliar voice in the mix of Betty yelling at the chickens.

I poke at Christa as the commotion grows louder. "Can you see what's going on over there?" She pokes her head around a tree. Looks like Betty is yelling at the damn birds again. She ought to just kill them and get it over with." Her sentence is no sooner out than rapid gunfire fills the air. "She must've finally gotten sick of them."

The kids run, falling and sliding until they are by our side. Men in black surround the Watson's house with weapons poised.

I take aim with the bow, finding a clear shot, but am uncertain if the arrow will travel the distance.

Christa swiftly knocks my aim to the ground. "If you shoot, you'll alert them to our position. We need to run...hide...something."

I motion for everyone to get low. "We can't very well hide our tracks. Our best option is to hide and take out as many as we can before capture."

Ella shakes her head violently. I slap a hand over her mouth before she lets out the scream that is building.

Tanner reaches for my gloved hand. "Are we going to die, Mommy?"

I cup his face, his eyes budding with tears. "I'll figure something out," I say, pulling him up the incline.

Our breathing is heavy when I hold a hand up to stop the group on the mountain just above the cabin. I've positioned us so that the small shack helps to hide our position, but we've gained enough ground to get a better view of the situation. We now have nosebleed seats to watch our new friends being led away with a group of ten or so men carrying off a large loot of guns, food, and valuables. One of them carries a painting and another a large vase.

"Do you think they'll follow our tracks?" Christa whispers, still panting.

"We'd better pray they don't."

Ella shakes beside me. I wrap my arm around her. "They want us to know what it's like," she says, abruptly turning still.

I bend to her level. "What do you mean?"

"I heard one of the guards say that when we were locked up." Her eyes fade like they had during our time in captivity.

"Did you hear anything else?" She recites the entire recording that played over the speakers in the storage unit. Christa's mouth gapes open and her eyes bug out of her head. They both could use an exorcism, I think as I grab Ella by the shoulders. "What does that mean?"

She shrugs. "Something about control."

"Obviously. What else do you know?" My tone is sharp, bringing back the color to her eyes.

A tear slips down her cheek. "We're switching places with them."

I try to process the possibilities as our enemy disappears into the distance. "With whom, exactly?"

She shrugs again, slumping to her knees as tears fall. I plop down beside her, careful to process my thoughts in my head before they become words others can hear. *Let's assume it* is WIN, *that makes total sense. Their country is shit and they want ours to start over. Are they planning on shipping us all over to their shithole and sending everyone there over here? Nah. That would be way too complex. Do they even have that kind of manpower? It would take more than one country to pull that off. Has the entire world banned against us? We'd be doomed for sure if they have. So, what exactly does it mean, that they want to 'switch places with us?'*

Crunching snow piques my senses. Normally, I wouldn't have paid attention to the sound, but this isn't a typical situation. All heads turn with mine. Eddie stops when we face him. He's wearing an unfamiliar black coat and hat. His gloved hands shift nervously to his pockets. Nobody moves. Nobody speaks. The chickens left at Ralph and Betty's cabin cluck, another fight breaking out.

Christa makes the first step, cautiously inspecting him. "Where did you come from?"

"It's a long story," he replies, opening his arms for Christa to step into.

"Try us," I urge, even as Christa welcomes his embrace.

He tightens our circle, running his gloved thumb and finger over a freshly shaved chin. "I've been worried sick ever since you left. I spent days looking for you."

"You mean they didn't find you in the cabin?" Christa's question hangs in the air while I motion for Sidney to take the kids into the tiny cabin while we sort this out.

He shakes his head as we watch them head down the hill. "I waited all day, hoping they would find me first, but nobody ever showed up. I thought you guys were overreacting. I was very weak for the next few days, but that oil really cleared up my arm and I started searching for you as soon as it healed."

"Your arm is better?" Christa tries to see, but the cuff of his coat prevents it.

I turn to the cabin in time to see Sidney scooting the kids up the porch. "How on earth did you find us?"

"I was out searching when I started hearing voices. I thought it was you at first, but I soon found out it was *them.*" He motions into the distance with his hand. "When I realized who it was, I followed them."

"Why would you do that?" Christa clings to his side. I wonder if she isn't putting on a show given our previous discussion.

"I thought maybe I could get some answers. You know, find out what was going on. Maybe where they had taken you. Where's Clint?"

"He and Jett headed to Canada with the husband of one of the ladies who were just captured," Christa offers. Either we really can trust him or she's incredibly stupid, I think as she waves toward the cabin with our kids. "Apparently, Ralph, the man who lives there knew where some men had hidden out at a campground."

"How long ago did they leave?"

"A few days ago," I say before Christa can reveal the truth of how long they've been gone.

"It's been longer than that," she says, looking at me like I'm interfering with an investigation.

"Time gets away from you when you're not in a routine."

"That's true," she agrees.

*Thank goodness she stopped there,* I think, but what I say is, "It does seem like it's been longer, but I'm certain it's only been a few days."

Eddie shifts on his feet. "Why don't you ladies head into the cabin. I'll check to make sure we haven't been followed then we can figure out our next move."

I pull Sidney to the side and fill her in on what Eddie has told us while we wait for him to join us.

"We should stay the night here," Eddie says, closing the door behind him. He takes one look around and adds, "Or maybe at the other place. This one's a dump."

"I'm with you on that," Christa beams.

"Here is better," I argue.

"The other place has been searched. They probably won't go back, but they haven't been here," Eddie counters.

"We can't risk starting a fire and this place has a room small enough to keep us warm."

"You have a point," Eddie says, ushering us into the small bedroom. "We'll leave first thing in the morning."

# Chapter 28

Our night is spent huddled together, freezing on blankets strewn on the floor with a cloud of fog from our breath circling our heads.

I wake before the sun, as usual, and begin my search for anything we can take back to our cabin with us. I don't know what Eddie has in mind, but I fully plan on returning to our haven where Clint would be sure to find us. There is nothing ready to eat in the cabinets aside from canned goods. I save a can of cinnamon apples for us to share for breakfast and sling everything else into a sheet. Tanner and Ella stumble in over their too-long coveralls as I'm tying the knot next to a flickering lamp. I strategically placed it in a corner where it wouldn't project too much light out the window. Their breath hangs in clouds over their heads, and they shiver despite their coats as I hug them. I open the can and hold out two forks.

"I'm cold," Tanner whimpers.

I run my gloved hands over his arms. "We'll have a fire tonight," I say. We can't go without one for another night.

Ella plunges her fork into the can. "Where are we going?"

"Back to our little cabin."

Christa and Eddie enter, Christa's hair showing the only signs of bedhead I've ever seen on her. Sidney is a step behind, looking like she didn't sleep at all.

"Looks like you missed breakfast," I say, noticing the empty can on the nicked table.

"We should get going anyway," Eddie says.

I remove my glove and run my finger in the shape of a *C* on the gooey inside of the empty can until it is clear.

Christa yawns. "Where we headin'?"

"To our cabin," I say as Eddie says, "South."

"The cabin is east," I correct him.

"If Clint headed north to get help, I think we should go south and see if we can find some help of our own."

I remember my talk with Clint about going to the Appalachian Mountains, but Eddie can't possibly be thinking of that. "We can't wander around the country with the kids looking for signs of help. We could fall into any number of traps. We should stay put. Especially this time of year." According to the Watson's calendar, it's December.

"We'll take a vote," he says.

I roll my eyes. "State your case."

"If we stay in one place, we risk being found. You've seen first-hand what they're doing—going door-to-door and taking prisoners. If we are on the move, we aren't as much of a target."

"If we're on the move, we don't have access to shelter and food like we have at the cabin. We can set up traps and alerts so we know when danger is near. If we take off on a wild goose chase, we have no idea what we'll encounter and there will be no way for Clint to find us. Plus, it will be easier for them to spot us with the bare trees," I argue.

"We lack the weapons to fight."

"We'll have to improvise."

He blows breath into his cupped hands. "Surely you've heard the expression, 'don't take a knife to a gun fight.'"

"Ever seen *Rambo* or *The Patriot?* We'll just have to outsmart them."

"Let's just vote. We're wasting time. All in favor of being heroes and finding others to fight alongside us—like Clint and Jett are doing—raise your hand." I shoot daggers out of my eyes at him as the kids raise their hands. "All in favor of going to the cabin, raise your hand."

I raise my hand and look at Christa.

Her hand rests at her side. "I vote that we stay at the Watson's."

"The kids are too young to vote, so they don't count." I hate the look of disappointment on their faces, but I have to find a way to overrule him.

"Typical," Eddie coughs.

"We're going to the cabin," I say firmly.

"We don't have a unanimous decision," Eddie counters.

"The democracy you're so obsessed with is based on who has the most votes."

"Fine."

All eyes turn to Christa.

"The Watsons have running water," she offers.

I nod slowly. "Until the gas for the generator runs out and that won't be long. We're better off being off the grid completely." Christa shifts nervously. "If your dad makes it into the country and isn't captured, where do you think he'll go?"

"That's ridiculous," Eddie says in a clipped tone. "All air travel has surely been stopped and even if it hasn't, he'd be taken the moment his plane landed."

"He has a private jet," Christa offers as a way to make Richard invincible.

"You don't think these people have access to private jets too? This thing is huge. There's no chance he comes back and resumes his life."

"You're probably right," she admits solemnly.

"Hey, nobody says we have to stay together. Christa, you can stay next door, Lexi can go back to the cabin, and I can go rogue," Eddie suggests.

Christa yanks on his arm like a child. "You can't go out there alone."

"She's right," I say. "It's not safe. Why don't we compromise? Clint said it could take a month to get to Canada. Why don't we wait at the cabin for two months and if they aren't back by then we can set out?" I cross my fingers that Christa doesn't open her big mouth about how long ago the men left.

"They've been gone a few days already so six weeks should be enough," Eddie says firmly.

I nod. "Six weeks." Even as I say the words, I know I don't mean them, but that argument can wait.

Eddie overturns the table.

Christa jolts out of the way. "What the hell are you doing?!"

"Making it look like the place has been searched," he says, going into the bedroom to dishevel it.

For once he has a good idea.

A waning moon hangs low in the sky giving way to the coming sun as I open the door to the brisk air outside. Smoke wafts faintly through the breeze as we stand frozen on the porch. Embers burn across the cove in what's left of the Watson's house. The brick entry lining the front still stands, but beams lie in flickering flames across the ground as it smolders.

"That's a hell of a smoke signal," Eddie chuckles.

"I don't know how we missed that." My voice is so low I'm not sure anyone hears my words.

"Could've happened in the middle of the night," Christa says, looking as if she may cry. "Maybe it was electrical."

I ignore her ignorance. "More like arson by terrorists."

"I suppose that makes more sense," she agrees.

I shift into ultra-survival mode. "We should take as many chickens as we can," I say, dropping my sheet and bow onto the porch.

Tanner and Ella chase the birds as they cluck wildly in attempt to escape. I corner one near the outhouse and tuck it under my arm.

"Let me help," Eddie says, taking the bird from me. He snaps its neck. Tanner has captured one but is reluctant to hand it over.

Eddie snatches it from his hand. "They'll be easier to carry this way," he says, twisting its neck.

I usher the kids back into the cabin while Eddie performs his solo massacre. Opening a kitchen drawer, I pull out dish towels and wrap them around the kids' faces, tucking the ends into their coats. Christa and I follow suit before heading back outside. The musky fabric barely blocks out the thick burnt smell, but without the Watson's house to raid, we have no other options.

With a pile of dead birds at his feet, Eddie wipes his hands on snow pants that are wet from the snow. "That's enough," he says, clutching the birds in his hands by their lifeless necks. Six in all, I note, counting their bulging bellies as they swing.

"You said you followed them to the Watsons, but how did you know to find us here?" I question as he takes the lead around the cove.

"I saw the tracks. They must've been too occupied to notice them. We have to be more careful."

"With any luck the temperature will reach above freezing today and melt this." I kick a thin layer of snow with the too-small snow boots Mrs. Watson had given me from her daughter's closet. Thankfully she had also been able to outfit the entire crew with snow gear and we were wearing them when we left their house. It will be too warm for all the layers by afternoon, but I now consider the early snowfall yesterday a blessing.

"I suppose you're right. We'll have to take our chances," Eddie admits.

"I wonder why they didn't burn both cabins," I comment as we begin the trek into the mountains.

"Maybe they didn't see the other one," Christa offers. "It's barely the size of a closet."

I roll my eyes. "It doesn't make sense with them being so close together."

"They were probably just following orders. Why question it? We got lucky and that's all that matters," Eddie says gruffly.

"I'm trying to figure this out. The more we know, the better prepared we can be."

"We have plenty of time to think about it," Eddie says, though I get the feeling he doesn't see the importance. It was just a matter of luck to him.

Static from the radio we had seized from the dead terrorist screeches on Eddie's hip. It only takes a second to remember we left Eddie before taking the radio. I already don't trust him, and this doesn't earn him any points. If he is one of them, how far will he go to protect his secret? I figure it's best to keep a close eye on him before taking my concern to the others.

"Turn that down," I sternly whisper.

"'*Aya hazin?*'"

I raise my eyebrows at the foreign words. Eddie fumbles with the device and slides over the call button as he works to turn it down. I've heard those words before, I vaguely recall.

"*Ailtazam balkht.*"

Eddie shrugs and picks up the pace. "Doesn't do us much good if we can't understand what they're saying," he mumbles, flicking the device with his index finger.

The Watson's cabin soon lies in front of us. Sidney runs ahead to search for anything salvageable. I position Tanner and Ella near a single rafter still burning and take a minute to warm myself before joining Sidney in her search. Eddie crunches a dainty tea cup as he walks through the debris and I'm glad Mrs. Watson isn't around to see it.

"Lexi!" Sidney waves her arms wildly at me from the nearby shed which was also torched. She shoves a large slab of shingles still burning on one end to the side and hoists the edge of a green paddleboard into the air. It's singed, but functional. "We can use this!"

I place a finger over my mouth to quiet her. "That should work great...until the snow melts."

"I'll look for some rope," she says excitedly and hurries into what's left of the shed. I almost faint when she returns with a bundle. "It was under the workbench near the wall." The smile on her face couldn't be wider than if she'd just won the lottery

"Didn't realize we were running a chauffeuring service," Eddie gripes as he and Christa join us.

"It will be faster," I growl.

"I don't see how."

"Let's just get on with it," Christa moans. "We can stop in a cabin along the way."

Eddie kicks a smoldering board into the ashes. "What cabin exactly? I didn't see any, did you?"

Christa motions for the kids to come to us. "Where's the map?"

I point to the rubble. "It's okay. I have most of it memorized." I wait for Sidney to tie the rope haphazardly around the green plastic before placing Ella behind Tanner on the board.

The makeshift sled jerks forward as she tests her work. "Maybe we'll get lucky and it will—"

"Don't you say it!" Christa barks. Giant flakes sprinkle around us, and we stare at the sky, wondering if they had been conjured. "This is your fault!" She squeals and stamps her foot.

"We could always stay there," I offer, pointing to Ralph and Betty's shack.

"This is ridiculous," Eddie curses under his breath as he spins in a circle. "Why can't women ever make up their minds?"

"It might be safer if it's going to keep—" I turn toward Christa as if I need permission to finish. Her lips press tightly together. "—snowing."

"They probably didn't have enough manpower to check that cabin earlier. I'm sure they'll be back."

I consider his words. "Why don't we just mark it?"

"With what?" His voice is sharp, and birds fly from their perch in a nearby tree.

"Clint had spray paint before he left. Maybe we can find some more."

"In this mess? I'll give you five minutes to find it before I'm leaving." He wraps his arm around Christa's waist. She shrugs into his shoulder.

"It's no use, Lexi. I saw the cans burned up when I was looking for rope," Sidney says, causing her mother's eyes to narrow.

Eddie wears a look of righteousness as he asks, "How did you find the paddleboard?"

"It had fallen against the outside of the wall. I don't think we got them put away after we used them, but whoever started the fire shoved them over so they would catch, I think. The other one is gone."

Eddie nods. "What's it going to be, Lexi? Are you coming with us or not?"

It's Sidney I turn to, not Christa. She nods. "Fine. Did you see a tarp or anything we could use as shelter if we get stranded?" She shakes her head. "Let's look for a shovel. We can use it even if the handle is gone."

Eddie and Christa huddle like reunited teenagers next to a beam still producing heat. Tanner and Ella catch snowflakes on their tongues while Sidney and I rummage for tools. I hand a rake to Tanner and place a shovel head on top of the sheet bag between the kids.

Sidney yanks on Christa's arm, urging her to make a shield as we inch past the bloody snow and chicken remains.

Travelling is faster with the makeshift sled but we're not covering enough ground to make it to the cabin by nightfall. We stick to the ravines because they're easier to navigate and I question my bearings when asked where we are.

"I'm hungry," Tanner complains as we round another mountain.

My stomach growls too. "Eat snow," I suggest even though I wonder how it's possible with the leaves and grass still poking through.

"Moooommm," he whines.

We have nothing to provide any sustenance without ingredients we don't have. Eddie had tucked the chickens into the straps on the board, but that won't do us any good without a fire.

"I'm sorry, honey. We can't stop and there's nothing to eat in the bag while we travel." He picks leaves from his gloved hand that scrapes along the ground and shoves it to his mouth, flecks of dirt and all. I trade Sidney the rope for the bow, and she adjusts her pace to match mine. Eddie and Christa are ahead of us, flirting heavily from what I can tell. She shoves her arm into his shoulder, causing her to slip in the slushy mess. Eddie swiftly reaches out to steady her, whispering something I can't make out as he does so. We crunch through the wet snow as flurries continue to fall around us. The fragrant aroma of smoke wafts through the air long before we see it. As we round the next bend, a cabin lies in ashes halfway up. It's not one on our map so Eddie hurries up to scan the soggy gray slush for anything useful. He returns empty handed. We continue our long trudge through the thickening snow as I try to remember how long it took us to get to the Watson's in the first place.

Eddie holds out his hand, offering to take the rope and pull. "Are we going the right way?"

I rub my throbbing thighs, "I think so, but I really need to be higher to tell for sure."

He nods for me to go on up and check. I motion for Sidney to come with me.

"I want you to stay where you can get back to them quickly," I tell her as we climb.

"Are we lost?"

I shake my head, but I'm not sure. I wish Clint were with us. "We're going to need to stop going through the mountains and start going over them."

"Want me to tell the others?"

"Not yet. I want to see what's over there. I'm looking for the tree with the knot in it."

"I've been looking for it too."

"I'm going up. You stay there where you can see us both."

I leave Sidney and trudge to the top. From the crest, I quickly check for Eddie and the paddle board, but it is out of sight. Sidney nods to me from her location and I head to the other side. A small lake lies in front of me in the next valley. Three cabins are smoking in ruins at the edge of the water. I quickly slide back down.

"We need to turn back," I say. "All the cabins are gone."

"We've come too far to turn back," Eddie says calmly.

"It's not going to do any good if the cabin is gone," I snap.

"There's no way they got them all. We'll find something."

"That could take days out here."

"You were able to find the Waltons." He hands the rope to Sidney.

"Watsons," I correct, taking the bow from Sidney.

"Whatever."

"We got lucky."

"We'll find shelter."

"Christa?"

She looks behind us then stares longingly in the distance toward the direction we are headed. I doubt she has any clue which way is up at this point. "We should try to get as close to civilization as we can so help will be close when this is all over."

I don't know why I expected her to be rational. Eddie has had plenty of time to pollute her brain. "There is no civilization." Sweat pours down my sides as I argue a pointless case.

"We won't know when that is if we are in the middle of BFE. Nobody will be able to find us."

"That's the point. Clint will know where we are, and he'll come get us when it's safe."

Christa stops, flipping her drenched, blonde hair over her shoulder. I don't know how she makes the drowned rat appearance look good, but it makes me envy her even more. "He might not come back, Lexi. It's very possible that none of them return."

I don't see how she can be so callous. I let her words hang in the air for a moment. "We need to start heading over the mountains instead of around them."

Without a word, we shift course, taking turns pushing and pulling up the side.

A thin sliver of moon hangs in the sky as the sun fades. We haven't covered nearly the ground we should've, but we're forced to stop for the night. If it had been a full moon, we could've pressed on from the reflection it would've cast on the glittering snow that's slowly growing past two inches deep.

"This is as good a place as any," I say, finding a spot high on the top of a mountain under the canopy of a large Fir tree. "There's some pancake mix in the sack. You can mix it with some snow."

"That sounds disgusting," Christa complains.

"I think there are a few cans of something in there. Take a look." I ignore the tightening of my stomach and shove my thick glove into my pocket for the knife buried inside.

"Take the shovel and move the snow aside," I order at no one in particular, knowing Sidney will be the one to follow through.

I work quickly to cut the smallest branches of pine needles my pocketknife will allow until we have a thick covering over the dirt Sidney exposed. Exhausted, famished, and worried, I slump onto the edge of the bed of green. Eddie takes the rope from the sled, tying one end around the chickens' necks. Another good idea from Eddie, I think as I watch him hang our future dinners from the tree. Reluctantly, I remove my glove and mix a paste in my hand from the box of Hungry Jack Christa passes me. Sliding the glob in my mouth, I twist my frozen nose in the air. One bite is enough. I swallow the lump and use snow to clean my hand and get the taste out of my mouth. Sidney closes the box and puts it back without taking any.

"We should get some sleep," I suggest.

Sidney, Christa, and I sandwich Tanner and Ella between us like a double decker sandwich while Eddie takes the outside. Even with the branches I saved to cover us, we will be lucky to not be hypothermic tomorrow.

# Chapter 29

The better part of the next day we spend aimlessly searching for our cabin. We zig zag across the mountains in hopes of finding signs of...anything. The trek is nothing I wouldn't trade for a cross-country trip on a bus full of first graders. Endless fighting and grumbling takes its toll until I am relieved to see the sun dropping from the sky. I dread another night outdoors, but at least it will provide enough silence for me to think. It's time to find an alternate plan. Something I can't do when I'm turning around every five seconds to tell Tanner or Ella to stop rolling off the sled. I finally threatened to make them walk if it happens again when Sidney stops us all.

"There it is!" She slaps her hand on her mouth while pointing with the bow.

"We're close." I smile, running to the giant knot in the tree. Taking my knife out, I carve a faint *E* just below it. "That way." I point in the direction of the cabin.

"I'm hungry," Tanner whines.

With renewed energy, I pull a chicken from the straps and hand it to Christa because she's closest.

"Start plucking. We're having chicken tonight." I can't keep the excitement from my voice.

She hands the bird to Eddie. Like a well-trained boyfriend, he starts plucking, leaving a trail of feathers behind us.

We cross the mountain and stop, knowing our cabin is on the other side of the peak facing us. That is *our* mountain. I inhale sharply, the brisk air refreshing my lungs and spirit. For a second I think I smell smoke but convince myself it's my imagination when nobody mentions it. The rest of our journey is done in silence. A wonderful silence filled with hope. We all know the possibility is there that the cabin is not more than ashes, but it isn't voiced. If our cabin is burned, it's likely the others we'd mapped out would be also.

Our breaths exhale as one when we cross over the side and see a roof still standing.

"I'll go down and check it out," Eddie offers.

"I'm coming with," I say, not wanting to relinquish control of the only weapon we have.

Without answering, he skids down the snow, creating small avalanches trailing behind him. My feet press into the toes of my boots as I follow his marks. His arms wave two fingers for me to go one direction while he goes the other. We meet at the corners of the porch and signal with a jerk of our heads that we're ready. The door is slightly ajar and, as I come around, I notice the large black *X* marking it. Eddie kicks it open, and I point the bow into the room. The table is overturned, and cabinet doors are ajar. Drawers hang from their tracks with contents spilling onto the floor. Eddie searches the table for a knife but ends up pulling his from his pocket.

The bedrooms and loft are empty, as I figured they would be after Eddie's boot thudded against the front door, but they are just as searched as the main area. The beds are cockeyed, and the dressers knocked over. A small pile of snow lies under the shattered window in my room but the window in the second room is intact as if it were too much effort to do more.

Eddie heads to the porch as I slam cabinet doors when Christa and Sidney follow the kids in. "The rest of our weapons are gone," I say bluntly.

Eddie walks in carrying a bundle of wet wood. "Going to be hard starting a fire with this."

"They took every last bit of food." I kick the table, sliding it several inches.

As if Eddie hasn't heard a word I'd just said, he picks up a chair. Raising it above his head, he slams it down in the middle of the room.

Christa sprints to her room as Eddie tosses the broken chair into the fireplace. I open the cabinet doors again, hoping I'd hallucinated their emptiness. A blood-curdling scream comes from the bedroom as I stare into the bare shelves. Eddie breaks another chair, ignoring the kids rushing to Christa's aid. She forces her way past them and plants her feet on top of the broken leg of a chair.

"My jewelry is gone!" Eddie tugs the wood from underneath her dripping boots. "Did you hear me?!" She slumps onto a chair as Eddie is about to grab it. He moves to the next one and breaks it.

"Eddie, that's enough," I say roughly, then more calmly, "We may need to save more for later."

"My gold Tiffany cuff is gone," Christa whines.

"Good. It was ugly," I reply coldly, despite not having a clue which one she's referring to.

Eddie glances in her direction as he piles the kindling into the fireplace. "The Peretti faceted one?"

I vaguely remember seeing a thick gold band around her arm when she arrived. "It looked like someone punched a piece of metal and called it jewelry," I say, turning the table upright. "Sidney, would you bring in a chicken and put the rest in the cooler outside?"

"My Coco Crush bracelet is gone too. And my diamond Cartier." I stop and face the woman who is about to come apart in the middle of a crisis over objects that will serve us no purpose in our situation.

"Stop right there, Christa." Her head falls into her ungloved hands and I'm certain she's hiding tears. "I have no idea what you're saying and, quite frankly, it does not matter. None of it matters. What are you going to do with that crap out here anyway? You don't wear jewelry like that to cut wood or hunt or anything else we need to do to survive. I don't know why you brought it in the first place."

Eddie steps between us. "Enough. Lexi is right, we have more important things to worry about right now. And Lexi, let Christa grieve for a minute. It won't hurt anything." He waves his hand to the fire he started.

My mouth gapes open. "How did you get it started?"

"The matches were still on the mantle. I used some towels to get it going," he says proudly.

"We can't be burning our supplies. Tomorrow we can cut some pine branches to use when we need to start a fire, but we'll have to try to keep it going."

"We'll have to bring wood in to dry out."

I nod as Sidney steps inside the door, holding a chicken's leg with two fingers. I smile and take it from her. Its frozen body cracks against the table as I plop it down. "Get me a pot of water."

"I'm hungry," Tanner says, planting his feet firmly next to mine. His stomach agrees with him, rumbling loudly. With tiny fingers he plucks two feathers from the bird Eddie held earlier.

"This is going to take some time. Maybe there's something in the bag to eat." I point to the corner where the sheet was dropped on the way in. He pulls out the pancake mix and places it on the table next to the bird. "Is that it?" I scoot it to the side.

"We ate everything else already." My pulse quickens at the thought of Eddie feeding them the canned goods while Sidney and I were on the mountain. The cans are missing from the pack which can only mean he left them to be found.

I fight tears as I rip a plume from the wing. Yanking the tough feathers from the wings, I put all my energy in not looking directly at Tanner. His big blue eyes will break me. Clint and I may struggle financially from time to time—which I'm sure I'll be mad about later, knowing we didn't have to—but we've always been able to provide the basic necessities for our family.

Tanner tugs on my snow pants. "What are we gonna eat, Mommy?"

When he doesn't stop, I look down. Shrugging, I slump onto the floor and bury my face in my frozen fingers. Ella curls into my side as the tears warm my cheeks. I pull them both close and whisper how sorry I am before I turn into a blubbering, sobbing mess.

"I was thinking about pizza all day so I'm not really hungry," Ella says. She reaches over me and smacks her brother on the head.

He doesn't respond until she clobbers him again. "Okay, fine. I ate a spaghetti in my head today."

I smile through my tears. They're using lines I'd previously used on them. "One spaghetti?"

"There was a big meatball. It was the size of my head." His arms open to gesture the size.

"Is that so?"

He nods into my arm. "And I had the biggest ice cream sundae you ever saw. It had sprinkles and a whole bag of chocolate chips on it."

I wipe my cheeks with the back of my hand. "I hope you ate your vegetables first."

"We had those for lunch."

"What else did you have?"

"Pudding. And not that lumpy kind Daddy likes," Ella chimes in.

"You don't like tapioca?"

She sticks out her tongue. "Yuck."

"I ate a big bowl of cereal and mashed 'tatoes," Tanner adds with a smile.

"I hope you didn't mix them together."

"You're silly, Mommy. And you made me the bestest Chinese bread ever. Thank you." He wraps his arm around my coat. I laugh into a sob at the mistake he made over a year before when he couldn't remember what French Toast was called.

The tears flow again. "I'm sorry."

"Didn't you hear us, Mommy? We're full."

I wipe my nose with my coat sleeve and don't even care that I've yelled at them for doing the exact same thing. They let it slide.

"Yeah, Mom, we couldn't eat another bite."

"Even if I made snow pancakes?" Sidney waves a plate over us. None of us had noticed the smell coming from the room or the pattering of her feet as she whipped up the dish.

"Well, maybe," Tanner says, jumping up.

I let her make plates for the kids and try to control the emotions flowing through me. I miss the usual scraping of forks on plates as they eat the thin discs with their fingers. My stomach knots with emotional sickness. I watch as Tanner and Ella reach for seconds. Sidney holds a small plate out to me. I shake my head.

"There's plenty," she says.

I smile. She's reading my mind. I shake my head again. "You guys go ahead. I'll wait for the chicken." Wiping my eyes with the backs of my hands, I lean back against the cabinet.

Tanner chews with his mouth stuffed as he sits beside me, holding a round cake out to me. "Try it, Mommy. It's not that bad. Not as good as your Chinese bread, though."

I wave it away. "I have chicken juice on me."

"The handle to the waterspout has been broken off. You'll have to use snow to wash," Sidney offers.

Ella pulls on my arm, urging me to stand. I give in and see the plate, still covered in snow pancakes. "See, Mom? There's enough. Sidney did good."

"Yes, she did." I head outside and take a deep breath into the biting wind. Placing my hands in the snow, which has doubled in amount, I grab a handful and place it against my face.

Feeling refreshed, I go inside and take the food Tanner offers. Normally, nobody eats anything Tanner touches, but I'm too spent to care.

I scrunch my face as I chew, thankful that Christa is a distraction from the bland batter used for our meal. She is draped in her clothing and Eddie is bringing each piece out of their room one at a time, holding it up to show her as if he is a model, and covering her with it.

I take another pancake and wonder how long the snow will last. Finally, Tanner yawns.

"I'm ready for bed," he says.

I glance at the table. The plate still has enough pancakes for another meal. "Aren't you hungry?"

"That meatball filled me up."

I tousle his hair and wipe his mouth before tucking him in.

# Chapter 30

Putting my pillow against the back of one of the large chairs Eddie hadn't burned, I sit next to the fire. I stare at the rising smoke and wonder if we're signaling our location to anyone. It's a chance we must take, I think, reaching down to make sure the bow is still propped against the maple wood. My arm drapes across it as I make a mental list of chores for tomorrow. *Cut pine branches while more chicken cooks, board up the window that is temporarily blocked by the dresser, find saplings and string to make traps, figure out how to make snowshoes, find another cabin in case we have to leave this one, get a sturdy piece of wood to make a shovel with the head we have, find a place to fish...*

Startled awake by something covering my body, I reach for the bow, but grab at air instead.

"I didn't mean to wake you," Eddie says, standing over me. A thin blanket covers me. Leaning over, I again prop the weapon against the chair. Eddie adds some wood to the fire and checks the chicken I've left cooking in a kettle.

"It should still have a few hours left," I say.

He pulls a chair from the table next to me and stares into the flickering orange flames. He wrings his hands, his mind clearly as heavy as mine.

"Did you get Christa calmed down?"

He runs fingers through his jet-black hair, tugging at the long ends. "I found a pair of earrings they missed. She really lit up when I showed them to her. She's sleeping in them now." I nod, irritated by her materialism and lack of survival instincts. "There's something I want to tell you," he says slowly, resuming his hand wringing.

"Oh?"

"I haven't had a chance to talk to you alone. I wasn't going to say anything, but I think you should know."

"What is it?" I sit up straight, pulling the blanket up to my chin.

"A while back, I overheard Clint tell Christa they had to talk privately."

"So?"

"Have you noticed Clint being protective of his phone or spending a lot of time texting—before all this?" I shrug, not wanting to admit any part of my personal life to him. I realize it looks bad but could really care less what he thinks. "A week or so before our lives were turned upside down, Christa got a text. When I picked the phone up to hand her, she yanked it out of my hand."

Irritated that he's interrupting my sleep, my words come out clipped. "Is that supposed to mean something?"

"It was from Clint. I caught part of the message. It said, 'Can't wait for next time.'"

"I'm sure it was about the kids."

"That's what I kept telling myself, but you've had to notice the way they've been around each other. It's like we're playing second fiddle."

"I'm sure there's a logical explanation," I say defensively.

"I'm not so sure now."

"Why?" My tone is emotionless. If he had brought this to me before Clint opened up, I would've already been at the conclusion he's getting at.

"I followed them. The way Clint wrapped his arms around her, it was pretty clear." He makes a fist and clenches his jaw. "She curled up into him. I couldn't hear what they were saying, but I'm almost certain the kiss he planted on her head wasn't the only one that happened."

"They kissed?"

He nods slowly. "I just thought you had a right to know."

I pull the blanket tighter around me as a chill runs down my spine. He squeezes my shoulder on his way from the room.

The thoughts he planted swirl around my head as I meander outside for chickens to pluck. Before the dawn breaks, I have convinced myself that Clint and Christa have been having an affair since he and I were newlyweds. It all makes sense when I play back his excursions across the state in my head. I angrily debone a bird, wishing Clint were here to confront.

Everyone but Christa shows up at first light for breakfast. I pass on the meal of leftover snow pancakes and chicken, my stomach too knotted up to digest anything. Telling the kids I ate as I pulled the meat seems to satisfy their concern for me. I've finished putting the mess from the terrorists back in order by the time Christa joins the living. Once again, her hair falls neatly over her shoulders and her makeup is done like she has somewhere to go. Past that, she's a mess. Her floral jumpsuit that reminds me of a painting smeared onto fabric is tucked neatly into her black Jimmy Choo boots. A cashmere sweater with gold and pink stripes covers the top of her outfit followed by a ruffled gray cardigan that bunches around her layers.

"This way they can't steal my favorite clothes," she says, wrapping her hair behind her ears to reveal the dangling diamond encrusted emerald earrings Eddie found.

I slam the door on the way out. Cursing myself for not grabbing my coat, I wrap my arms around myself and stomp through the snow to the nearest pine tree. I shake the powder from its branches and remove my knife. The bitter air stings exposed skin, but anger keeps the chill from reaching my bones. My fingers are numb by the time I cut the first branch free. Tossing it to the side, I move to the next low branch and work on it. With shaking hands, I slice through it and move to the other side of the tree. Blowing on my hands to warm them, I fight the cold working its way into my body. The knife glides swiftly into the soft bark as I saw back and forth. My hands are so brittle I see blood on the snow before the slight warming sensation trickles over my index finger. Squeezing the gash and pulling the skin away, I gauge the depth at just over an inch. Enough to need stitches. I tuck the knife away and drag the three branches with my uninjured hand.

Dropping the limbs on the porch, I head straight to the sink and watch the blood plop onto the metal. Tanner and Ella stop their game of acorns and rush over to inspect the wound.

"Sidney," Ella calls. "Mommy needs you."

Eddie and Christa stop flirting in the corner and join Sidney at the sink. Everyone watches the blood drip until I feel slightly claustrophobic.

"I'll find medical supplies," Sidney says, backing away.

Christa's face pales. "I can't watch whatever you're about to do," she says and heads back to her room.

Eddie's eyes light up. "My turn to do stitches?"

"There are no medical supplies of any kind," Sidney announces after digging in the closet.

"Get me a bowl of snow," I tell her, taking a seat on the floor next to the fire. "I'm going to need a towel," I tell Ella. She scurries for the stack of drawers I've piled on the counter to fix.

"You're not going to do what I think you're going to do, are you?" Eddie's expression is mixed with concern and amusement.

"Cut me off a strip from a bedsheet." My voice has gone monotone and, by the looks I'm receiving, everyone thinks I've lost my mind.

Sidney returns with the snow and I shove my finger in it, warming my other hand by the flames. By the time Eddie returns with two strips of fabric, my right hand has regained most of its feeling. I pull out my knife and carefully stick it in the biggest flame. Sidney, having picked up on my actions, ushers Tanner and Ella into the bedroom with Christa.

"You don't have to do this," Eddie says, watching me wave the blade over my shaking hand. I shove the towel into my mouth and touch the tip to the corner of the wound. With a painful groan, I leave it pressed against flesh for a second before removing it. Eddie puts his hand on my snow-soaked knee as I shove the blade into the fire once more. Taking a deep breath, I cover the gash with the full length of the blade. I stifle a scream into the towel as the smell of burning flesh fills the air.

Eddie pulls my hand away as tears fill my eyes. "You've got to be the bravest damned woman I've ever seen," he says, carefully inspecting the singed skin. My breathing is sharp and quick, and I don't fight when he tenderly offers to wrap the finger.

After the drama is over, Eddie and I look at the waterspout and decide there's nothing that can be done until spring. With that out of the way, I follow him as he cuts saplings for snowshoes.

I point to a sapling, "Can I ask you a question?"

"Ask away," he says, cutting into a tiny tree.

"Why are you not more upset about Clint and Christa's affair?"

He holds a branch out and moves on to the next tree I've pointed out. "We're kinda stuck out here together. Besides, I have a lot to lose."

"You're willing to turn a blind eye just to keep the lifestyle?" He nods, handing me a second branch. "I couldn't do that."

"That's why I told you."

"Then you're trying to be a homewrecker?"

"Not at all. I like to have all the facts when making a decision. I get the impression you do too."

I nod. "But we have kids involved."

"Worse things have happened to children than divorce."

"I know."

I let the conversation end at that and spend the rest of the time thinking about the consequences of my actions. The divorce papers have been drawn up, but it seems unfair to not get Clint's side of the story. Still, I can't help but wonder if he deserves to tell it. My finger throbs as I carry the armload of twigs into the cabin.

We spend the afternoon tying fishing line around the bent branches and finish the day with bland chicken. I know I'll need to hunt in the morning but worry about how my finger will hold up.

"You'll split your finger open," Eddie argues with me in the dim light of the oil lamp. We face each other, both in our warm snow outfits, prepared to take the hunting responsibility.

"It will be worth it if we have food on the table," I snap. The sun is hours from rising and our voices carry farther than they should.

"You need to let it heal."

"Dammit, Lexi," Christa says, emerging from her room wearing her fluffy pink robe. "You don't always have to be in control. Let him help you."

I jerk my head to face her. "I'm a better shot."

"My finger isn't injured," he replies, yanking the bow from my grasp.

"You don't want to risk an infection," she says. "My oils are gone and we don't have any medical supplies."

"You know how to use it?" I ask, refusing to admit Christa's valid point.

"Aim and pull the trigger," he replies sarcastically.

I roll my eyes and watch him strap on our homemade snowshoes and walk out the door. Without saying a word to Christa, I head back to my room and crawl into bed for a few more hours sleep.

Sidney is mixing the last batch of snow pancakes when heavy footsteps fall on the porch. I reach for my knife and position myself behind the door. It slides open, casting a large shadow on the floor. I prepare to strike from behind until an outstretched hand produces two rabbits.

"Look what I got," Eddie says happily as I discretely sheath my weapon.

"You kill it, you clean it." I grab the bow and inspect it. "Where's the other arrow?"

"I missed the first shot and it was too cold to go searching for it. We have more."

"Four! We have four more! We've lost more arrows in the last couple months than I've lost in my entire life."

"I'll go back out later and see if I can find it."

"You would've had a better chance if you looked while you were there." He drops the rabbits in the sink and moves over to the fire to remove his boots. "What happened to the snowshoes?"

"They fell apart."

"Really?" I grab the set by the door and inspect the tight knots.

He nods. "Wouldn't stay on my feet so I ditched them."

"Why wouldn't you bring them back so we could revise the design?"

"Where would I have carried them?"

"You guys fight like an old married couple," Christa says, coming from her room dressed in more ridiculous layers that don't match.

I turn my attention to her. "Are you going to continue wearing half your wardrobe all at once?"

"I'm thinking of starting a new trend when this is all over," she says, twirling her way to Eddie. He wraps his arms around her delicate waist and plants a kiss on her cheek.

"Breakfast is done," Sidney announces.

# Chapter 31

The next week is grueling. Despite my best efforts to wake up first, Eddie is up before me every morning, beating me to the task of hunting. The small amount of game he brings back shortly after sunrise barely sustains us for the duration of the day. The metal traps were lost in the snow by the time we returned from the Watson's and I am forced to spend two days rigging up traps with sticks like I'd watched Clint do. I don't put much faith in the fishing line I'm stuck with using, but it's all we have so I faithfully rebait the same spots each morning and evening with chicken guts I'd kept. Several of my traps break within days and others disappear completely. The ones still intact leave no evidence of a struggle. The bait is simply gone.

"What are you doing?" I drop the remains of a broken trap on my way back from checking them on a particularly frigid night.

Eddie crouches near a tree where I'd set a trap minutes before as if he's inspecting something in the ground. "Thought I saw something. Turns out it was nothing."

I point to the bow in his hand. "I'll do the hunting tonight."

"Actually, Tanner was asking when you'd be back. He wants you to tell him a story." I sigh. "Besides, I'm feeling lucky."

"I hope so," I say, feeling defeated, and trudge back inside.

We still have no food the next morning. Chicken guts are all that remain of the food from the Watsons. We're now relying solely on what Eddie has been shooting. So far, that has amounted to just enough to get us through each day but still leaves us going to bed hungry. Gathering guts in a rag, I head out alone to check the traps. The first two traps are empty and the third is missing altogether. My stomach growls as I approach the next one. My body is getting weaker, fatigue making me force myself onward. Hoping for the best, I watch for signs of tracks, but all I see are the ones I've made in previous days. Fresh snow has fallen, leaving my compacted prints as my trail. It's as if nothing lives nearby. Except something has to. The broken traps prove that. It still doesn't explain why I don't see tracks, but it gives me hope that one day I'll catch something. I'll have to revisit my design, I think as I head back to the cabin with empty hands.

Snow has started falling again in giant, wet flakes. The laughter I hear as I approach the cabin lifts my spirits. Sidney is helping Tanner and Ella make a snowman. Eddie lurches from the side of the cabin, hurling snowballs in their direction. They stop to make their own to chuck back before continuing with the snowman's head. I want to tell them they've made an obvious sign that the cabin is occupied, but figure anyone with any sense isn't going to be out here in this weather looking for us.

"Mommy, come help us," Ella says, dragging me to the completed figure. "He needs a face."

Eddie whacks her with a snowball. I quickly scoop a ball into my hands and hold it out for her. He walks into it as she throws it and drops to the ground. "Grab your acorns while he's down. Hurry! I'll hold him off."

He plays along as I hold two snowballs over him until she rushes back. She and Tanner place them in the shape of a mouth. "He needs eyes," Tanner yells, laughing. "He looks silly."

"Better go find something while I've still got him," I call as Eddie pelts me with a snowball to the stomach. I lurch one into his face. "He's going to get away."

Eddie sneaks a handful of snow into my boot as I'm watching them run into the house with Sidney. He backs away as I try to remove it.

"He's on the loose," I yell as they barrel off the porch.

With a quick glance around, they make a beeline to their creation, getting pelted by snowballs as they go. They squeal in delight, poking a butter knife above the mouth.

"Where did you get those?" I ask as Ella puts two cabinet knobs in the place of eyes.

"In a drawer."

"Good thinking." We stop to toss snowballs at Eddie, who has appeared with sticks.

"He needs arms," he says, shoving them in the sides.

"Now he's just missing the magic hat," Tanner says with a small pout.

I pull mine from my head. "He can borrow mine."

Tanner swings his arms around me. "Think he'll come to life?"

"I sure do. He's going to stand guard out here to keep us safe."

His tiny face turns serious. "What will he use to protect us?"

"His nose, of course."

Tanner flashes the smile he uses when he knows I'm feeding him a line of crap. "We need to make a whole army."

I touch his red nose. "We'd better get inside for a bit. We're not made of snow."

He runs to the snowman, carefully wrapping his arms around its large belly. "We'll get you help later. Stay strong, buddy."

We link arms and head to the warmth of the fire.

"I should head into town," Eddie says after an unsuccessful hunting trip the next morning.

Christa stabs her fork into a sliver of rabbit. "Don't be insane."

"We're going to starve if we don't get more food."

"It's too risky to make that kind of journey. Maybe if the Ranger's tires hadn't been popped, but there's no way you can make it on foot."

"I forgot about that." He hangs his head, staring into his empty plate.

My stomach growls even as I slide my plate to Tanner. "We need to find a fishing hole."

"I haven't seen any bodies of water since we left the Waltons."

"Watsons."

"Whatever. I think it would be safer to head back into town rather than wander around these mountains. At least we know the way there. You wouldn't want to get lost out there in this weather."

"We have to do something," Christa says. "We're going to starve to death if we don't."

"I can't believe you haven't seen a deer," I say, looking at Eddie. "I'll go out tonight and see if I have better luck."

"I think the deer are hibernating."

His expression is so serious I almost laugh. "I know how to track them. I should've been doing that instead of wasting my time on the traps."

"I checked those again this morning. I don't think the line is strong enough or something. The bait was gone, and we still caught nothing."

"That proves there is food out there. There are enough guts from these rabbits to put one last batch out tonight."

"Clearly there's a problem with the traps."

I place one hand on my hip and stare around the room as if what I'm looking for will materialize. "It would work if we had some actual rope."

"I'll pick some up while I'm in town."

"There's over a foot of snow on the ground. Nobody is going to town."

He takes his empty plate to the sink. "Would you rather we all starved?"

"Give me one day to find food and, if I don't, you can go into town."

"Deal."

"You shouldn't go alone," Ella chimes in.

Christa shakes her head. "I'm not walking that far in these." She kicks her expensive boot into the air.

"I'll take Sidney," he says.

I clear the table and head to the shed for the fishing poles. Finding them all snapped in two, I kick the wooden wall. Turning, I give a good kick to the slashed tire on the Ranger. I want to scream but that might be dangerous.

Sidney stands in the doorway watching my fit. "Mind if I join you?"

I motion to the useless vehicle. "Kick away."

She lightly taps the tire with her foot twice before really giving it a good kick. "I hate this."

I place my hand on her shoulder. "Me too."

She slumps next to the broken rods. "Mom and Eddie are driving me nuts."

I take a seat beside her. "I know the feeling."

"They're always sneaking off." She sighs. "I just wish she'd pay that much attention to me. I'm up here too. And Jett is gone."

I pull her into me. "This is an adjustment for us all. I'm glad you're here. I've really enjoyed getting to know you. And we're learning sign language," I add for emphasis. "It's like we have our own language."

She laughs and puts her arm around my shoulder. "I'm glad you're here too. I always wondered what you were like."

"You're only saying that because you want to eat." I give her a quick squeeze. "We never really got a chance to know each other before. I'm sorry about that. I know it's not enough, but things will be different when this is over."

She reaches for a splintered pole. "Hey, there are still hooks on these lines."

Our gazes meet. "We could make some old-fashioned poles."

"Let's do it!"

In ten minutes we have tied lines to a couple thick sticks and my pocket is full of rabbit guts wadded in a rag.

"I want to go fishing," Tanner says, tugging on my pants.

I bend down. "I need to find a place first. Sidney is going to help me look. Once we find something, I'll be sure to take you next time."

He pouts. "I want to go this time."

"I need you to stay here and help Eddie take care of the girls."

"They can take care of themselves."

I run my hand over his hair. "Maybe Christa can cut your hair."

He scrunches his face. "I don't want a stinking haircut."

"I can make you all handsome for when your mommy gets back," Christa says. "And we can paint our nails," she says, reaching for Ella as she comes to hug me.

"Won't that be fun?" I try to make it seem that way while Tanner wrinkles his nose. "And when you're done, you can find the perfect sticks to use for poles. They'll need to be big like these," I say, showing him the long branches we'd sawed from a nearby tree.

"Okay," he concedes.

"We'll be back before dark," I tell them, grabbing the bow. "What happened to the vanes?" I glare at Eddie, inspecting the torn yellow flaps on the arrows.

"I shot into a couple bushes trying to get a...raccoon...I think."

"Why were you trying to shoot a coon?"

"There's three times as much meat on it than a measly rabbit."

I run my hand along a slight curve in one arrow. "This is precisely why I wanted to do the hunting. I would never have taken a shot that could've damaged an arrow. You've made the task so much more difficult."

"I was hungry. I thought you were too."

"We'd better hope Clint has some spares around." Scowling, I swing the bow over my shoulder.

"You should leave us an arrow. What if we're attacked?"

Tanner clings to my leg at the thought. I hand Eddie the damaged arrow.

Sidney and I strap on our snowshoes on the porch. Our feet sink into the snow as the twigs we used to make them crack.

"Well, that was a waste," I say, taking them off before reaching the tree line.

"It was a good idea," she agrees, removing hers.

"Not good enough."

We head down the mountain, sliding most of the way. "When this is over, I'm going straight to the beach," Sidney says, brushing snow off her gloves.

"That sounds wonderful."

"There's this one beach in the Maldives that looks like the night sky. Dad should've brought you the last time we were there."

"I don't remember what I was doing," I say, not wanting to reveal the bombshell she's just dropped on me.

"I think he said you had a work thing."

It's been a while since I've had 'work things' but I don't want her to know this is the first I've heard of the trip. "I might have."

"Next time you'll have to go."

"Why don't we plan a trip somewhere you *haven't* been." She looks thoughtfully at me. "I'm guessing that's a short list?"

She shrugs. "We've never been to India. Mom says it's not clean enough."

I laugh. "We'll go to India then."

"Can we go to the Taj Mahal?"

"How can you go to India and *not*?"

Her smile turns into a laugh when her stomach growls loudly.

"You're gonna wake the bears with that thing," I say with a chuckle.

"We'd better find some water then."

I keep my eyes open for signs of deer trails as we wind around the next mountain.

"If we can find tracks, they'll lead us to water," I tell her. "Keep your eyes open."

"How did you and Dad meet?" She asks, looking around for footprints.

"We've known each other since kindergarten, but we were never friends during school. Then, one day I decided to go fishing. And guess where I bought my bait?"

"At Boats 'N Bait?" I nod. "How romantic."

I laugh. "I know. You'd be surprised at how many people met their spouses in a tackle shop around here."

"So, what happened?"

"I started fishing more. He offered to take me out on his boat. The rest is history, as they say."

"Water!" I jump at her exclamation but am relieved to not have to answer any more questions.

"Wait," I order as we come to the edge of a small lake. "Let me test the ice."

Walking out, I motion to her that it's safe after reaching a depth good for fishing, but close enough to shore that the ice is thin enough to break. I jam the end of the bow into the ice until I've made a small hole. Reaching into my pocket, I pull out a liver and tear off a small piece. She looks at me and reluctantly holds the browned bit in her hand. Watching as I thread my hook, she follows my lead.

We sit on the ice for a long time with our lines in the water. Finally, I get a bite. I pull on the line, moving backward to help reel the fish in.

"Damn," I scream when the stick breaks and slides into the water after our dinner.

"Is nursing school hard?" Sidney asks as we settle back in with only her pole in the water.

"It's rewarding."

"That doesn't answer my question."

"There are days when I don't know why I do it," I admit.

"Oh."

"Why?"

"I thought maybe I might want to do that after high school."

"I see. There are days when you save someone's life and it all makes sense."

"You've saved someone's life?"

I smile and nudge her shoulder. "The doctors don't deserve all the glory. They couldn't do it without us."

"The whole 'it takes a village' thing?"

I nod. "Kind of like what we're doing out here. Teamwork is key. I know I struggle with that a lot."

"Like when Eddie wants to help?"

"I'm better qualified is all."

The corner of her mouth rises in a crooked smile. "I can't argue that."

She jumps when her line tugs. I leap to my feet and grab the string. She falls backward as I wind the tightening line around my glove. Thankfully there's only about twelve feet to reel in and I quickly have the fish on the ice. It flops around so much that I slip, allowing it to slide back into the water. My foot glides into the hole as I try to regain my composure. With a final tug, I secure its head against the ice. I reach in and grab him by the gills.

"That's a nice one," I tell Sidney, tossing the three-foot Northern Pike onto the snow.

"Not bad for a first fish, huh?"

I shake the water from my leg as moisture seeps into my sock. "How is that your first fish?"

She shrugs. "I don't know."

"I'm having strong words with your father."

She laughs as I pull my knife out. "Please do." I stab the fish's brains. "On second thought, don't."

"Afraid he'd make you do this?"

"A little."

"The first one's always a freebie." I toss the line back in the water and hold the stick for Sidney to take. She shakes her head. "Oh, come on, I know you got it in you."

With a reluctant smile, she takes the makeshift pole. "Where do you think Dad and Jett are?"

"With any luck, near the border by now."

"Do you think they're okay?"

I put a gloved hand over hers. "I have to. Hope is all we have." She nods. "And I can't bear the thought that they aren't."

"I'm worried about them."

"We all are. Your dad isn't one to give up. I know he can do it."

"What do you think will happen when he gets there?"

I shrug one shoulder. "The Canadians will send troops over, I reckon."

"Do you think he will come straight back?"

"He'll come back when he can."

The line sways in the water as a hawk floats over the cloudless sky. We patiently wait for a bite that doesn't come. After nearly an hour, I rise, stretching my cold, stiff muscles.

"We'd better head back before we turn to ice."

"But we don't have enough food."

"Maybe we'll find something along the way."

"You're not going to stab anything else, are you?"

I smile. "I'm not making any promises."

We begin the long trudge back, talking about the boy she'd been interested in before this all started. As she tells me about him, I can tell she's questioning her attraction to him in the first place. I let her talk more to herself than to me as she figures out her tastes have now changed.

"I think it's important to have someone who can protect you in certain situations," she says.

"I think so too. But you think Miles wouldn't?"

"He once pushed a kid out of the way during a fire drill because he thought he smelled smoke. I mean, what if we had been on a date and someone tried to mug us? I don't think he would worry about me. I think he would want to get away."

"I hope you never have to find out."

"But there's this other guy who likes me. He's always asking me out, but Mom says he isn't good enough."

"What do you think?" I place a hand on her arm, letting her know it's okay to form her own opinion.

"He only goes to our school because his grandparents pay the tuition, but that doesn't make me any better than him. He's a nice kid. A little goofy, like he knows he doesn't quite fit in."

"I can relate to that."

"When the fire alarm went off, he was the last one out of the room and when I tripped over someone's dropped bookbag, he helped me up, even though there was a sea of people trying to get around us."

I smile proudly. "Which one would you rather bring home to your dad?"

The light fades from her eyes. "He's not White."

"Your dad doesn't mind purple people. As long as they don't eat people. You have to watch out for those purple people eaters."

Her smile returns, and she playfully shoves me. "He's Black."

"Do *you* have a problem with that?"

She shakes her head. "Mom said Dad would go ballistic."

"Your mom is engaged to someone who isn't completely White. Is he Mexican?"

"I think so. He never really said."

"Character is what your dad will be looking at when you bring someone home. Color doesn't matter."

She wraps her arms around herself. "You think he'd be okay with it?"

"If the guy treats you right, it won't matter what he looks like."

"What about Mom?"

"She doesn't have a card to hold on the race issue."

I hold up my hand to halt her, pointing to the deer tracks that cross our old ones. We turn our course to follow them, Sidney taking the fish so I can shoot, if possible. Within twenty minutes we have weaved our way back toward the lake. I spot a doe in the clearing near the water's edge. Sidney stops as I tiptoe to the side, trying to get a clear shot. The deer twitches her ears. I freeze. She looks around, sniffing the air. I slide the bow over my shoulder and flip the safety. My boot crunches as I sidestep to line her in my sight. The noise attracts her attention but not enough to spook her. I wait patiently for her to move into position, aiming in the direction she should head if she goes for the easy watering hole. She sniffs the air and I know she must smell us from the distance, but she doesn't seem to mind. One more step and her neck will have a red dot in my scope. One hoof moves then the second. I press lightly on the trigger, the arrow whizzing through the air. She wobbles as she heads for the protection of the trees. I wait for Sidney to rush over.

"Looks like luck is back on our side," I say, slinging the bow over my shoulder. "Let's go get her."

"How far can she go?"

"She'll bleed out in a few minutes. We just have to follow her trail."

We cross the lake and follow the blood-stained snow into the woods.

"There," Sidney points as the crimson dots curve around a large pine. The doe lies ahead of us, motionless, next to a fallen tree. The arrow has been snapped in two, the end dangling from a thin thread and still moving slightly.

Out of habit, I check for a pulse. Finding none, I turn to Sidney. "You might not want to watch this."

Pulling out my knife, I run it along her belly, spilling intestines and organs onto the snow. Steam rises from her empty cavity and the mass of guts on the crimson powder.

Standing, I wipe my hands on my pants, leaving blood smears along my thighs. "You're gonna have to help me carry her."

"I want to argue," she says, her stomach growling loudly. "But my stomach won't let me."

"Which end do you want?"

"I feel like that's a trick question."

I look to the sun for an idea of how much time we have. Sidney stares at the lifeless creature before us. "We don't have much daylight left," I say, pointing to the west where the sun threatens to sink.

"How much does it weigh?"

"I'll tell you when you pick an end."

"I don't know."

"Head or tail."

"Tail."

I shove the fish into the deer's body and sling the bow over my shoulder. We grab a set of feet and step over internal organs still steaming on the ground. I'd like to take them for bait but know the extra weight will be a burden we don't need. "She's about one-ten, one-thirty."

"And we have to carry her all the way?"

"If you want to eat."

We're about to the spot where we first saw the doe's tracks when Sidney drops her end.

"I need a break," she pants.

I remove my glove and shovel snow into my mouth. It has been dry for quite some time but I didn't want to risk being caught out here after dark so I refused to stop.

"We have to keep moving," I say, shoving the glove over my wet hand.

"There's something I should tell you." Her tone is quiet but stern.

"Sidney, unless you're about to tell me you're having a medical issue, it's going to have to wait."

She scoops snow into her mouth and shakes her head. "I'm fine, but it's important."

"I promise you as soon as we get this back to the cabin, you'll have my undivided attention."

"I can't tell you in front of Mom."

I hoist my end of the deer and wait for her to do the same. "That's fine. We can slip outside...or use sign language."

She smiles, but it quickly fades. "I really think I should tell you now."

"Let me ask you this—is it more important than getting food?"

She exhales slowly. "I guess it can wait a little longer."

"Is there anything I can do about it before we reach the cabin?"

"No."

"Then please, let it wait. We may not make it back before dark the way it is."

"Okay."

Sidney is silent as we trudge along. I know I've hurt her feelings, but the extra energy it takes to talk while carrying a deer uphill isn't something

I have. The full moon hangs in the eastern sky while the west displays a stunning orange and pink combination beyond the trees. An owl screeches overhead. The weight of the deer shifts with Sidney's abrupt jerk to the startling noise. Whatever is on her mind has her so deep in thought she's unaware of her surroundings. I know I should stop and let her unburden, but we're not going to make it back before dark at the rate we're going and that is more dangerous than whatever it is she has to say. The half of the deer behind me thuds to the snow.

"Sidney, we have to keep going," I urge.

"I can't. My arms feel like jelly," she says, shaking them out.

My arms ache and I'm a little light-headed from exhaustion and lack of food. Wolves howl in the distance. "If we don't keep moving, the wolves will have dinner before we do."

Her eyes expand. "Can't we send Eddie back for it?"

"The wolves would get to it before we reach the cabin."

She reluctantly picks up the stiff legs and we make it the length of a football field before she drops them again.

"Sidney," I growl.

"I'm sorry. I just can't."

I drop onto the cold ground, trying to catch my breath. The sun has dipped over the horizon, leaving only the light of the full moon to dance over the glittering snow. I shove my fist into the powder, sinking my arm up to my elbow.

"You could wait here with it and I'll run back and get Eddie," she offers.

"I don't think so."

"Can we drag it?"

"Worth a shot." Sidney lifts one front leg and I reach for the other. A set of eyes carefully watches us. "We've got company."

Sidney bolts upright, letting the leg drop. "Where?" She spins in a circle as I point.

Slowly, I reach into the deer's belly and retrieve the fish. "Hold this." I hand her the Pike and slip the bow off my back.

"There's another!" She points a few feet to the left of the first. "What are they?"

"Wolves. They'll have us surrounded in a minute."

"What do we do?" Her voice quivers as she asks.

"If they get any closer, throw the fish as far as you can." She trembles as a low growling fills the air. With steady, but quick movements, I move to the tail of the deer and pull my knife out. Grabbing hold of the hind quarter, I begin sawing away at the meat. I can't hear it, but I know the pack is making their way to us.

"They're getting closer," Sidney whimpers. "Do I throw it?"

"Not yet." I roll the carcass over and yank on the leg. A bone cracks and the hair on the back of my neck prickles despite the sweat building. I manage to free the second quarter as the wolves prepare their attack. I clutch the raw meat as if it were a prize.

"Be prepared to toss the fish," I tell her, finding us surrounded by hungry beasts. I urge her forward with a single step. Behind us, the wolves snarl as we move out. "We're going to have to pass a couple. When you see them, toss the fish behind you and run."

She lets out a muffled cry. "I really have to pee," she says with a terrified laugh.

"Move!" I step powerfully forward, leaving her no choice but to keep up.

Hungry eyes watch us as a fight ensues behind us. Just as I had said, we're met by three wolves eager to join the feast. Eyes are skillfully trained on the meal I'm holding, but Sidney's distraction works, and they pass us with merely a growl.

# Chapter 32

The welcoming smell of fire greets us as we approach the cabin. We're out of breath and shaking from our adventure. Sidney's smile is contagious as she points to a new snowman standing guard with the one we built. I drop the giant leg portions on the porch and reach for the door handle. Sidney sweeps me into a hug.

"I'm going to go pee now," she says. "I'm sorry I lost the deer."

"We wouldn't have made it far with them on our trail anyway."

She nods and leaps off the porch. I know she's beating herself up, but we'll have to deal with that later. My stomach is in knots, my insides feeling like they're about to eat themselves. I prop the bow next to the door of the outhouse, knowing Sidney will be more comfortable walking back with it. Swinging the cabin door open with my foot, I hold the furry legs up like trophies. My mouth drops, along with dinner. Sitting on the table next to the oil lamp is Eddie. A pistol rests on his lap and he swings his legs as if he hasn't a care in the world. I open my mouth to warn Sidney. He shakes his head, halting me. My legs wobble and my heart courses blood so rapidly I think it may burst a vein.

"Make a noise and I'll put a bullet in your head." His tone is cold, as if he's talking about taking out an enemy he's never met. "Where's Sidney?"

I force air through my lungs as I try to plot my next move. With any luck, Sidney will be alert when she enters. But will she be able to get the shot before he does?

"Eddie, what is going on here?" I ask, hoping to buy some time and diffuse the situation.

"We'll have plenty of time for that once Sidney is safely inside."

I almost laugh at the hilarity of his statement but control myself as to not set him off. "What's one more wolf?" I mumble.

"You'd have been better off if you'd gotten lost today." He hops off the table and moves to the door, keeping the gun ready.

*No. You'd be better off,* I think as footsteps pound the porch.

"Did you tell them about the lake?" Sidney stops in the doorway and stares at Eddie. I could lunge at him, but he'd easily overpower me and regain control. It's best to wait, to come up with a plan, I convince myself as Sidney studies him. "Where'd you get the gun?"

"Had it the whole time." His tone is snarky. I've never wanted to hit him more.

"That would've been useful. Especially today. Did Lexi tell you about the wolves?" She is clearly misreading the situation.

He nods, understanding my earlier comment. "She mentioned one."

"One? There were at least eight. That's why we only got part of the deer."

"Put the bow down, Sidney."

She leans it against the wall. "Will you help clean the deer? I'm famished." She looks at Eddie when he doesn't answer right away. Her face pales as her eyes connect with mine. "What's goin...?"

"Plans have changed." Eddie interrupts.

I pull Sidney next to me. She looks around the room. "Where is everyone? Are we going back home now?"

"Not exactly." He motions to the only two remaining chairs. "Sit."

"Not until you show me where Tanner and Ella are," I demand.

He points to the loft with his gun. My foot slips off the second rung as I fling myself upward.

My two helpless children sit on the bed with duct tape over their mouths and their hands bound to the wooden bars of the headboard. Ella's eyes are red and puffy from crying. She wiggles her legs as she tries to reach me. Tanner's face is also stained with tears and his arms are red around the gray tape. He tries to pull toward me, but the restraints make it impossible for him to move. I rush to them, throwing my arms around their tiny bodies.

"It will be okay," I whisper between their heads. "I'll get us out of this."

The metal barrel of the gun jams into my back. "You've seen them," Eddie growls. "Time to go downstairs."

Sidney takes my hand as we stand at the bottom of the ladder. "Where's my mom?"

Eddie kicks the bedroom door open, revealing a slender body lying peacefully on the bed. Christa looks as if she's playing the part of damsel in distress. *Probably waiting for Clint to rescue her,* I scowl. Her hair falls neatly over her shoulders and her eyes are red, but dry. Her clothes aren't wrinkled and she's still wearing the earrings Eddie produced nights earlier. Aside from the tape over her mouth and at her wrists on the headboard, she looks like a willing participant in this horrific game. The only sign that this is real is the look of horror that fills her green eyes when Sidney steps inside the room. They hold such sorrow I know she's as caught off guard as we are.

"Your turn," Eddie says, pointing the gun to the other room.

Sidney clings to my hand and we squeeze through the narrow opening.

"It's okay," I whisper. "Just do what he says."

He tosses her a roll of duct tape from the table. "Tape her arms to the chair," he orders. I nod, more to comfort Sidney than to appease him. I take position in the chair and wait for Sidney's hands to stop shaking enough to perform the task. Muffled wails float from the loft as the tape screeches.

Pointing the gun is all the prompting Sidney needs to take a seat. He tucks the weapon in his waistband and tightly bounds her without a fight. After slapping a strip over her mouth, he returns to me. He reaches for my waistband and the knife concealed there. Satisfied, he smacks a gray sticky slab over my mouth.

With nothing else to do, Sidney and I watch Eddie's long gait as he slinks out the front door. He leaves it open behind him. Sidney whimpers through the tape, her eyes wide with fear. My heart is pounding so violently I wish there were tape over it to help keep it in place. A loud groan comes from Christa's room. I'm hit with a sudden compassion for the woman in the next room who doesn't know if her daughter is being hurt. There's no way for us to signal her so I hope the silence is a comfort. Tears stroll down the teenage girl's face—a look I've seen many times in my line of work, usually by patients and family members who know death is coming for them. I've learned there is not much I can do in these situations.

The frosty air blows a wispy powder inside the cabin. I stare into the darkness, where Eddie has gone without a light, and watch the fresh flakes fall heavily. The wind flickers the oil lamp on the table, threatening to send us into darkness. The oil is dangerously low anyway and the flame struggles for power against the storm brewing over the threshold. Eddie is gone for several minutes that seem like both an eternity and seconds at the same time. I am certain he has backup somewhere in the cover of the trees where only the most determined people would spend any time. Maybe he has them in the shed, I fear as we wait. Although, they should've been back by now if that were the case, I tell myself as an imaginary clock ticks in my head. Tick. Tock. Tick. Tock. Tick. Glock.

Sidney pulls against the tape on her arms. Her eyes ask why I'm not doing the same. I shrug, knowing it's futile.

Bare branches dance eerily through the window against the light of the full moon. They claw their way across the table like long, black fingers scratching toward their victim.

Footsteps pound the porch, and Eddie kicks the door closed with his foot, the force taking the light out. He laughs, a deep sound coming from the pit of his stomach. It's the evil laugh of a villain waiting for the hero to show up for battle. Except he knows there isn't one. He drops a large duffel bag on the table, leaving me to wonder what kind of torturous devices it holds. Through the moonlight, I follow him as he moves to the fireplace. He throws another log on and reaches for the matches. There is enough light to maneuver about the cabin, but clearly, he has an ulterior motive by lighting the lamp again.

"You're going to want to see this," he snarls. "I think we should have a party." With that he whips out my knife and heads for Christa's room. I strain against the layer of tape on my right arm as muffled screams come from the next room. Christa is forced through the door with Eddie's arms wrapped around her and a knife poking into her neck. A slow trickle of blood creeps toward her cardigan. She's still wearing multiple layers of mismatched clothing and strains her neck away from the blade as he demands she move toward us. He places her in a vacant chair and I wonder if it's a coincidence that he left four chairs. After securing her with duct tape, he heads up the steps to the loft. I stand with the chair awkwardly attached behind me, desperate to figure out how to use it for a weapon. Ella sobs heavily as they descend the ladder with her slumped over his shoulder. Her feet have been bound and her arms are flailing about, trying to get loose. He forces her into a chair as she beats on him until her arm is twisted backward and taped to the round rung on the back. He stomps up the ladder again after making sure

Ella can't get free. I groan to get Sidney's attention. Nodding toward my hand with my head, I use sign language to spell out 'knife' and 'table,' thanking my lucky stars we all know a bit of sign language due to Sidney's teaching. She makes her way awkwardly toward the kitchen knife, the chair legs scraping against the floor as she goes. Eddie leaps off the second rung with Tanner still bound at his feet. He tosses him to the floor, thudding his behind on the wood. I motion with my head for him to make a dash for the door as Eddie hurries to the knife. Stabbing it in the table, he moves Sidney away while Tanner slowly pulls himself toward the door.

Scooping him up, he says, "There's something I want you all to see." After taking his time taping Tanner to the last chair, he lines us up so he has an audience for his one-man show. He yanks at the zipper on his bag and hops onto the table again. I fully expect to see a menagerie of torture tools spill out. Instead, he grabs a bag of Cheetos and displays it proudly. The popping of the bag resonates throughout the room. He hops off the table and places the bag under Tanner's nose then takes it down the line so we're all forced to smell the cheesy snack. Once he's done, he hops back onto the table and pops one in his mouth, crunching loudly. His legs swing in amusement as he finishes his refreshment.

"I suppose you have questions," he says, wadding the bag and tossing it onto Ella's lap. "Who's gonna go first?" He points his finger around like a kid doing Eenie-meenie-miny-moe.

"I'll bet *you* have questions," he says, stopping in front of me. "But first, let's hear from Christa." In a swift movement he rips the adhesive from her mouth.

"Ow!"

Eddie presses the tape over her mouth, patting it twice. "That's all the time we have," he says, smiling wickedly. He's gone mad, I think as he steps in front of Sidney. "What about you?" He pulls at her tape slowly, leaving it hanging from her cheek.

"How could you do this to my mom...to us?" Her voice lacks emotion, and I can only hope mine will if he gives me the chance to speak. I have so many questions, but I need to know if this was premeditated or if he just snapped. It's quite possible our circumstances made him crazy. I know Clint would give him the benefit of doubt, but I'm not sure I can.

His evil laugh fills the room and I'm sure any creatures stirring nearby run from the sound. "You think I have some deep connection with your mother?" The question is clearly rhetorical. He yanks the ring off Christa's left hand. "I have no idea where this came from, but it wasn't from me." He flicks the ring into the fire. The act has no effect on Christa. Maybe she's lost enough jewelry out here that she no longer cares, I think as my eyes burn into hers. Of course, it's probably insured for more than my house, but it doesn't stop me from wondering what the story behind it is. Could be that she wore it only because she didn't want to leave it behind. Then why the facade about being engaged? The answers will have to wait.

Eddie leaves the tape dangling from Sidney's face and reaches over to yank the covering from Christa's mouth. "Tell everyone the real story of our relationship," he urges. Her mouth gapes open. "Do it!"

"I was so scared," she says, her lip quivering. "I had gone to the city to shop and, just as I walked out of Bloomingdale's, I noticed the chaos in the streets. People were running in all directions as those big military trucks pulled up to block traffic. There was one on each corner and they were shouting over loud speakers for everyone to surrender and get in the trucks. Shots were fired as people refused. I didn't know what to do." She sobs and shrugs her shoulders as if we might take sympathy on her.

"What *did* you do, Christa?" Eddie torments her, hopping onto the table and clapping his hands.

"I slipped into an alley."

"What happened there?"

"I ran into you," she growls.

"Then what happened?"

"You said you could get me out of town and back to my family." Her voice is so full of sorrow I almost feel sorry for her, like *she's* the victim instead of the cause of this.

"Don't leave out the best part," he taunts.

"I offered to pay him a large sum of money," she admits.

"It will go a long way to aid our plan."

So, he hasn't gone mad. I'm sick at the thought and wonder how much she paid. Eddie takes care of that by saying, "Tell them how much."

"A hundred thousand."

"Plus another fifty thousand to get you out here," he adds.

"I can't believe you hired a stranger with something so important," Sidney spews.

"It was the only way to get to you and keep you and your brother safe," she chokes behind tears.

"And look where we are," Sidney snaps.

"He was supposed to leave once we got here safely," Christa says defensively.

"But when you found out your ex-husband and his wife were here, you decided you wanted to play a game with him, so you agreed to pay me another grand per day to play the part of your doting fiancé," Eddie says, rubbing his hands together. "I guess it doesn't matter; we would've come back for you anyway."

"Mom!" Sidney's eyes burn with anger. "You told us he was a friend. We trusted *you*. You said he was a friend that you bumped into that day, then you told us you had secretly been dating and he had asked to marry you, but you wanted to wait to tell us. We trusted you." A tear streams down her reddened cheeks as she glares at her mother.

"Clearly it was a mistake," Christa says as if that makes it all better.

For an instant I'm glad I can't get my hands on her because I'd probably strangle her.

"What's the total up to now? Got to be over a hundred. But I lost count. Why don't we just make it one fifty?"

"You'll not see another cent. You weren't even around for two or three of those weeks," she boldly states as if the extra thousands will bankrupt her.

Eddie slides in front of Sidney, placing the knife to her throat.

Christa slaps her hand against the wooden arm of the chair. "Okay, fine!"

"I thought you'd see it my way." He hops onto the table and opens a can of tuna. The aroma fills the small room as he takes a pinch between his fingers. "I'm sorry. Am I being rude?" A fire burns inside me like I've never felt before as he holds the can out to Tanner and Ella, letting them grab a bite. Tanner tries to figure out how to get it to his mouth but ends up dropping it when his neck doesn't reach. He whines through the tape and stares at the meat on his leg. Lifting his leg, he tries to make it reach his hand. Ella, on the other hand, realizes the cruel joke that has been played on them and keeps the food in her fingers. Tears well in my eyes watching them suffer from the stupidity of Christa's selfishness. I try to put myself in her shoes but can't manage to see how she came to the conclusions she did. I guess I could understand taking his help getting to her house, but she shouldn't have trusted him with the location of the cabin.

"Eddie, I beg you to not take this out on them," Christa pleads. "If it's money you want, I'll get it to you, but please leave Lexi and the kids out of it. They had no part in this."

"I'm just following orders, honey."

"Orders?"

His head moves up and down as if to degrade her intelligence. "To bring in stragglers."

"What kind of lame job is that?" I glare at Christa. She obviously doesn't care about keeping him from losing all control. "I mean, really? Were you not qualified for a better job?"

Eddie slams the can he's holding onto the floor. The fishy liquid sprays over me and Christa. Chunks fly in the air, one sticking to Christa's forehead. If I weren't so angry, I'd laugh.

"It's a respectable job. With the size of our mission, subjects were bound to slip through the cracks. I was supposed to blend in and bring you in."

"Why didn't you then?"

"You offered a large sum of money—which has helped our cause tremendously—so they thought you'd make a good decoy."

"Decoy?"

He taps an index finger on his temple. "For the other people out here. They'd trust you before they would me. After you drew them out, I'd tell my leaders where to find them."

She gasps. "Is that how they found the Watsons?"

Eddie nods with an evil grin spread across his face. "I followed you then reported the location." He shakes his head. "They kept getting lost so it took longer for them to find you. I'll bet I made ten trips between here and there."

"Why didn't you tell us how to get back then?"

He shrugs. "Thought it might be fun to see how long you could wander out there before one of you froze to death."

"You're evil," she snaps, spitting in his direction.

"What did you expect?" He opens a bottle of Gatorade from his bag. "I'll tell ya though, you're pretty lucky you were gone when they showed up. If that old man hadn't told them you'd gone for supplies, they'd still be hunting you."

"Luckily, they had you to find us," Christa snarls. "They knew we'd trust you."

"It all worked out so well," he responds smugly.

"I've got more cash at the house. I can get it to you. Just let them go and I'll take you to it."

"Even if we hadn't already seized everything, you'd just try to get help to stop our mission."

"Clint is already on his way to do that," Christa boasts.

"I wouldn't be so sure."

"Did you do something to Clint and Jett?" she asks, her tone suddenly worried.

"Our men up north were waiting for the group. Last I heard, they'd been taken into custody."

Christa stomps her foot. "I thought you were our friend," she growls.

"Friend? We met in an alley, and you paid me to be your guide. If I was really your friend, do you think I would have let you pack all the ridiculous things you did? Although, I must admit, the jewelry came in handy."

"*You* stole it?"

"You're starting to get it. I almost had you completely disarmed and waiting for capture, but Clint got impatient. I should've taken him out when I had the chance." He laughs from the pit of his stomach. "Wouldn't have taken long for the rest of you to starve to death with all the work I did to keep the traps from working."

Since I was trying to trust him, it didn't cross my mind he was sabotaging the traps. Part of me actually felt relieved it was nothing I did that kept us from eating.

"How did you expect to live if you were trying to keep us from getting food?"

He taps his bag. "I buried this the night you cut me."

So that's what he was doing by the tree!

He takes a long, slow swig of his orange drink. "Don't be so angry. I saved you the day they had you surrounded out here."

"You weren't even there," she says, full of confusion.

"Didn't have to be." Producing a high-tech walkie talkie, he says, "I called them off."

She shakes her head. "Why would you do that?"

"I was the one who put up with your crap—the whining, the high-maintenance bullshit—I wanted to be the one to deal with you."

"You're sick," she barks.

"That's why I burned down all those cabins," he gloats. "It was especially fun to sneak out and start the fire at the Waltons, knowing you'd find it when you woke up."

"What's going to happen to them?"

"They'll be taken to a camp where they will be trained in the ways of our ancestors." He spins on his heel in a complete circle. "That is, if they aren't executed."

"No!" Sidney's shriek echoes throughout the tiny room.

I fight the tape holding me to the chair, growling against the adhesive on my lips.

Eddie skips two steps to me and yanks the tape. "Is there something you'd like to say?"

"We never treated you like an outsider. We fed you and protected you like one of our own. What would've happened if I hadn't stitched your arm?"

"Are you forgetting how that happened?"

"You scared me half to death. It was an accident."

"And my oils helped with the infection," Christa chimes in like she should be awarded a medal. "Those weren't so silly to pack, were they?"

"Those stupid oils didn't do anything but smell up the place. The infection was mild. I used the radio to get antibiotics delivered and was back on my feet in no time."

"You've done a great job of fooling us Eddie, I'll give you that. Why don't we part ways now? You can untie Tanner and be gone before he gets us free. We'll forget we ever saw each other," I offer.

"I don't think so," he snarls.

"What if we promise to stay here and you can come check on us from time to time?" Christa offers.

He shakes his head. "Can't do it. You know too much."

"Take us to one of your camps then," I suggest, hoping to deter him from killing us and leaving our bodies for Clint to find, on the chance that he's lying about his capture.

"Can't do that either. You'll be resistant to the drug."

"What drug?"

"Its street name is 'Brainwasher.' Lame, but effective. It's pretty self-explanatory. We ground it into a fine powder and put it in water. It's flavorless and virtually undetectable. Why do you think you were so willing to accept me?"

"Christa didn't have the drug."

"Consider the source," he says lightly.

"Why didn't it work on me before I escaped?"

"You were on high alert then. We ran into issues with some people. Sometimes we have dosing issues on the strong-willed or crazies. Which are you?"

"I'm definitely not the craziest person in this room."

His hand hits hard against my face. "It's also not as effective on people who aren't well grounded. You know, the ones who always have their heads in the clouds, but—combined with the recordings—it should've worked on everyone." He shrugs. "I guess nothing is one hundred percent."

I don't like where he's going with this. "I bartended during nursing school. When you hear the same song fourteen times a night, you learn to tune things out," I explain.

"You just got lucky, but that's about to run out."

"You said we'd be resistant to the drug—what makes you think that? What if we don't fight it?"

"You've built up a tolerance to it for one thing. I've been slipping it in your water bottles, but with all this snow I've been unable to get supplies, so I had to cut back on your normal doses. Luckily, you'd already come to trust me. If I take you back, you'll try to alert the others. It shouldn't matter now, but we still can't take the chance." He moves to the far side of the table and rummages in his bag.

"If I'm going to die, I demand you tell us what your agenda is. I'm assuming you're with WIN?"

He pulls a long syringe out of his bag, his villainous laugh cracking in the air. "You would think that. They get all the credit." Glass clinks against the wood as he lines vials on the edge of the table. "Although, we did set them up."

"Why would you do that? Don't terrorists want to take credit for their heinous behavior?"

He puts a needle to the vial but doesn't fill it. "It was a joint effort. The Worldwide Islamic Nation invokes fear in name alone. Our organization has been kept undercover so much that we wouldn't be taken seriously if we took credit for the attack."

"That doesn't make any sense. We take all attacks seriously."

His evil laugh reverberates throughout the room. "But this one has been orchestrated right under your noses. We've been working on it for decades. It's finally time to turn the tables."

"What does that mean?"

"It's time to take our land back."

There's no way that can mean what I think it means. "*Your* land?"

"You've had it long enough." Liquid fills the syringe. "You thought sticking us on some Reservation would be good enough, but we're finally standing up and taking back what is ours."

"You're Indian?"

"Does that surprise you?" Clear liquid seeps from the tip of the needle as he taps it. "Did you really think we were going to let you get away with destroying our land like you did?"

"It's been more than a hundred years," I argue. "*We* didn't do anything to your People."

"And yet you still treat us as if we're beneath you."

I wrinkle my brow. Until today, if I'd ever encountered a Native American, I'd not known it. "What exactly are your plans for our country?"

"We're going to restore it." He places the needle carefully on the table and hops on top of the oak.

"What does that mean?"

"We're giving it back to nature." He rubs his hands together in pure enjoyment.

I wonder if this is a well thought out plan but, clearly, they've gotten pretty far with it. "How does that work?"

"First, we start by making the White Man undo all the work they've done. And that's a lot. Cities to destroy, factories to dismantle, that sort of thing."

"What happens then? I mean, there has to be a government. You'll have to interact with the world outside the United States."

"Our Chief is already working on that. It's all going to fall together."

I furrow my brow, trying to understand. "And how does WIN fit into this?"

"We offered them every rifle we don't need—and that's a *lot*—in exchange for a treaty stating there will be no further attacks on this land."

"Do you really think that's smart? How will you defend yourselves?"

He makes a circle around us. "Our warriors are skilled. And, thankfully, they've adapted over the years. We'll keep enough of your military extravagances to protect our People."

"So WIN isn't a threat, but you're okay with the rest of the world being against you? They'll attack, you know."

"WIN has our back. We're going to be unstoppable."

"I don't feel like this has been properly thought out."

Eddie jumps off the table and I know I've offended him. "How do you figure?!"

"You don't have the numbers to make a plan like this work."

"I beg to differ."

I shrug. "You've made it farther than anyone would have imagined; I'll give you that."

"You don't even know the half of it. It'll be years before anyone realizes we've been hiding under the guise of the Mexican Brotherhood."

"Why the ruse?"

He shrugs. "Less chance of being discovered. It's a shame you can't stick around to see how it all turns out. I think you'd like it." He grasps the needle, agitation obvious in his movements. "Christa, you'll go first. I know you don't want to stick around and learn how to turn animal hide into clothing."

Christa scrunches her face.

"What's in that?" Sidney asks timidly.

"The same thing used in lethal injections." A frown develops across his face. "I hate to use such a White Man tactic, but there are children involved."

"Thank you for not being a savage," I say softly, hoping to stir ancient history.

"The Chief thinks if anyone stumbles across your bodies, they'll be scared back to town if they think you died of starvation."

"I have one other question," I say loudly as he moves toward us with the needle. "Do you honestly think your ancestors were innocent? That they behaved in a way that made White men feel like they had a choice?"

He looks quizzically at me. "They shouldn't have come here in the first place."

"They had no way to know anyone was here. I'll admit a lot of things were handled unfairly and I'm truly sorry for that, but it was so long ago."

"So you'll agree this is long overdue?"

"There was a better way then. And there's a better way now."

"Our great-great grandchildren can discuss it." He shrugs as if the idea suits him.

"Why not do it now?"

He puts the needle to Ella's arm. Terror and hopelessness consume me. She thrashes wildly against the tape, muffled screams filling the air. I jump my chair forward, though I know there's little I can do but watch. Eddie calmly moves away from her kicking legs and sticks her skin. "This won't hurt a bit."

"Wait!" My scream halts Eddie.

"What now? I have work to do and all your questions are taking up valuable time."

I look to Christa and Sidney for help. Christa's eyes bulge, and Sidney trembles like a toddler.

"Don't you want to be better than *them*?" Sidney asks through quivering lips.

He retracts the needle and I'm afraid my exhale will distract him from being distracted. "People will be hurt in the process. But I promise it's all for good." He hesitates the syringe over Ella's arm.

Sidney shakes her head. "I really want to know why the guy who helped make snowmen wants to kill us. What happened to make you so hateful?"

"Don't pretend to care."

"We need to understand, Eddie," I plead.

Eddie's eyes turn softer, the evil seeping from them as he places the needle on the table. He takes a seat next to it. "Our stories were passed down from previous generations and, as a kid, all I ever wanted was to live life like they did in the old days. Now's my chance."

"Eddie, it doesn't have to be this way," Christa whispers.

"I'm afraid it does."

"You could live off the land in these mountains and nobody would know you were here," Sidney offers.

"I could. But what about the rest of my People?"

"Maybe we could increase Reservation land," I suggest.

His laugh booms through the room. "That's what we're doing. Don't worry; we'll drive you like cattle to California or somewhere. You can live there for two hundred years." He grabs the needle, holding it like a knife. "Let's get this over with."

"I still don't understand," I say cautiously. "Even if you managed to recruit every Native American in the country, you still wouldn't have enough manpower to pull something like this off."

"Turns out, there are plenty of minorities willing to help get revenge. Slavery ring a bell?"

"You have supporters. I get it."

Christa squints her eyes at the window. "What is that?!"

Eddie whips around and bolts over to check it out. Christa swings her head to Sidney. She violently whips it downward like she's possessed. Sidney seems to understand the meaning. I shrug my shoulders to let them know I'm clueless.

"I don't see a thing," Eddie barks.

Sidney spells with her hand. She wants me to duck. Christa points to the window discretely with her index finger. I strain my eyes but don't see anything.

Eddie turns to face us again. "Where were we?"

"You were about to explain the Spanish I heard coming from the radios. Why not use your native tongue?"

"Spanish was easier. Most people are at least familiar with it." He steps to the window once more.

Christa strains her neck. "Tip chair back," she whispers through the side of her mouth. I pass it on to Tanner as Eddie continues. My son's nod is so slight, I'm not sure he understands. Christa holds up three fingers quickly and puts them down.

Eddie runs his fingers through his hair. "We should've fought harder when there weren't so many of you."

I watch Christa with slight glances, unsure of her mysterious plan. Seconds tick away as I wait for the signal.

Eddie steps toward me, needle poised. "You're a nurse. I think I'll take it out on you first."

My skin is clammy as he goes straight for my jugular. From the corner of my eye I see the sign I've been waiting for. I kick Eddie's shin. He stumbles backward, and our chairs fall to the floor. The synchronized movement puts him on alert. He spins around and hits the floor, falling before we hear the shot ring out over the shattering glass.

Christa and Sidney's screams fill the room, drowning out whatever noise Tanner and Ella are making. Blood seeps onto the floor inches away from our feet. I hope whoever took him out is here to help because we're now no better than turtles that have flipped over. My pulse races as we wait for the door to open or to find out Eddie still has a pulse. My breath sticks in my lungs as I watch for signs of movement. His eyes are open and staring straight at me as the door cracks.

# Chapter 33

A lanky man dressed in a three-piece suit and a white Stetson stops in the doorway. A large oval belt buckle sticks out like a sore thumb with a *B* heavily embossed over an eagle. Further down, brown cowboy boots lie underneath the cuffs of his navy slacks that contain a hint of dirt, but no wrinkles. He rests his hands on his hips, his finger still over the trigger of a .45 Colt.

"Where's Jett? And Clint?" The man asks, frantically searching the room.

"Put the gun away, Daddy," Christa says calmly. "Clint and Jett have gone for help."

My breath escapes in a large gasp and tears spill from my eyes as Richard kicks Eddie's foot. Satisfied, he pulls a knife from his inner jacket pocket and makes the rounds slicing tape.

"You must be Lexi," he says, helping me to my feet.

"Couldn't have come at a better time, Mr. Bennett." Sidney and Christa swarm him while my children cling to me. "Tanner and Ella," I say, pointing to my attachments.

He bends. "I'm Sidney and Jett's grandpa."

Tanner tugs on my arm after shaking Richard's hand. "I'm still hungry," he whines.

Placing them at the table, I scavenge the bag for food. Gas station snacks litter the bottom. I toss a handful on the table and watch them grab like vultures before taking the deer outside to skin. Sidney quickly jumps in to remove the lethal objects, placing them on top of the cabinets. Ignoring Christa's woe-is-me story, I slip outside.

An extra set of footsteps on the porch is comforting, given what we've just been through, until I realize they belong to Richard. His eyes burn into me as I skillfully remove the skin from the second quarter.

"Don't believe I've ever seen a woman do that," he says.

"Don't believe I've ever seen a man in a tie wearing boots and a buckle," I reply coldly.

"I get the feeling Clint has poisoned you against us." His hands move to his hips as if he's trying to appear superior.

"You've done a fine job without his help."

"All stories have two sides, Lexi."

"And all children need their fathers."

He scratches the thin stubble of his gray beard. "They tell me Clint and Jett have gone to Canada—or tried to go—why didn't you wait for me? Surely Christa knew I'd come."

"This is a problem money can't solve." I run my knife along the bone.

He removes his hat and runs a hand through thinning hair and replaces it. "Look, I know we have issues, and we'll work on them, but right now we have a body to move. I'm not eating with a corpse at my feet."

I stab my blade into the wood and stack the meat. "I'm only one man. Let me get dinner started then I'll worry about your daughter's fiancé." Maybe I should choose my words more carefully, but I'm over pretending everything is okay when it isn't.

The color drains from his already pale face. "Come again?"

"That story is almost as good as the one where you made Clint sign an agreement that kept him from his kids." I slip inside before he can respond.

I toss the meat inside the iron skillet and move it over the flames. Sidney removes the tape from the chairs and wads it into a ball. She nods to me, signaling that she's taking responsibility of her siblings while I tend to business. She motions them over, starting a game of catch in the small living room space.

"I'm taking the trash out," I announce, grabbing hold of Eddie's ankles. Blood smears the floor as I drag him for the door.

Richard shakes his head as the body lumps over the threshold. "Is this a one or two-man job?"

"Two, if you know one that could help," I retort.

He catches Eddie's arms as they are about to slide off the steps. "I'm grateful you were all able to meet out here and help each other."

"Yeah, that's how it went."

"Christa and the kids have had it pretty easy and they probably weren't prepared for this situation."

My foot sinks in a drift, bringing out more irritation in my voice than I mean to expel. "You think?"

"I brought Christa out here a few times when she was a kid. Man did she hate it...until she turned twenty-one."

"I heard about that."

"Maybe I didn't handle things very well after that."

"Mr. Bennett, let's cut the crap. I can understand why you didn't want your daughter to have a child out-of-wedlock, but punishing Clint for being who he is, was crossing a line," I pant. "Forcing him to be separated from his children because he couldn't handle that lifestyle any longer, that's...insane, for lack of a better word. He sacrificed so much because you used money—something you knew he didn't have—that's not even fair. Did you know he offered to bring Christa out here with him and she refused?" I slip as the body stops behind me.

"I didn't know that. She told me he left her because he couldn't stand the social functions and she refused to go without him. She never said a word about going with him. I thought it was an excuse."

"Clint needs space. Not space from people—he needs nature, a place to fish and hunt."

"We came up here often." We start moving again, but I detect a slight smile before I turn. "He's actually the one who taught me to shoot. I won the land up here in a poker hand just before Christa was born, but I'd never hunted until I met Clint."

It's my turn to laugh. "He said you couldn't hit the broad side of a barn."

"When I met him, I couldn't. I'd bring business associates up here and, while they hunted, I worked. Clint changed all that for me. I was hooked after he got me out here."

"I guess that explains the belt buckle."

"My redneck side came out a bit."

I stop, dropping Eddie's boots into the snow. "Why were you so against the kids coming to our house then?"

"That was Christa. She hated it here. I guess she wanted to punish him for leaving."

"She sure had a grand time of making him drive across the state at the last minute."

"Every once in a while she would get to feeling sorry for herself and demand he do something lavish. I tried to get her to stop, but I think she was jealous."

"Jealous of what?"

"Of what you and Clint have. We should've done things differently."

"It's not too late to start."

He drops his arms, letting Eddie's head hit the thick powder. "You're right. I'll drop the arrangement we have and you all are welcome to make decisions as a family. And if Christa gives you any trouble, I'll take care of it."

I roll my eyes and walk past him, leaving the body where it is. "How generous. And speaking of generous, the money you've been giving Clint will be coming back to you. We haven't spent a dime."

Snow crunches in quick increments as he catches up. "What do you mean?"

"We don't want your money. That includes the trust funds for Ella and Tanner. I want them to know the value of hard work."

He matches my stride. "I don't mean to be rude, but without my money, you've got to be barely making ends meet."

"We were managing."

"I admire that. Listen, keep the money and the trusts. It's the least I can do for the trouble of you letting your husband pretend to be married to another woman."

I freeze in my tracks. "Say what?"

He pretends like the statement was public information. "Oh. I shouldn't have said anything. It wasn't my place."

"I'm so damned tired of being kept in the dark. I need the full truth. Now!" An owl screeches as it leaves its nearby perch. I picture the ring Christa was wearing and couldn't be happier that Eddie tossed it in the flames.

Richard watches its powerful wings propel it away from our disagreement. "I didn't want Christa's reputation tarnished so I made Clint agree to keep up appearances. You know, at parties and select social events."

"Isn't that why he said he was leaving? That doesn't make any sense."

"Christa didn't want her friends to know what really happened, so we told everyone Clint was moved to a job within the company that required him to travel a lot. He only had to show up for candid vacation shots and Christmas parties occasionally. That sort of thing." He shrugs as if that's not too much to demand.

My chest pounds violently. I wonder how much I can take in one night. "That's why he missed Tanner's first Christmas?!"

"I'm sorry. Our agreement was so iron-clad that if he messed up, even once, he'd lose everything—including the store." I nod and take off as fast as I can toward the cabin. For a man his age, he catches up quickly. "None of this was his fault. He was also ordered to keep it quiet. If we ever found out that you knew, the same rules applied."

"We may not have much, but we'll fight you if you try to take the store."

He blocks my path. "Relax, Lexi, I'm not taking anything. That includes the money and the trust funds. You said it wasn't too late to change. This is me doing that."

"What were you going to do if I had stumbled across a picture of my husband and Christa online? Most women would've started digging years ago. Lucky for you, I'm not like that."

"Would I be way off base in thinking you either gave Clint an ultimatum or filed for divorce?"

I push past him. "That is none of your business," I snap.

"Clint risked losing a lot by telling you the truth."

"Congratulations to him. I still didn't get the whole truth. What else don't I know?"

"I've told you everything I had my hand in. Anything else is on him."

My boot slides into a footprint from our trip out. "Why should I trust either of you now?"

"I'm a man of my word—Clint can attest to that—and I'm telling you once I can get my lawyers to revoke the agreement, I'm going to."

"Why would I take Clint's word on your character after all the years he's been lying to me?"

"I don't think you understand how much Clint risked by telling you. Not only would he lose Boats 'N Bait, but the trust funds were going to disappear. And that's just to start. I told him I'd make sure you got custody of the kids if you chose to leave because of it, which he was certain you would."

I shake my head in disgust at the whole conversation. "All I really wanted was the truth."

We walk the rest of the way in silence as I try to process the secrets he's thrust on me.

I stomp my boots on the porch. His hand lingers on the door handle.

"I need a word with Christa," I say, refusing to get out of the cold.

"I'll send her out."

I wipe my dripping nose with the back of my gloved hand. Tears warm my cheeks in tiny trails, and I wonder how long I've been crying. Christa steps outside wearing her dad's oversized fur coat. I motion for her to have a seat.

"In other circumstances, I'd slap you, but my hand is frozen and it would probably snap my fingers." She nods from her chair. "I've finally learned the truth and I hate you for what you've done. You robbed Clint of memories he'll never get back. You made the kids miss getting to know each other. If it weren't for the terrorists, they wouldn't have the bond they do now and, I swear, if we all make it out of this, you're not going to take that away from them. Do you understand me?"

"Can I explain?"

I cross my arms, a frown forming. "Is there anything your father may have left out that I should know about?"

"He said he told you everything."

"I better not find out otherwise."

"I—"

"No. You don't get to talk. You're going to listen." She nods like a scolded child. "What you robbed us of, we can't get back. It stops now. I'm done loaning out my husband. I'm done sacrificing all of our children, mine and yours, from time with their father. When we go back home, we will all sit down and work out arrangements for visitation of Sidney. We'll want her half of the summer every year and every other school break. Jett is old enough to make decisions on his own and we'll expect you to not interfere. You'll also explain this all to them when the time is right. I won't have them thinking ill of their father when his hands were tied. I don't care why you did what you did, but it's over."

"I was embarrassed," she squeaks.

"Don't care. Now, we're going to go back inside and figure out a way to get along. It's going to take time for me to forgive both of you and I expect you to understand that. I can't say I would make the same decision under other circumstances, but it is what it is. I'm not going to dwell on it; however, it will take time for me to trust either of you. With that being said—things *will* be different from now on."

# Chapter 34

Six Months Later

"Tell us again how you saved us, Grampa Richard," Tanner says in the new chair he helped Richard build once the weather broke.

Richard smiles, and I can't help but join them in giddiness at the sight. Tanner and Ella had never known their biological grandparents and I'm glad they get a little taste of it with Jett and Sidney's. Tanner had taken to Richard right off and I was surprised at how easily I gave in when he asked if he could call him 'Grampa.' Richard was softened by the two young kids and Tanner was almost always by his side. They were up before dawn to catch the fish sitting on our plates.

"That old story again?" Richard removes his hat and places it on Tanner's head. "Well, it all started with my trip to Europe. I flew out the week before—"

"Skip to the good part," Tanner urges impatiently.

"You don't want to hear about my business deal?" Tanner wrinkles his nose. "Okay, okay. We were just about to head home when we received reports about the airports here."

"The good part," Tanner whines.

Richard uses a knife to cut the fish Christa had cooked to a perfect tenderness that required no utensil but a fork. She had taken to cooking shortly after her father arrived and was getting quite good at it. He chews slowly, watching Tanner's anticipation grow. I know he's mentally going through the steps in his head again. Though he's told the story enough that I have it memorized, he still frets over the fact that if one thing changed, the outcome would've been different. He skips over the part about the incoming planes' passengers being forced into camps and returned empty. He leaves out the time it took for the world to put it together and shut down all travel to The States. I wonder what he's going to add to this rendition. Each time he tells the story, it grows. I think that's what Tanner likes best.

"You remember me telling you about my pilot, Philip?"

Tanner shoves a bite in his mouth. "Wife's name's Rita. Has twin daughters. Come on, get to the fighter planes," he says with his mouth full.

Richard laughs at the squirming boy. "We had fought about the flight," he says, taunting Tanner.

"Yeah, yeah. He wanted to get back home to find his family and you wanted to fight it another way."

"Yes, but the Europeans were taking too long. Said they had to gather evidence."

"Money talks and you were able to find out what was happening. That's when you knew you had to come home," Tanner says quickly, trying to hurry the story along.

"I knew Clint would make sure his family got here," he says slowly. "He wouldn't sleep until he made sure his family was safe."

"You flew from London to Saint Kitts to refuel," Tanner says with a thudding toe tap.

Richard is clearly amused, his voice dramatic as he picks up the story. "We were over land mere minutes before Philip alerted me we had company."

Tanner throws his hands in the air. "The fighter jets!"

Richard's hands turn to airplanes soaring across the table. "There were two on our tail. We tried to dodge them by getting low—so low we chopped the top off one tree—" Embellishment number one. "—but we couldn't shake them. We adjusted our course to the south and headed higher. They had missiles and were faster. We thought we were doomed. Then we spotted one of their camps. Men worked in the fields with tractors. We could see tents set up where our people were being held inside fences with barbed wired at the top. We crossed New York City and it looked as if life was going on as normal, but we knew it was only an illusion."

"So, you flew up to Canada."

"And they were waiting for us when we crossed over into Michigan."

"That's when you realized Detroit was gone."

Richard nods. "The Middle East looked like paradise compared to Detroit. Men, who looked like little black ants, stood atop the fallen buildings as our citizens were forced to load dump trucks with their backhoes and excavators. Philip pointed out the courthouse that was still standing."

"He took out the flag!" Tanner gets so excited, he leaps from the chair, waving his arms like a plane. Embellishment two, I count as I clear plates from the table.

"You should be telling this story." Richard laughs.

"He likes seeing what new detail you're going to add," I explain.

He smiles, swooping Tanner into his arms. "We couldn't leave the Mexican Brotherhood flag flying on our land."

"Then they started shooting!" Tanner breaks free and soars around the room with his arms spread wide.

I take a towel from the drawer and dry dishes as Christa washes. "How much of this do you think is true?"

Christa hands me a dripping plate. "Philip was able to fly in under the radar. They were never even detected."

"Tanner sure loves the story though," Sidney says as she takes the plate from me. Putting it in the cabinet, she whispers, "Looks like Ella is enjoying it too."

Ella has taken her position as the bad guy and shoots imaginary bullets from her fingers into Tanner's body as he spins around. The story finishes with a lot of shooting and a landing only the movies can provide. The three of them take a bow after Richard recounts how he encountered a cougar—a new addition to the story—on his way to rescue us after parting ways with Philip.

Christa claps. "I'm just glad you looked in the window before opening the door."

Richard picks his hat from the floor where it fell when Tanner was 'shot.' "Me too."

I stare at the boarded half of the window, playing a different scenario of that night in my head. Lost in my delusive thoughts, the flickering light in the distance sends me into a state of panic. I reach for my bow beside the door and nearly shove Sidney out of the way to get back to the window. Richard is beside me with his gun drawn in an instant.

"Do you see that?" I point, but the light is gone. The window suddenly becomes crowded. "Get back," I instruct the kids.

"I don't see anything," Richard says, holstering his weapon.

"There!"

Richard's gun points into the darkness.

"I see it," Sidney whispers.

"It's Clint," Richard says, withdrawing his gun.

"How can you tell?"

"Morse code. Thought all rednecks knew that," he says with a smile.

"Not this one," I reply with a small laugh.

The room erupts into cheers and Christa rushes for the door.

"Wait for him here," Richard orders, grabbing Eddie's spotlight from the duffel bag in the closet. Covering the lens with his left hand, he sends a message into the trees.

Christa rises to her tiptoes, trying to see over Richard's shoulder. "What's he saying?"

"He wants to know if we're safe. I told him we were." He flashes another message. "He says he's plus two and ten out."

"I'll start cooking the rabbits Lexi caught," Christa says happily.

"They aren't so hard to catch when my traps aren't being sabotaged," I say lightly.

"I still can't believe I let the enemy get so close to us."

I shrug. "Water under the bridge."

I smile as she heads out the door. She'd been pulling her weight since Eddie's death and it had made it easier to forgive her. She runs back in and looks out the window next to her dad.

"What'd I miss?" Christa watches the light exchange for a second before returning to her task.

"He wants to know what you called him the first time you met." Richard glances from me to Christa.

Her confused expression matches my own. "It's rather embarrassing."

"He wants proof that he isn't walking into a trap." He waves his hand over the light.

I shrug. "I called him a baboon." All eyes turn to me. "What? We were in kindergarten and he stole my crayon."

Richard nods and waits for Christa.

She stares at the floor. "Sexy beast."

Tanner giggles as Richard coughs uncomfortably.

"Sexy baboon beast it is," he remarks, flashing light through the remaining glass. "What can we ask him so we know we aren't being set up?"

"Ask him the name of the bait shop," I suggest.

"No, that's not personal enough," Christa says. "Ask him his mother's middle name."

"He says Ramona." No wonder she suggested that, I think, surprisingly not jealous she knows a part of Clint I don't.

Richard turns to us for confirmation.

Christa passes high-fives around.

Ten minutes later, Clint stands on the doorstep with two men, all equipped with guns and wearing military camo. Helmets come off as they push their way inside. Clint is attacked with friendly arms swarming him while the other two stand awkwardly to the side. I let the kids flock to Clint and shake the hand of the taller of the two accompanying men.

"Where's Jett?" Christa shrieks.

Clint breaks free from the kids and takes Christa by the arms. "He's fine."

"Where is he?" Her tone is demanding as she motions for the men, except Clint, to sit and eat.

"You're not going to like this, and there's no easy way to say it. Our military men and women were taken to the Reservation, where most of them were shot. It's hard for us to rebuild our troops in the midst of all this, but Jett wanted to volunteer. He and I had a long talk on the way to Canada and he said he wants to be a soldier."

"And you just let him?"

I place a hand on each of their shoulders. "You must be proud. I know I am." I wrap my arms around Clint, squeezing him tightly.

"He's turned into a fine man," Christa admits, tears pooling in her eyes.

"I agree." Richard slaps Clint on the back. "Richard, didn't expect to see you here."

"Got here just in time."

Clint searches the room. "Where's Eddie?"

"You're gonna want to sit down for that one," Richard responds.

"Thank you," I say quietly to the men scarfing down food. They stand as I extend my hand to the other man this time. "I'm Lexi."

"Bart," a short, stocky redhead with a wiry beard says and points to the larger man. "Stone."

"First name's Rock," he says with a smirk.

I laugh nervously as arms fold over me and whisk me around. Clint's lips plant firmly on mine, melting away everything bad between us.

"Everything's okay," I whisper.

"It is now."

# Epilogue

Salt spray from the ocean spritzes my cheeks as the wind blows my hair in the warm breeze. Clint holds Ella at the bow so she can pretend to be Rose on the Titanic. Richard walks over with a beer in each hand. He holds one out to me while watching Jett help Tanner at the wheel.

"Thank you for inviting us out...for everything," I say.

"You've done so much more for us than I can repay you for."

"You saved our lives. It doesn't get much bigger than that."

"You saved our family." He reaches his beer forward to clink mine. "Here's to new beginnings."

"Amen to that."

Christa struts over in a tiny pink bikini, revealing stretch marks I never would've thought she would possess. My bathing suit isn't as revealing as hers, but I suddenly don't feel self-conscious in it. She points to Sidney and Tyrell, the boy she'd mentioned to me. They are flirting heavily over a tray of fruit on the long bench near the starboard side.

"I'm glad you opened my eyes to that. I let myself forget money isn't everything. You made me remember that. Clint and I loved each other once and I threw it away." Not knowing what to say, I sip my Coors Light. "Don't get me wrong, I'm glad he found a woman worthy of his love. I was angry for so long and I held that against Clint...and you. I wish I could give you back the time I stole."

I place my hand on hers. "Christa, all is forgiven. The kids moved past it easily; I don't see why we can't do the same."

"I don't deserve it." She sips on a pink liquid in her martini glass, complete with pink umbrella. When she moves to a bench near the kids, I follow, needing to feel the rays on the last day of summer.

I remove my shades and face her. "Everyone deserves a second chance."

"Except the terrorists."

"I'll drink to that." We raise our glasses as Sidney leans over the railing next to Ella. Clint drapes an arm around each of them as they watch the dolphins jump in front of the forty-three-foot Alliaura sailboat.

"I wonder what's going to happen to them," she quietly whispers, chewing on her straw.

"I saw on the news that they are being held in military prisons."

She slurps to the bottom of her glass and motions for me to follow her to the bar. "I can't bear to watch it. The news, radio, papers—it all reminds me of the nightmare."

Jett sidesteps, keeping his eye on Tanner at the wheel. "The ringleaders will be thrown in maximum security prisons. The rest will probably get away with it. It's sad really. I understand the motives behind the whole thing. That's what makes this so hard. But I still want to do my part to keep this country safe from anything like this happening again."

"We need to find a way to make Natives feel like this is still their home," Clint says, reaching into the cooler for a Capri Sun. He tosses it to Ella. "When do you ship out?"

"A week from today," Jett answers. "The President says our top priority is border security around the Reservations. Apparently there are already riots. He's also increased bonuses for new recruits due to the extreme losses we suffered. Our allies are coming in to help train and protect while we reestablish."

Clint nods, opening a bottle of Bud Light. "I still can't believe they were able to ground Air Force One before he could take off."

"They had people on the inside. Luckily, they shuffled the President through the mess to Agent Winthrop's cabin in Vermont," I say, tossing my bottle into the trash.

"I'm surprised he wasn't found. There had to have been hundreds of men looking for him," Christa says, shaking a silver decanter.

"I think the only thing that saved him is the fact that Winthrop didn't actually own the cabin at the time. He had just looked at the place the week before and hadn't made a bid on it yet so there was no paper trail to follow. It was all kept on the D-L because it was supposed to be a surprise for his wife. Turns out, it saved their lives."

"Kind of like you and the bow," I say. Clint lunges for me, whisking me off my feet and making Christa dodge my swinging legs.

"I think I'm going to need a boat like this," he says, planting a kiss on my lips. "It may save our lives someday."

I pull his mouth back to mine. "Don't even think about it," I whisper into his lips.

"Burgers are done," Richard calls from the grill. "Have you seen all the stories pouring in on how people survived?"

Clint squirts ketchup onto a bun. "One lady gave birth in the Everglades while she and her husband were hiding out there." He raises his burger in the air. "Glad we weren't stuck there dodging gators."

Richard flops a patty onto Ella's plate. "One guy in LA escaped to the sewers, did you see that?"

"Daddy, we're eating," Christa shrieks, turning up her nose.

"Sorry." He shrugs. "There was a whole village in the Appalachians that had no idea anything was even going on," he offers as an apology.

Clint and I exchange a friendly smile.

"Guys, look at this," Jett says, waving a tiny phone screen at us. "London's letting off fireworks to celebrate our victory. It doesn't feel like much to celebrate, though. Not when we have a whole minority so oppressed."

Clint throws his arm around his son. "We're going to do better from now on."

We gather around to watch as a broadcaster announces plans for countries around the world to show a display of fireworks in support of our regained freedom and the fight on terrorism. It may be Labor Day, but it certainly feels like the Fourth of July, and I couldn't ask for a better family to spend it with.

# Acknowledgements

I can't thank my husband and kids enough. From giving me time and space to write and dealing with my moodiness when the words wouldn't come, I appreciate your sacrifices and understanding through this process.

I never would've made it this far if my mom hadn't shown me the joy of reading. I sincerely apologize for every time I interrupted your book.

A huge thank you to Eric, Jenny, and Travis who answered my questions about hunting and trapping during this process. I couldn't have done this without you. Sara and Maria, thank you for helping me with all things way over my head in the fashion industry. Christa is definitely better dressed because of it.

Lori and Kim deserve the greatest of thanks for reading the first draft and urging me on.

To the Pitmad Hatters—thank you for dealing with my neediness. You guys are the best!

And, to anyone whom I may not have mentioned, you are not forgotten. I appreciate all of you who have answered random questions or provided inspiration, whether you knew it or not.

# About the Author

Erin grew up in a small town in Indiana and dreamed of getting away after high school, but instead she went to work in a factory and later became a waitress at a local restaurant while earning an Associate's degree in Office Administration from Indiana Business College. The thrill of exploring new places was once filled by reading until she discovered her passion for writing.

Erin is married and has three children, three bonus children, and six bonus grandchildren. She has put her days as a waitress behind her and now helps her husband with his appliance business.

# Connect with Erin

Website
www.erinpickettbooks.com[1]


Twitter, @erinlpickett
www.twitter.com/erinlpickett[2]


Facebook, Erin Pickett, Writer
www.facebook.com/erinpickettbooks/[3]
Erin Pickett Books - BookBub[4]

---

1. http://www.erinpickettbooks.com

2. http://www.twitter.com/erinlpickett

3. http://www.facebook.com/erinpickettbooks/

4. https://www.bookbub.com/authors/erin-pickett

# Also by Erin Pickett

*A Place on the Porch*
(2022; Women's Fiction)

Elliott Norton is struggling to escape her grief after the death of her husband and son. Determined to move forward with her daughter, she relocates with the hope of leaving the past behind. When a rundown house calls to her, she's unprepared for the waiting torrent of emotional turmoil.

Befriending a neighbor who offers to help her remodel, Elliott bonds with the hunky man over their shared tragic losses. But her fresh start comes to a crashing halt when she discovers a devastating town secret.

Will she risk renewed heartache for the sweet joy of watching a sunset together?

*The Adventures of Logan and Scruffy*
(2020; middle grade)

The kids at Logan's new school laugh at his cowboy boots. Who wears cowboy boots in New York City? No one at Van Buren Elementary, anyway. But with the help of a talking dog, Logan learns how to stand up to the bullies and even makes a few friends along the way.

Copyright © 2020 by Erin Pickett. Published by Erin Pickett. All rights reserved.

# Thank You

Thanks for reading *The Takeover* by Erin Pickett.

I hope you enjoyed the story! Please remember to leave a review at your favorite retailer.

To learn more about other Erin Pickett publications, please visit her website at www.erinpickettbooks.com.

# Don't miss out!

Visit the website below and you can sign up to receive emails whenever Erin Pickett publishes a new book. There's no charge and no obligation.

https://books2read.com/r/B-A-UNPK-CCYIC

**BOOKS 2 READ**

Connecting independent readers to independent writers.